HARD
AND FAST

D0920900

Also by Raven Scott

Hard as Ice

Published by Kensington Books

3 1526 04730530 2

HARD
AND FAST

RAVEN
SCOTT

Dafina
BOOKS

Kensington Publishing Corp.

http://www.kensingtonbooks.com

To the extent that the image or images on the cover of this book depict a person or persons, such person or persons are merely models, and are not intended to portray any character or characters featured in the book.

DAFINA BOOKS are published by

Kensington Publishing Corp.
119 West 40th Street
New York, NY 10018

Copyright © 2016 by Raven Scott

All rights reserved. No part of this book may be reproduced in any form or by any means without the prior written consent of the Publisher, excepting brief quotes used in reviews.

If you purchased this book without a cover, you should be aware that this book is stolen property. It was reported as "unsold and destroyed" to the Publisher and neither the Author nor the Publisher has received any payment for this "stripped book."

All Kensington Titles, Imprints, and Distributed Lines are available at special quantity discounts for bulk purchases for sales promotions, premiums, fund-raising, and educational or institutional use. Special book excerpts or customized printings can also be created to fit specific needs. For details, write or phone the office of the Kensington special sales manager: Kensington Publishing Corp., 119 West 40th Street, New York, NY 10018, attn: Special Sales Department, Phone: 1-800-221-2647.

Dafina and the Dafina logo Reg. U.S. Pat. & TM Off.

ISBN-13: 978-1-61773-541-7
ISBN-10: 1-61773-541-8
First Kensington Mass Market Edition: January 2016

eISBN-13: 978-1-61773-542-4
eISBN-10: 1-61773-542-6
First Kensington Electronic Edition: January 2016

10 9 8 7 6 5 4 3 2 1

Printed in the United States of America

To all the amazing women in my life that are smart, strong, ambitious, feminine and beautiful. Thank you for inspiring me to strive for the same.

Acknowledgments

Scott, thank you for letting me pick your brain and drive you nuts with all of my questions. Thanks to Sha, Renee, Dinesha, Natasha B, and my sister Natasha J for being my trial audience. And finally, thank you to the real Marco Passante for letting me use your exciting company as the backdrop for this story.

CHAPTER 1

Lucas Johnson strode purposefully through the entrance of an apartment building in downtown Chicago. While he looked casual and relaxed in dark blue jeans and a lightweight charcoal blazer over a black shirt, his eyes were sharp and alert. A pretty, full-figured woman passed him in the lobby, giving him an open look of interest and appreciation. At six feet two inches tall with a lean, athletic build, he was hard to miss. Lucas flashed a wide, flirty grin and she winked back. His pretty face and disarming smile suggested a naughty playboy, not a brilliant and lethal former government agent.

"How far are you from the target?"

The question came from Raymond Blunt through the tiny earpiece in Lucas's ear. Raymond was an agent at Fortis, the full solution security and asset protection firm owned and managed by Lucas and his two best friends, Evan DaCosta and Sam Mackenzie. They had a team of twenty-two highly trained and uniquely skilled field specialists, technicians, and operations analysts with experience from all branches of elite government service.

Lucas had three men with him on the ground for this operation. Their objective was to shut down a small-time black hat hacker named Timothy Pratt who had tried to infiltrate their client's secure computer system with a sophisticated Trojan horse program.

"We're inside, heading into the stairwells," advised Lucas.

The other two Fortis agents were entering the building from different access points and linked into the connected earpieces.

"Okay, the signal is coming from the fifth floor," confirmed Raymond from his position providing surveillance support from their rented truck parked down the street. "According to the building schematics, you're looking for the third unit on your right from the west staircase."

Lucas was now at the base of the staircase closest to him.

"Ned, you take the east stairs," he instructed. "Lance, take the elevators and I will approach the target from my end. We'll converge on the apartment door. I'll make contact, with both of you as backup in the wings."

"Got it," confirmed Ned Bushby. Like Lucas, he was a former Secret Service agent.

"Confirmed," added Lance Campbell, an ex–Army Ranger.

Lucas ran up the staircase, two steps at a time. The hall on the fifth floor of the building was empty, except for Lance as he exited the elevator. Ned came through the other exit door only seconds later. The three men crept swiftly and quietly to apartment 514. Ned and Lance took positions next to the door, hands hovering near the grips of their concealed pistols. Lucas gave them both a signal with his hand and knocked.

There was no answer.

The men looked at each other. Lucas knocked again.

"There's no answer, Raymond," Lucas stated in the earpiece.

"Well, the system's on and running, so it may be an automated program," Raymond replied. He came to Fortis after twelve years with the NSA, and next to Lucas, was their top systems and security specialist.

"Do we have any activity from the target?" asked Lucas in a whisper.

"Negative. No cellular phone usage since nine forty-three a.m.," Raymond confirmed. "And the phone's GPS signal is still in the apartment."

It was now almost eleven-fifteen on Friday morning. Lucas looked at his two men, putting up two fingers to indicate their plan B. He then took out a small, pointed tool from his back pocket, inserted it into the door lock, and picked the standard residential lock in under twelve seconds. The deadbolt took another ten seconds. The three men slipped into the apartment silently, guns drawn and ready for any situation. They quickly fanned out from the front entrance into the small, messy studio apartment, checking in the closets and bathroom. The abandoned food containers and discarded clothing everywhere suggested the place was well occupied, but there was nobody home. A laptop was set up on the kitchen counter.

"Raymond, we're in," Lucas confirmed. "The computer is here."

"Boss," stated Lance from the living area. "He couldn't have gone far. His cell phone and wallet are on the coffee table."

Lucas nodded. He was already turning on the laptop to assess the tech.

"Let's be out of here in ten minutes," he told Ned and Lance. "You guys see if you can find any info that can identify his motives. I'll need at least seven minutes to clone the system and shut down the Trojan."

He did a quick inspection of the equipment, a standard, off-the-shelf laptop connected to a wireless modem. The operating system was another story. Lucas quickly bypassed the secure login and accessed the system administrative functions before connecting a small jump drive to one of the USB ports. It contained a highly complex program that he had designed, meant to wirelessly transmit a cloned version of the desktop, operating system, and hard drive of the target system. It also left behind a passive rootkit software that would allow Lucas and the Fortis team undetected access to the computer and connected networks.

"Raymond, I've started the clone," he advised.

"Yup, the data is coming through here," Raymond confirmed through the earpiece.

"Good, we're at forty percent transmission. It should be done in three minutes."

Lucas did a few more configurations to the programming code in the admin program, then backed out of the system, erasing all traces of his presence until not even the most elite intrusion detection specialist could sniff his activities. He put the computer back in sleep mode just as the data transfer was complete.

"Got it, Lucas," noted Raymond. "The info looks complete."

"Good. We'll be out of here in one minute." He turned to the other agents as they completed their careful search of the apartment. "Anything?"

"Nothing," Lance replied.

"I got this," added Ned, holding up a couple of empty, used bank envelopes. "Whatever Pratt's up to, he's being paid in cash."

The team did one final sweep to ensure everything was as they found it. Then they exited, locking the door behind them, and split up to meet with Raymond at their rented truck a block down the street. Ten minutes later, they were headed out of the city, back to the Fortis chopper grounded at a private heliport fifteen miles outside of the Chicago city limits.

"So, what are we dealing with here, Lucas?" asked Lance. "From what we saw, Pratt looks more like a messy college kid than a corporate hacker."

"He is a kid," added Raymond. "He just graduated from Johns Hopkins a year ago, with mediocre grades and an unremarkable college life. Up until January, he was doing tech support at Best Buy in Maryland."

"So what happened three months ago and why's he in Chicago trying to break into the computer network at Magnus Motorsports in Toronto?" continued Lance.

"Hactivism maybe?" asked Ned.

"I don't think so," Lucas replied. "Magnus is a relatively small player in custom race car components. Their latest project is a high-performance, fuel-efficient hybrid engine. Not really something to upset any political or social groups."

"When Marco Passante hired us last year to set up a secure computer network and data backup system, was it just the timing of their new technology, or was he worried about a particular threat?" Raymond questioned, referring to the president and owner of Magnus.

"At the time, he suggested their technology had the potential to be revolutionary, and highly coveted in the auto industry," Lucas told them. "He talked about general concerns that his competitors would try to steal or destroy the work. Something that happens pretty often in the racing industry, apparently."

"Well, Pratt's not good enough to have built that Trojan we just shut down. He has no online portfolio or footprint to suggest he's an active hacker," Raymond added. "Looks to me like someone has set him up as a script kiddie for several months to go after information that has to be worth a big return on the investment. So either Passante had great foresight, or there is more to this client engagement than we thought."

"Raymond, my man, you've read my mind," Lucas concurred as they arrived back at the small airport in north suburban Chicago. "Once they've detected that we've shut down this attack, whoever's funding Pratt will have to find another way to get what they're looking for. Since the full Magnus network is self-contained in a local, private system within their building in Toronto, any additional attacks will be directed on-site. So, I need to have a more transparent conversation with our client and rescope this project."

They all piled out of the rented truck and began loading up their chopper.

"Question," interrupted Lance while they worked. "What the hell is a script kiddie?"

Lucas and Raymond exchanged looks of disgust.

"How do you not know this stuff?" demanded Raymond with a shake of his head.

"Because I'm not a geek," the ex-Ranger shot back.

Lucas grinned, and Raymond shrugged since neither was the least bit offended.

"A script kiddie, or a skiddie, is not skilled enough to design their own programs," explained Lucas. "So, they use tools and scripts built by other hackers."

"Got it," Lance replied, looking even less interested in tech-talk than before. "So maybe Pratt's just a lackey here. Maybe we should be looking for the person that developed the program he used."

"Not necessary. I already know who designed the Trojan program," Lucas stated with a dry smile. "It's called AC12 and it's been around for a while."

The others looked at him with various degrees of surprise.

"AC12?" repeated Raymond. "Are you sure? I worked on a few instances at the NSA. It's an ugly fucker, nearly impossible to disarm without wiping your whole system clean."

There was a pregnant pause.

"I'm sure," Lucas finally confirmed. "I build it in my freshman year at MIT."

Two days later, Lucas landed at the Billy Bishop Airport on the Toronto Islands in Lake Ontario. He headed straight into the city to check into his hotel, a short block away from the Magnus Motorsports shop and offices. A couple of hours later, he was unpacked in his room and seated at a table in the hotel's lobby restaurant for dinner. He was scheduled to meet with Marco Passante first thing Monday morning.

Lucas was not a big fan of hotels. During his career as a cybersecurity consultant with the Secret Service, he'd spent many nights in cold, cramped rooms around the world. Even ones as nice and fancy as the five-star Metropolitan didn't come close to the comforts of home. The only advantage they offered, hopefully, was a decent restaurant and a selection of imported beer. Maybe a beautiful stranger to share the bed with for a night or two.

Like the woman who just walked into the room, he thought. Now there was someone who could make this trip more enjoyable. Around five feet eight inches tall, this woman was slender in a tight dress, long, bare legs, and stiletto heels. Since it was April and raining hard outside, Lucas concluded she was a guest at the hotel, possibly alone. Perfect circumstances and exactly his type.

He took another drink from his beer bottle,

watching unobtrusively as the hostess directed the attractive woman to a dinner table across the room from his. Her hips swayed gently with each step, and she tossed her long brown hair with confidence. He relaxed back again, patiently anticipating how the evening would unfold. If she remained alone, Lucas would invite her to join him for dinner.

"Sorry! I'm just going to steal this seat for a second," announced a feminine voice. "These boots were definitely the wrong choice for tonight."

In the chair across from him, all he could see was the flat of the woman's back. She was bent over, doing something under the table, muttering swear words like a trucker. Lucas's lips quirked and he took another sip of his beer.

"Who designs these torture devices?" she added while straightening up.

He followed her hands as she gestured to her legs encased in a pair of very high and very sexy black leather boots. They went past her knees, but the table cut off the rest of his view. Lucas had to resist leaning forward to see where they ended, but his imagination was now fully engaged.

"Definitely a man," he replied smoothly.

She finally turned in the chair to look at him. Lucas paused, caught by the intensity in her large golden brown eyes. He also noticed her creamy caramel skin, pink shiny lips, and a mass of jet-black, curly dreadlocks falling well below her shoulders.

"What?" she asked, clearly confused.

"Those boots were definitely designed by a man," he stated with a wide smile.

She finally blinked, then looked back at her feet.

"You're right. Explains why I can't stand in them for more than an hour at a time," she muttered.

"I don't think they were meant for that kind of action," Lucas added, giving her a wicked grin.

The woman looked at him again, assessing him intensely. Her frank stare was strangely unnerving, but he fought the urge to look away.

"You're pretty," she finally said. It didn't sound like a compliment. "Thanks for letting me get off my feet for a minute."

"Stay as long as you'd like," he offered casually, sipping his bottle again.

Her eyes narrowed, and her gaze lowered to his lips. Lucas felt the start of a low, familiar pulse in the base of his stomach. She licked those plump, pink lips, and the pulse deepened.

"I'm Lucas, by the way," he added when the silence between them stretched uncomfortably.

She blinked again, then smiled broadly. Lucas stopped breathing, while the pulse deepened to a full throb. Wow, she was gorgeous.

"Thanks, Lucas, but I'm good now."

She stood, allowing him to see her full length. Lucas rose to his feet also, noted her height and soft curves. The boots ended a few inches above her knees where shiny, latex-covered thighs continued, topped with a white crisp men's-style button-down shirt. But only her eyes kept his attention. They widened with surprise as he stepped closer, topping her by at least six inches. Her brows knitted, then she brushed past him without another word. Lucas turned to watch her walk away as the scent of sweet vanilla and brown sugar lingered softly in her wake.

"Lex! Nick's leaving," he heard, as a man from the group at the bar waved in her direction. She was swallowed into the crowd of people.

Lucas looked back at his table, wondering what had just happened. There was no way he had imagined the physical chemistry between them, or her subtle reaction. His body was still humming at a low frequency.

Lex.

In all likeliness, she was here with another guy. Someone from the private party milling around the bar. But the night was young. With any luck, he'd have a chance at round two. Particularly since the other options in the room no longer held any interest for him. Lucas sat back down and ordered another beer as his prime rib dinner arrived.

Over the next forty minutes, he got several glimpses of black locs within the group of noisy men. She talked and laughed with many of them, but none seemed to have a claim on her. He finally drained his second bottle of beer, charging the tab to his room, and headed in her direction.

He was only a few steps from her position against the bar when she said something that must have been very clever, because the three guys around her roared with laughter, one of them almost choking on his drink. Lucas took in her bright smile and the teasing look in her eyes, wishing he could share the joke. He brushed her shoulder lightly as he leaned toward the bartender.

"Stella Artois, please. And whatever she's having," he requested, pointing to Lex's empty cocktail glass.

She glanced at him from the corner of her eyes. He met her gaze steadily.

"Thank you," she said softly when the fresh drink was placed in front her.

"Club soda?" Lucas quizzed.

She shrugged with one shoulder. "I'm driving."

He nodded. There was a pause. Lucas intended to wait for her to make the first move, ideally to indicate she also felt the attraction and his attention was welcome. It was usually a pretty easy strategy at a bar. But the seconds ticked on and she just watched him with those curious eyes. He cleared his throat and caved.

"How are your feet doing?"

She smiled.

"I'll survive for a little longer, I think."

"Good. But I'm happy to help you out again if needed." His grin was meant to be charming and flirty, but her raised brows made him doubt its effectiveness.

"Really? And how exactly would you do that?"

Suggestive words sprang into his mind, like the offer of a soft bed to rest on and a long foot rub to ease any discomfort. The direction of his thoughts must have been clearly written on his face because she finally looked away. Lucas leaned forward so he could whisper near her ear.

"I'm a gentleman, so I'd do whatever you need me to do."

"I bet you're good at that," she shot back, playing

with the frosty condensation at the side of her glass.

"At what?" he probed, now facing her with his elbow resting on the bar. His fresh mug of Belgium draft beer remained untouched.

She rolled her eyes, suggesting he knew exactly what she was referring to. "At doing whatever a woman needs."

"I can only try my best."

Lex looked at him again.

"So, Lex, is it? Are you from Toronto?" he finally asked.

"Born and raised. But I can tell from your accent that you're American. Visiting for work, I take it?"

"That's a pretty accurate guess," he conceded.

"A man like you, alone in a downtown hotel bar on a Sunday night, and looking for company? Not hard to figure out."

"Ouch," Lucas stated with a grimace. "I'm pretty, and a cliché."

"Sorry, I didn't mean it as an insult, just an observation," she added. Her eyes twinkled with amusement, taking the sting out of her words. "Unless of course, you have a wife and kids back in . . . where, New York?"

She took a sip from her drink.

"Alexandria, actually. Born and raised in New Jersey, but I live in Virginia now," explained Lucas, lifting up his left hand as evidence. "No wife, no kids. Not even a girlfriend."

There was a silent pause as they both continued to assess each other.

"Lex. Is that short for something?"

She smiled wide again, her eyes sparkling.

"Alexandria, actually."

Lucas laughed.

"Now, that can't be a coincidence," he replied, leaning a little closer so that her intoxicating scent teased him.

"Hey, Lex, this dude bothering you?"

Lucas didn't take his eyes off her, but from his peripheral vision, saw that the guy asking was a couple back in the crowd, standing over six feet and big, almost as big as his friend Evan. But he looked slow and well into multiple cups of alcohol.

"Are you bothering me?" she asked with a big smile. She was enjoying the conversation. Lucas felt encouraged for the first time.

"I hope so, if you don't mind," he replied with a grin of his own.

"I'm good, Adrian, thanks," she told the other man before facing Lucas again. "I'm leaving now anyway. Thanks again for the drink."

"So early? We were just starting to get to know each other," Lucas protested.

"Sorry, I have to be at work early tomorrow."

Lucas followed her as they made their way through the crush of people pressing close to order drinks.

"All right, I'll walk you to your car."

Lex gave him a funny look.

"Okay, if you insist," she conceded.

"I do. I'm a gentleman, remember?"

They were silent as she handed in a coat-check ticket and got back a long red raincoat that tied at the waist. He escorted her out of the restaurant.

"My car is in valet parking, so I'm just going to the front entrance. There's really no need to accompany me," she added.

Lucas looked down the long expanse of the hotel lobby, with the main doors at the opposite side. There was plenty of real estate for more conversation.

"No biggie. It's on my way to the elevators anyway," he dismissed with a shrug.

"Giving up on the night already?" she teased with raised eyebrows. "You're walking away from a lot of potential."

"Who says I'm giving up?" Lucas shot back. His gaze said very clearly that she had all his attention.

Lex let out a short bark of laughter, her lips spread wide in a big smile. He was now certain she was enjoying their banter as much as he was.

"Exactly what is it that you think you'll accomplish on this short walk?"

"Nothing. I'm just enjoying your company, that's all," he lied smoothly while he plotted the right words to say that would convince her to stay with him for more of the evening. Maybe even all night.

"Liar. You think you can talk me into sleeping with you tonight," Lex shot back, her voice still soft with humor. "And I bet you're successful with almost all the women you meet. But, unfortunately, I really have to be up early in the morning."

Her blunt assessment caused Lucas to stop his slow stroll. His expression showed a mix of surprise and intrigue. Lex stopped two paces ahead and faced him.

"And as tempting as whatever your offer is, I'm not what you're looking for. I'm the exact opposite of what you want, Lucas."

He heard two things in her statement: she remembered his name and she was tempted. Lucas smiled, slow and sexy.

"I haven't made you an offer, Lex," he clarified.

"Not yet, but you will."

"Touché," Lucas conceded. He continued their walk, slightly slower than before, and she fell in beside him.

"What do you think I'm looking for, and why is it not you?" he finally asked, genuinely curious.

"The answer to the first question would damage your fragile ego, pretty boy. And the second is way too complicated."

Lucas snorted, not the least bit insulted.

"Try me. I'm tougher than I look, and I've got time."

She looked him up and down, her eyes lingering in some interesting places. Lucas felt like straightening his back and flexing his chest. But he resisted the juvenile urge. Nothing he did would demonstrate just how strong or lethal he really was.

"Okay. But I don't think I can handle it if you start crying," she shot back, her lips twitching with the effort to hold back a grin. "You're looking for someone fun, easygoing, comfortable with a casual hookup. A girl that's not going to have expectations beyond a night or two. A week, tops. And all on your schedule."

She wasn't asking for him to agree, and he wasn't offended. The summary was pretty accurate.

Casual sexual encounters required honesty and clarity at the onset or they were bound to go disastrously and uncomfortably wrong. A complication that he never had time for.

"And that's not something you're into," guessed Lucas. "I can respect that."

"No, I prefer casual, actually," she clarified, surprising him with the transparency. "And I'm partial to pretty men without expectations. But I need it on my terms, too. My available time is limited and I don't like to waste it. And that's where it gets complicated."

They had both stopped walking, and now stood side by side in the middle of the marble-tiled hotel corridor. A small number of people walked about around them, but neither noticed.

"I'm pretty sure that's not going to work for you, pretty boy," she continued.

"Let me be the judge of that. I can compromise," he replied softly, completely captivated by her frank statements and overall energy.

She looked back at him speculatively, her bold, golden eyes piercing into his. Lucas found himself holding his breath, willing her to see what she needed in order to make a connection between them worthwhile.

"Was that an offer?" Her expression was deadpan, but her tone was teasing.

Lucas laughed. He liked her. "I believe it was."

"Thanks, but I have to pass," she finally replied. "I don't compromise very well. One of my character flaws, I've been told."

She started walking again, much faster and more determined than before, and Lucas could only fall in step. He felt much more disappointed than he cared to admit. And it was more about the end of their conversation than a spontaneous roll in bed.

"Well, there's no need to decide so quickly," he added when they reached the large revolving door at the hotel entrance. "I might be here all week."

Lex turned to face him, then backed into the open section of the turning door and pushed herself out of the building, her eyes fixed on his. Lucas shoved his hands into the pockets of his jeans, experiencing a rare moment of indecision. She'd already turned down his invitation and was walking away. It was just unmanly to chase after her further. Yet, a minute later, he was following her outside, ignoring the damp, windy night air that easily blew through the fine wool of his sweater.

The valet attendant had already taken her ticket and they stood waiting silently for her car to be brought up. He looked at her profile, then felt her look at his. Their eyes finally locked before the deep, low rumble of a powerful turbo engine vibrated around them. Lucas turned to watch the slow arrival of a late-model Porsche 911 Carrera, tricked out with sexy skirts, matte black sport rims, bright red brake calipers, and a slick storm-gray paint job. It was a beauty.

"This is me," Lex said at his side, and he turned to find her watching the car as it rolled to a stop. Pride of ownership was written all over her face.

"Wow," was all he could say.

She laughed, throwing back her head. Lucas couldn't help laughing also.

"I was serious about my offer," he added seconds later, feeling helpless to stop her from walking away.

Her lips quirked again, and she stepped to his side, close enough to brush against his arm, but still a breath away. Lucas looked down at her face, locked on those incredible eyes, and did what he wanted. He leaned down until his face was close to hers, then paused to gauge her reaction. Lex lowered her lashes and tilted her chin up an inch. His mouth covered hers without a plan of attack, only the irresistible need to touch her, explore the powerful attraction, taste her flesh before she disappeared into the night.

The kiss was open-mouthed and instantly hot, giving her a glimpse of what he had to offer and taking more than he was entitled to. Lucas was rewarded with her quick response. Lex leaned in until her soft curves pressed into his side. Her tongue met his, swirling around with arousing strokes. Lucas Johnson, elite security specialist and practiced bachelor, felt his knees go weak.

His lids were still closed when she pulled back, stepping out of his reach. His breath was caught somewhere between his stomach and throat, dreading what came next.

"Nice to meet you, Lucas," she said softly.

He opened his eyes to watch her walk around her car and slide into the low driver's seat. He was still standing in the cool night air, hands buried in his front pockets, as the sports car disappeared down the street.

CHAPTER 2

Alexandria Cotts entered her town house about twenty minutes later and tossed her car keys on the console table near the front door. She leaned against the wall and slowly unzipped her boots, her mind lingering on the night's encounter.

Lucas. She should have taken him up on his offer. She could have gone up to his room, sweated out her frustrations in his bed, and still be home before eleven o'clock. What was the worst that could have happened?

Alex sighed while placing the boots and her jacket in the front closet, then walked farther into the house carrying her purse. In the kitchen, she turned on the gas stove to heat up the kettle. Her cell phone beeped with a text message and she took it out of her purse, and then tossed the purse on one of the kitchen chairs.

It was from her brother, Adrian, who was checking to see if she was home yet. Her twin was only a few minutes older than her, but still acted like he needed to take care of her. It was both sweet and exasperating.

Alex replied with a message to let him know she was safe and sound.

"Hey, Lex. You're home early."

The statement came from her cousin and roommate, Noelle Cotts, as she came down the stairs from the upper floor of the house.

"Yeah. I need to be in the office early tomorrow," Alex explained. "Want some tea?"

"Sure. How was it?" asked Noelle, joining her in the kitchen.

Alex shrugged. The evening had been a bachelor party for her best friend, Shawn Hampton.

"It was okay. Typical stuff. They're on their way to the strip club nearby, so I'm pretty sure Adrian's happy I couldn't stay," she told Noelle with a wicked smile. "The last time I went along with them, I completely ruined his fun."

"Yeah, well, you're the only straight girl I know that can enjoy watching female strippers with a bunch of guys. It's weird."

Alex shrugged. It wasn't the first time she'd heard similar comments, and it wouldn't be the last. Other than Noelle, all her friends were male. It's the way it'd always been since preschool. And having three older brothers certainly didn't help.

"Don't worry, Nick was a good boy. He left the party before I did," added Alex. Nicholas Carter was Noelle's boyfriend and a member of Alex's group of friends.

"I wasn't worried," Noelle insisted, but it was clear she had been.

"Yeah, you were. I'm sure he'll call soon to check in."

Noelle ignored Alex's ribbing. As cousins, the two women looked a lot alike in the face, with similar caramel skin, expressive brown eyes, and shapely lips. But that's where the physical similarities ended. Noelle was five feet six inches tall and slim, but Alex barely hit five feet four, with lean limbs and curves that were more than a handful.

They also had vastly different views. While Alex was very liberal about lifestyles and relationships, Noelle lived with tightly held boundaries of right and wrong. And her boyfriend had to fit in or move on. It was the source of many hot debates over the years.

"So who was the guy you left the restaurant with?" her cousin asked above the whistle of the steaming kettle.

Alex waited until she had poured hot water into two mugs.

"Am I under surveillance now, or something?" she mumbled, adding bags of green tea and honey to each cup.

"Adrian had sent a note to Nick while I was talking to him before you got home," explained Noelle as Alex sat beside her at the kitchen table and slid over her drink.

"Wow, Nick really is well trained. He checked in right on schedule," retorted Alex, but Noelle ignored the jab.

"They asked if I knew who you were meeting up with," she told Alex. "Which of course I don't. I haven't met anyone you've dated for at least three years. Maybe four."

Alex shrugged. It was true, and on purpose. Her life and relationships were complicated enough without adding the opinions of her six closest friends; five of which were dominating males with the emotional maturity of a thirteen-year-old. And that's not including her two oldest brothers.

"So," persisted Noelle. "Who was he?"

"No one. Just some random guy that I met in the restaurant. We chatted a bit and he walked me to my car."

"Hmm. That's it?"

"What else could it be?" Alex shot back with a sardonic smile. "There was hardly time for a quickie— I'm good, but not that good." There was no point in mentioning that toe-curling kiss.

Noelle rolled her eyes, pretending to be offended by the suggestion, but was unable to stop her lips from quivering with amusement.

"Did you get a number or anything? Are you going to see him again?"

"No, and probably not."

"Why? You're not seeing anyone else right now. You said things were finished with that French driver, right?"

"What's with all the questions about my love life, Noelle? Are you reporting back to Aunt Nadine? 'Cause I'll just tell you what I told her last weekend: boyfriends are not my thing. They are more work than what they're worth."

Noelle sat back and raised her hands in a defensive gesture.

"I was just asking, Alex. That's what girlfriends do. They talk about boys and their relationships. There's no conspiracy," the younger cousin insisted, more than a little annoyed. "Geez, I thought we covered this lesson on being a girl back in high school."

Alex shrugged. Maybe she had overreacted a little. But Alex wasn't convinced that all the questions weren't somehow instigated by her very loving, but very insistent aunt. The woman made it her business to monitor all the feminine aspects of Alex's life since public school.

Most would agree that it was attention that was much needed, since Alexandria was the only girl in a house full of uncouth males while growing up. Her mother, Arleen Cotts, had died from complications within days of giving birth to the twins, and Hubert Cotts was not at all equipped to be a single parent of four kids. It had never occurred to him that his only daughter would need anything different from her three brothers. In fact, she had been known as Alex for most of her childhood. And, according to Nadine, who was married to Hubert's brother Clifford, no one in the neighborhood even knew there was a girl in the house until her aunt had taken control of the situation.

Then, every other Saturday, Aunt Nadine took her for the afternoon to do "lady" stuff with her cousin Noelle. Most of it didn't make any sense to Alex. She would much rather have played football or soccer with her brothers, or helped her dad do stuff in the garage. But it seemed so important to her aunt, and her dad couldn't discuss it without blushing, so Alex went along with it.

By the time she was headed to college, Alex looked like every other girl. She wore the right clothes, dabbled with makeup, and could have a conversation about the typical female interests. But most of the time, it was just a public facade. At heart, she'd rather talk about cars or sports while wearing a hoodie and sweatpants. By the time she'd entered the working world, Alex was pretty good at balancing the two personas to suit the circumstances.

The cousins sipped their tea in silence for a few moments.

"So what's going on at work? Why do you have to go in so early?" Noelle finally asked. She was always uncomfortable with silence.

Alex stood up from the table and walked back into the kitchen with her empty cup.

"We're taking the race car up to the track for road tests. But I have to do some work before that," she explained.

"Wow, I can't believe you've finally built the hybrid car, Alex," Noelle replied as she followed Alex and added her mug to the full dishwasher. "I remember when you first told me about the idea, and now it's real."

Alex couldn't believe it either. Two and a half years later, she was finally testing a new, high-performance electric drive motor. As an automotive engineer, it was a dream come true and a career-building moment. Most of her former classmates who wanted research and development work had joined one of the big car manufacturers. They were still proving themselves in various departments, waiting for the chance to contribute to new designs. Even then, they were often assigned to small components, tweaking or updating pre-existing technology. It was really the only path available for new graduates, and the one Alex had also anticipated on completion of her degree.

That was until she took a co-op role with Magnus Motorsports in her senior year at the University of Waterloo. It was a small shop that designed and built custom components for high-performance sports cars. She had spent four months that spring doing every menial task, from lunch runs to cleaning everything in the shop. By the end of the first week, Alex was in love with the industry. Then, after demonstrating obsessive dedication to her job, she managed to secure a permanent position as a junior engineer that started right after her final exams.

Now, almost five years later, Magnus was a rising force in motorsport racing, with products ranging from small components to end-to-end customizations. Alex was their lead design engineer and they were about to start the testing phase of her latest prototype, the Cicada hybrid.

The Cicada hybrid was high-output dual-powered technology that could revolutionize the auto industry and would make or break her career. The early projections, based solely on the design schematics and very conservative estimates, suggested her design could outperform almost anything like it in the marketplace today. As a woman, and still very young compared to others in automotive engineering and design, Alex could not afford to under-deliver on the projected capabilities. If the Cicada failed relative to the expectations, she would be laughed out of her field, doomed to perform oil changes at Walmart for the rest of her life.

But Noelle didn't know all of that. Her cousin really didn't understand Alex's job beyond the drawing of intricate pictures of machinery, building prototypes, and the supervision of the final construction. The rest was highly confidential to those other than her boss, Marco; one outside consultant; and a small group of investors. Not even her team knew the details of the Cicada project to this point. But that would all change tomorrow.

"I won't be around much this week either," Alex added once the kitchen was clean. "So don't make any dinner for me."

"But you're still going to Kate's shower on Friday, right?" asked Noelle.

Kate Nguyen was her friend, Shawn's fiancée, and the bride-to-be for their wedding on Saturday. Alex was the best woman for the ceremony.

"Yeah, I should be there. I'm staying with Shawn at the hotel that night anyway," Alex confirmed.

Her cousin raised her eyebrows, clearly expressing her disapproval.

"Really, Noelle, it's the twenty-first century. I can sleep in the same room with Shawn without having sex with him the night before he gets married," scoffed Alex. "He's been my best friend since ninth grade. If we were at all interested in each other, I'm pretty sure something would have happened by now."

It was an old debate, and one Alex really had no interest in having over and over. There was no way to convince most of the women she knew that a man and a woman really could only be friends.

"I didn't say anything," Noelle retorted, but her

mouth was still twisted with disapproval. "Anyway, I picked something out for you from the gift registry. I figured you'd forget to buy her something."

Alex had forgotten. She gave Noelle a guilty and grateful grin.

"I know, I know, I'm the best girlfriend in the world," her cousin added while rolling her eyes.

"Thanks, babe," Alex told her with light punch to the arm on her way out of the kitchen. "I owe you."

"Yeah, you do. One hundred and twenty dollars to be exact."

"'K, I'll send it to you tomorrow. Good night."

Upstairs in her bedroom, Alex dressed for bed in an oversized Indy 500 T-shirt. It was the only thing left from her last relationship. While brushing her teeth in front of the bathroom mirror, she thought through all the things that needed to be done at work in the coming week. Not the least of which was a very extensive systems security review.

There were many projects similar to hers currently in the works all over the world. But her development of hybrid fuel technology with high-performance output was the most advanced that they knew of. Marco was concerned that any leaks about Alex's design and the Cicada schematics could destroy their efforts to be first to market. As a small Canadian player in the global arena, they couldn't afford to lose that advantage. Every effort had to be made to keep their information secure, including new information security protocols and a full audit and document cleanup. Everything related to the new engine had to be filed within one secure server on the network or destroyed.

There was a lot of tedious, time-consuming work and it needed to be done before they started a very aggressive testing schedule this week. Which meant tomorrow would be hectic and intense. The official product launch was two months away, but if there were any delays to the initial testing timeline, it could put her team behind schedule.

With all that could go wrong in the coming week, it was possible that Alex would not be able to attend Kate's bridal shower Friday evening. That didn't bother her too much. She was only going out of obligation to Shawn and so Noelle wouldn't have to attend alone. Worst-case scenario, Alex could apologize afterward with a gift in hand, thanks to Noelle's foresight.

Satisfied with her backup plan, Alex climbed into bed and turned off the night-light. She took a deep breath and tried to let sleep take over. But other thoughts interrupted. The plans for the upcoming weekend meant she would be back at the Metropolitan Hotel Friday night, then all day Saturday for Shawn's wedding. That led her mind back to earlier in the evening, when she sat down to rest her feet and found herself in front of the most beautiful man she'd ever seen up close.

Lucas. With the sexy eyes, smooth cinnamon skin, and panty-wetting smile. Never mind those lips. And that kiss. That kiss had sent shock waves through her legs and left her wanting more.

Alex shifted under the sheets, trying to get comfortable on her stomach. She took another deep breath and blew it out slowly. Sleep came swiftly, as did the shadowy dreams of a strong embrace against a tall, lean, lithe body.

The next morning, she was up and out the door in thirty minutes, dressed in her standard black yoga pants, Ferrari logo-ed T-shirt under a warm spring jacket, and thick socks in work boots. The Magnus Motorsports shop was located in an industrial area of downtown Toronto. She was the first in, other than Oliver Poulton, the overnight security guard.

"Morning, Alex," stated Oliver as she entered the lobby at the front of the building, her hands filled with two large cups of coffee. The walls were lined with framed Magnus car parts, design drawings, and custom race cars.

"Hey, Oli," she replied with a bright smile. "I brought you a treat. Caramel white mochaccino with whipped cream and chocolate slivers."

Oliver beamed at her as his round, pale face flushed with pleasure.

"Sounds yummy. You're a lifesaver," he declared as he stood from behind the reception desk and took one of the cups from her. "I was just about to make a fresh pot in the kitchen, but this is way better."

"Well now I've saved you the trouble," she quipped with a grin. "See you later."

Alex went through the hallway that led to the business offices. Hers was the last room on the left, right next to the large body shop at the rear of the building and across from one of the meeting rooms. It was a small office, dominated by a big desk in front of a bank of windows covered in vinyl blinds, with a view of the parking lot. Inside, she placed her purse and black coffee on her desk, then hung up her coat and stepped into one of several gray overalls hanging in the closet, all stitched with the Magnus logo along the right shoulder. Sitting behind her large desk, she turned on the powerful computer and the three HD screens that lined up on the surface. While they booted up, she took her iPad out of her purse and opened the notes and action plan from her meeting with Marco on Friday afternoon.

Last week, someone had tried to hack into their computer systems. There was no sign that they had accessed anything critical yet. But according to the security consultants, the attack was very sophisticated and aggressive, and after something more valuable and specific than their library of patented designs. As a result, Magnus was implementing a new network protocol with very specific data storage and backup criteria. The security consultant would be in their office this week to complete the implementation.

There was no question that the Cicada design was the target of this attack. From the moment she had outlined her idea to Marco almost three years ago, they both knew its success was dependent on a high level of confidentiality. Even her team was kept in the dark through the design and build of the prototype. Each engineer was assigned a component of the engine, based on tweaks to current patents, but only Alex worked on the electric motor schematics. And she had hired an external physicist to provide newly developed technology in rechargeable lithium-ion battery power. It was the key component in what made her hybrid different from anything known today.

Alex had also worked alone over the last six

months to put the prototype together and run it through the engine-testing equipment after hours. Today, they would start the road tests before more fine-tuning and detailed calibrations. It was time to bring her team into the fold and document every step of the process. And the risk of a security breach was now exponentially higher. It was now mid-April, and any leaks about the strengths or weaknesses of the Cicada design could sabotage their official launch, scheduled in June.

So Alex only had a little time through the day to finish organizing her classified files before the Magnus computer network went on lockdown.

CHAPTER 3

Lucas arrived at Magnus Motorsports at about eight thirty on Monday morning. The eight-thousand-square-foot design and fabrication shop was in a one-story building of an industrial plaza. There were seven custom sports cars parked in the front, and several more in the back parking lot, in various stages of customization and repair. While the company was making its name in racing components, the bread and butter of the business was the tuning, repair, and maintenance of high-end sports cars. Of the twenty-one employees, nine were mechanics licensed to work on everything from Audi to Lamborghini to Porsche, and everything in between. Six design engineers worked on the large library of Magnus-patented components, and another three had been hired within the last year to join the Cicada team, led by the lead engineer, Alex Cotts.

Lucas was very familiar with the organization structure at Magnus. Nine months ago, he had designed a new, highly secure computer and network system for the company, with the sole purpose to protect all the Magnus designs and intellectual property. The most sensitive of which was their high-output hybrid-engine fuel design, though it was still a concept at the time. He set up role-based permissions with very specific access perimeters for each employee based on the job requirements. Then, Fortis sent Raymond Bloom to Toronto for several weeks to implement the system, working with several local, highly recommended consultants.

With post-implementation network administration and support, the Magnus case was a relatively simple assignment, compared to most of the security work that Fortis managed. Or it was, until last week when someone went through a lot of trouble to try hacking their system.

"Mr. Johnson?"

Lucas turned to the woman walking toward him the moment he stepped into the front entrance of the shop. She was short and full-bodied, wearing casual cotton slacks and a light sweater. Her hand was extended in greeting.

"I'm Norma Stavros, Marco's office manager."

He shook her hand firmly and flashed a disarming smile. Her grip strength almost matched his.

"Nice to meet you, Norma."

"Marco's running late at another appointment, but he should be here in about an hour," she explained as she turned to walk through the main showroom. "He's asked me to set you up with a space where you can work."

"Okay, thanks. Can you also show me to your server room?" Lucas asked.

"Sure, it's near the entrance to the auto shop."

She opened another set of doors at the other end of the large space, leading to a long hallway with offices and meeting rooms running along its length. "Would you like some coffee or anything?"

"No, I'm good, thanks."

Norma turned into the first doorway on the left, a small conference room with a round table, four chairs, and a phone on top. There was a large whiteboard mounted on the side wall.

"You can use this room for as long as you need," she told him.

Lucas set his laptop bag on the table and removed his cell phone from the inside pocket of his blazer, then slipped it off to hang it over one of the chair backs. He unzipped the leather bag and pulled out an iPad and a few network cords.

"Ready whenever you are," he told her.

She smiled and led the way down the hallway and through another exit at the end. Before they went through, Lucas glanced into the auto shop through the glass wall that ran the full length of the hallway. There were five men working on several high-end cars at one end of the large space. Another three were standing around a big contraption, watching a readout on a computer screen, while a fourth appeared to be crouched low behind the machine. All wore full-cover gray overalls.

"Is Alex Cotts in there?" he asked Norma, who was waiting patiently in the doorway.

"Yeah, in front of the motor-testing machine," she replied.

Lucas nodded, then followed Norma through to a locked door with a touch-screen access panel. She entered the eight-digit numerical code and led him to a small equipment room, with the compact stack of high-storage servers, and other network and electrical equipment.

"It's not very fancy, I'm afraid," she stated wryly as they both looked around the dusty space. "No one has access but Marco and I, and neither of us know what anything is."

"No worries," Lucas assured her. "Everything important is well protected."

"I'll take your word for it," she laughed. "Let me know if you need anything else. My desk is just beside the showroom, and I'll have Marco call you when he arrives."

"Thanks," he replied with a grateful smile. Then he got to work.

An hour later, he was back in the small meeting room, on a call with Evan DaCosta.

"What are we looking at?" Evan asked, referring to the expanding scope of the Magnus assignment.

"I haven't met with Passante yet. But from what we know already, I sent Passante a new mission outline for an on-site security detail in addition to the systems lockdown, until the official launch of their product," Lucas stated.

"When's the launch?"

"I'll confirm this morning, but their plan was for mid-June."

"Eight to nine weeks," Evan estimated. "Who do you want?"

Fortis had eleven field agents with a wide variety of specialized and military training.

"I'm thinking of Ned, Lance, and Michael," Lucas suggested.

Michael Thorpe was from the FBI, and Ned and

Lance were already familiar with the mission from the assignment in Chicago on Friday. All three were highly skilled in physical security detail and close contact combat.

"What about the network? Raymond is working with Sam and me on a couple of other projects, but we could free him up if needed."

There was a knock at the meeting room door. Lucas turned to find Marco Passante standing in the entrance.

"I'll call you and Sam this evening and we'll finalize the team," Lucas told Evan before they ended the call.

He then walked forward to meet his client.

"Lucas Johnson? I'm Marco." He was a slim man in his midforties, about five feet ten inches tall with a full head of long curly hair and a goatee. "Sorry to interrupt your call, but I wanted to let you know I'm available to meet whenever you are."

"No worries, I was wrapping up anyway," Lucas replied smoothly as they shook hands. The two men had spoken many times by phone and video chats over the last eight months, but this was their first meeting face-to-face.

"Thanks for coming into town to meet so quickly. I hope Norma was helpful is getting you settled," Marco stated.

"She was great. I got access to everything I need so far," Lucas told him.

"Good, good. Everything in order?"

"All's good with your on-site systems, based on the strategy we implemented last year," replied Lucas. "We can modify as required, if you agree to the proposal we sent you on Friday."

A cell phone rang, and both men looked at their devices. It was for Marco.

"Sorry, it's Alex," he told Lucas before accepting the call. "Hey, how are you guys making out?"

Marco walked back and forth as he listened to the response.

"What time will you guys get there?" Marco asked into the phone, looking at his watch. "Okay, we won't be far behind."

Marco listened intently for another few seconds before he hung up.

"Do you want to go for a ride?" he asked Lucas with a boyish grin.

"To where?" Lucas responded, unfazed by the change in direction.

"Alex and the team have just left to take the Cicada prototype out for the first road test. There's a track a few miles north of here," explained Marco. "You could see the new engine in action, and we can talk about your proposal on the way."

"Sure," Lucas agreed with an easy shrug. "How long do you think we'll be out?"

"I have a meeting a four o'clock, so I need to be back by then anyway," Marco explained as he led them out into the hallway. "But, we can certainly come back sooner if you need to."

"No, that works."

It would give Lucas plenty of time after to get Evan and Samuel up to speed.

"Good," replied Marco with a big smile. "My car is parked out back.

The men walked through the hallway, into the auto shop, and out the back entrance. As they walked to Marco's car, a top-of-the-line BMW, something slick and gray caught Lucas's eye. It was a Porsche 911 with matte black rims and shiny red calipers, identical to the one that had pulled up to the valet parking last night at the hotel. The one owned by a very sexy and intriguing woman named Lex.

"Your first time in Toronto, Lucas?" asked Marco, interrupting Lucas's musing as they entered his car.

"No, I've been here a few times for work," he replied, leaving out that it had been on Secret Service business. "It's a beautiful city."

"Well, we'll make sure you see more of it while you're here."

Marco pulled out onto the street behind the building. The traffic was busy, but moving smoothly. They took a couple of turns, then entered the freeway going north about ten minutes later.

"Like I told you on Friday, Marco, you will need more than just the updated network security plan I've outlined," Lucas stated once they were cruising.

"But you said you've shut down the hack into our network, right? Once you upgrade our systems, won't that stop the attacks?" asked Marco, giving him a quick glance.

"I've done a full review of your local servers this morning. Everything looks secure, for now. But, based on what we discovered on Friday, someone has invested a lot of time, effort, and money to try infiltrating your network. Experience tells me that they aren't going to stop because we shut down their first attempt," Lucas explained. "When you hired Fortis, you made it very clear from the beginning that your highest priority was the confidentially of your new prototype. So we designed your computer system and network to be completely self-contained, with encrypted storage and backup on your local servers. All cloud-based or hosted solutions have inherent security vulnerabilities. The hosting company and its employees would have access to your information, even if it's hidden behind layers of security algorithms."

Marco nodded with agreement.

"But, that means the only access to your network is through your servers, or if we grant it through the collaboration portal," Lucas concluded. "If someone wanted to steal your information, they would need to get into your location to do it."

Marco was silent as he tapped his thumb against the steering wheel as the reality of the situation became clear.

"They'll try to break into the shop," the older man stated.

Lucas shrugged. He didn't want to scare his client, but his job was to prepare for all scenarios.

"It's a real possibility. Or someone in the company could do it, with the right incentive. It's why I've suggested expanding our assignment to include an on-site security team," Lucas explained. "Have you reviewed the new plan?"

Marco nodded.

"Yes. It's fine, of course," Marco replied. "I was actually thinking of hiring my own security team. Right now, Oli is just there after hours. But with the engine built and going into testing, I've been worried about keeping it secure twenty-four seven."

"Good," Lucas stated.

"How did they plant the worm in our network?" asked Marco.

They had just exited the highway and Marco continued north on a two-lane regional road.

"It wasn't a worm, it was a Trojan horse. Most worms are meant to destroy computers or shut down a network," explained Lucas as he glimpsed the confused glance on Marco's face. "A Trojan hides on a file, acting like a back door into a system to get undetected access to all the files."

"Okay. So how did they do it?"

Lucas checked the map on his cellular phone, noting their location on the more rural roads.

"It was through that professor you guys hired, North," he explained. "The Trojan was attached to an encrypted document he shared last week. Once the doc was accessed inside your network, the trap door was opened."

"Adam North was involved? That can't be true," insisted Marco with a look of shock on his face. "He's a highly acclaimed physicist, and an associate professor at the University of Illinois."

"We don't think he knew anything about it. Someone just used him as a point of access, and we suspect they had been tracking his movements for some time." explained Lucas.

"Alex started working with him months ago," Marco recalled.

"Back in December," confirmed Lucas. "They could have been tracking him from the start, looking for an opportunity to gain the access they need. But we only gave North the ability to upload locked files onto your collaboration portal. He couldn't save anything from Magnus on his own computers or to a drive. So, they had to find another way to access your information."

"Shit!" Marco muttered. "They've been targeting us for that long?"

"We can't be sure, but it's very possible," Lucas conceded.

The two men sat quietly for a few seconds before Lucas got to the second purpose for this meeting in person.

"Marco, I need to know what exactly your Cicada engine is, and why people with a lot of time and money want it." His client sat up higher and looked a little intimidated by the directive tone of Lucas's voice. "And don't tell me it's just a hybrid. I'm pretty sure Tesla and others have already been there and done that."

Marco cleared his throat and checked his mirrors. There were no other cars near them.

"I'm not asking out of curiosity, Marco. I need to clearly understand the scope of the threat in order to effectively neutralize it."

Marco let out a deep sigh.

"It is technically a hybrid, but completely different from anything commercially available now for passenger cars. Most of them use the electric motor to run at lower speeds, for a few hundred miles, then the gas engine charges the battery and takes over when the motor is out of charge. They're designed mostly for economy, not power."

"How is yours different?" Lucas probed.

"In almost every way. Only Alex can really explain

the technical details, to be honest. But in the end, it will be lighter, run faster and longer on electrical power. The battery will charge in minutes with gas fuel, not hours," Marco explained, his voice vibrating with energy and excitement. "For racing, that means higher velocity. Possibly record-breaking speed."

"And for the consumer market?" asked Lucas, already sensing the possibilities.

"In an average sedan, we think a twenty-gallon gas tank could last two months. The rechargeable battery would be efficient and durable enough to last the lifetime of the car."

Lucas stared at the profile of the other man, his brain running various analytical calculations at genius-level speeds. If what Marco was describing was just half-accurate, it was serious business, with implications way beyond the car racing industry.

"Who else knows about the specs, besides your employees?" he asked in a calm tone.

"Up until this morning, Alex and I were the only ones who knew everything. But the racing team would have been brought up to speed before they left for the road test," explained Marco. "Other than that, we have three investors that we've been providing monthly updates. But even they think we've only focused on building a lighter and faster hybrid for the race at the Sea-to-Sky Highway in June."

"What is the Sea-to-Sky Highway? Is this an event Magnus participates in?" Lucas asked.

"It's an open race up the steepest part of the Sea-to-Sky Highway to Whistler in B.C. We've sent a racing team for the last three years, but haven't cracked the top ten spot yet," he detailed. "But it wasn't until Adam North shared his battery technology that Alex saw the broader possibilities. Her engine and his battery show potential on their own, but together, they are a game-changer."

The puzzle pieces all fit together, and Lucas was buzzing with alert energy. Magnus Motorsports was a small, independently owned custom fabricator for car parts with impressive results in racing components. It didn't make sense that they would be a target for the type of funded cyber attack that Timothy Pratt had been fronting. Sure, small businesses had their fair share of intellectual property thefts, everything from client lists and marketing strategies to trade secrets and design schematics. But, it was almost always at the hands of disgruntled employees or business partners. They were typically crimes of opportunity, with only a little planning or forethought.

Pratt's setup suggested something much more far-reaching and big-budget. Based on what Marco had now revealed, there was no telling who or what companies were willing to steal the Cicada.

"The only way to fully protect you is to figure out who's trying to steal your design," Lucas explained. "Before that, we need to make sure everything related to the Cicada is now stored beyond the VPN and firewall on your network and backed up."

Marco nodded as he turned into the entrance of a large parking lot.

"I met with Alex on Friday after you had sent me your recommendations. We should be all set by tomorrow morning."

As they drove into the pit entrance of the field, Lucas looked around at the large open area. There were several grandstand seating structures along the three-mile asphalt track, with the largest at the starting mark, on the other side of the pit stop. Only one car moved around the track at racing speed.

Marco parked in the gravel near the track, and they both stepped out of the car. Lucas followed him toward the edge of the track where two men were standing, wearing matching gray coveralls, looking through a folder. He recognized them from the shop floor that morning.

"How's it going?" asked Marco as both of the engineers looked toward them.

"It's crazy," one of the two men replied, looking confounded.

"Lucas, meet Randy and Niles, two of the engineers on Alex's team," explained Marco, gesturing to the stocky, middle-aged man he first spoke to, and the second younger, more slender guy who was holding the folder. "Guys, this is Lucas Johnson, with our security firm, Fortis."

Lucas shook hands with the engineers.

"Where's Cotts?" Lucas asked. "I was hoping to get some more details on the work with Adam North."

Marco laughed as they all looked back out onto the track. "You'll have to wait until she's done testing her baby."

She? Lucas looked at him with a frown, but was distracted seconds later when a dark blue race-engineered Mitsubishi Lancer Evolution zipped by them, clocking at least one hundred and forty miles per hour. The sound of the wind wake and tire traction hit him in a flash, but the motor and exhaust were whisper-quiet.

"That's your Cicada motor inside the Mitsubishi?" he asked, still feeling the power vibrating through his bones.

Marco's eyes sparkled like a schoolboy at Christmas.

"That is it."

The four men stood and watched the car complete another couple of laps, each seemingly faster than the previous. Before the last pass, the older engineer, Randy, whipped his hands in the air.

"They're going to do a final lap at max velocity," Marco explained.

Lucas nodded, then stepped forward with the others to witness the results. He could feel the energy and excitement as the race car increased its speed coming out of the last curve of the lap.

Suddenly, there was a loud bang and dark smoke surrounded the car. Sounds of tires squealing were mixed in with muttered and panicked curses from Marco and the two engineers. Within moments, they were all running toward the Mitsubishi, now spinning out in crazy circles up the straightaway.

CHAPTER 4

The area was immediately filled with the scream of an emergency siren as a geared-up red 4x4 truck pulled out of a garage at the far side of the field. There was too much commotion for Lucas to see the cause of the explosion, or the damage to the vehicle and the people inside of it. But his instincts were heightened, and he scanned the open area for any sign of threats, attacks, or hiding culprits, prepared for all possibilities.

Within a few seconds, the car pulled out of its dizzying spin to skid across the pavement until the rear end slammed into the short wall with a loud crunch. It was a chilling sound, prompting Lucas to refocus on the probable injury and damage to the people and assets inside. With his long, fast strides, he was well ahead of the others, reaching the collision site first, just before the safety team vehicle arrived, with a full firefighting system set up in the bed.

The smoke had thinned out, revealing a shredded rear tire. But, knowing how highly flammable racing fuel was, and how unpredictable collisions could be, everyone was clearly prepared for the worst-case scenario—a gas leak that would come in contact with the extremely hot exhaust system, triggering an instant fire, maybe even an explosion. The safety crew got busy, quickly setting up the required equipment.

"Alex! Bobby!" Marco was yelling from behind Lucas, and the firefighters and paramedics were shouting instructions to each other.

The driver's-side door opened just as Lucas was about to reach for the handle. A young man, no more than twenty-one years old, climbed out from between the heavy white bars of the full roll cage. His angular face was ashen and clammy.

"We're okay," he whispered, though only Lucas was close enough to hear.

"Alex?" shouted Marco, still several yards away. "Bobby, is Alex okay?"

The young driver nodded, then bent over as though to prevent himself from fainting.

"You all right?" Lucas asked the driver.

He nodded again, coughing. A uniformed female paramedic jogged up to help.

"Any injuries or pain?" she asked, quickly guiding him away from the car, and got him to sit down at a safe distance.

Lucas turned back to the still-open passenger door, very aware of the danger to the other person in the car with every second that went by. There were no signs of smoke or sparks now, but that did not reduce his concern. He hunched down low enough to look into the interior. Whatever he expected to find, it wasn't the large, golden brown eyes that stared back at him, round with panic.

"What . . . ?" she stammered, clearly as surprised as he was.

But Lucas's analytical brain was working parallel to his instinctive actions.

"Are you okay?" he asked calmly.

The woman he knew as Lex blinked rapidly.

"Yes," she finally stammered. "But I can't get out. My door's too close to the wall, and my seat won't slide back any farther."

Lucas could see the safety crew rushing around the vehicle, hear them yelling questions to the Magnus team about the specifics of the car and fuel. But he stayed focused on Alex as the seconds ticked by. He'd already mentally calculated her size, the dimensions of the space inside between the roll cage and various other large custom, fixed equipment installed between the two bucket seats.

"Okay, I'm going to pull you out through this side," he explained, and she nodded quickly. "Ready?"

"Remove the steering wheel," she told him, her voice now stronger, steadier.

Lucas followed her instructions without hesitation, and the large wheel slipped easily off the steering column. Someone beside him took it off his hands immediately. Then, he grasped both of Alex's outstretched hands. Within three heartbeats he easily pulled her out of the vehicle headfirst until they both landed on the ground. Several people helped them to their feet and a member of the safety crew guided them over to where the driver was still sitting, drinking from a bottle of water.

"Are you okay, Bobby?" Alex asked him.

"Yeah, just a little dizzy," he told her. "You? Were you stuck?"

Marco and the other three men surrounded them at that point, all asking questions at the same time, and sounding winded and panicked. Lucas did another discreet reconnaissance of the area, while Alex provided a multitude of answers and explanations. He even examined the road within causative range of the blowout, but there was nothing there to suggest sabotage.

"Lucas," Marco called a few minutes later, waving him over with big arm gestures.

As Lucas jogged back to the site of the collision, the Magnus team was still assessing the damage, but the car was now running again. Alex was standing in front of the open hood.

"What's the damage?" he asked.

She looked up at him, but barely long enough to make eye contact before she was back inspecting her engine.

"Surprisingly little," Marco told him from where he was now crouched at the back end of the car. "It needs some panel work and the bulbs are busted. But other than that, we're in good shape."

He heard the car hood slam shut and turned to face the woman who had been an annoying disturbance to his sleep the night before.

"Alex Cotts, I presume," he stated with a cocky smile. "I've heard a lot about you."

"Really?" she shot back, expressionless as she

walked toward him. "And yet I know nothing about you other than a first name, Lucas."

"Glad you remembered," Lucas continued, then winced imperceptibly. It sounded like a completely inappropriate flirt, even to his ears.

"Are you sure you're okay?" he added. "That was a pretty close call."

"I'm fine," she replied with an exasperated eye roll. "It was just a tire blowout. It happens. So, why don't you tell me what you're doing here?"

Marco interrupted their conversation.

"Alex really knows how to make a first impression, doesn't she?" he said to Lucas, looking back and forth between them.

Now that the emergency was over, with minimal damage, the excitement about their motor's performance was obviously returning.

"I try, Markie-Mark," she replied to her boss, tapping his cheeks like he was a child. "Now, who is it that I'm making an impression on and why is he at our road test?"

Marco laughed, not the least bit offended by her nickname or playful teasing. She could tell that he was flying high with adrenaline. She felt the exact same way.

"This, Alexandria, is our security consultant, Lucas Johnson," Marco stated as he dropped an arm around her shoulders. "Lucas, meet Alex Cotts, our lead engineer and inventor extraordinaire."

Alex closed her eyes in a long blink as all the pieces fit together.

"We met last night, actually," she told Marco, seeing no reason to pretend otherwise. "In the Metropolitan, at Shawn's bachelor party."

Lucas Johnson looked back at her with those pretty eyes, rimmed with long, inky lashes. A trace of his flirty smile still lingered on his lips.

"She makes a pretty good second impression, also," he finally stated to Marco. "Nice to meet you, Alexandria."

"Alex, please," she insisted on reflex.

Still feeling uncomfortable about his presence in her "work" world, Alex turned back to the car and to business.

"Did Randy and Niles share the data?" she asked Marco in a soft, discreet voice. "Zero to sixty in four-point-nine seconds, Markie! That's just right out of the gate! Then Bobby got it to about one-sixty-two down that last stretch. Once we've cleaned it up a bit and dialed it in, I think we could hit one-eighty, no problem."

Even saying the words sent chills down her spine. One hundred and eighty miles per hour for a race car with a turbo-charged engine was noteworthy, but it was unheard of for an electric-drive hybrid.

"Jesus, Alex! You don't mess around, do you?" replied Marco, throwing his head back from the weight of her words. "That's insane!"

"I know," she agreed.

"Are you guys done here?" Marco asked.

"Yeah. Once the tow truck has the car loaded in the race trailer, we're going to head back to the shop," she explained.

"Okay. I'm going to head back now, but Lucas needs to get some information from you about the

Cicada and your work with Adam," explained Marco. "Can you meet with him when you get back?"

"Sure," Alex immediately replied. She completely understood the security concerns.

"Good, thanks. I'll have Norma order us some lunch to celebrate," he added. "Great work, Alex. I always knew you could do it."

He gave her shoulders a tight squeeze as he made the last statement. Alex was touched by his words, but tried to make light of it.

"I'm glad one of us did," she shot back dismissively.

This time, Marco rolled his eyes before walking back to where Lucas Johnson stood talking to Bobby Chiu, the youngest member of her team. She watched the two men talk briefly. Lucas looked relaxed and unaffected by what had happened, but Alex didn't miss the way he routinely scanned the area around the track, or the very sharp diligence in his eyes. While it was an unsettling surprise to have him walk into her professional life, his presence as a security consultant made her feel a little more safe.

"See you guys back at the shop," Marco told her team a few minutes later as he and Lucas started across the asphalt toward Marco's car.

"See you in a bit, Alex," Lucas said simply as he walked by her.

She nodded, then got back to work. But it was very hard not to watch the tall, lean length of his body as the two men walked away.

The tow truck for the speedway arrived a few minutes later. Alex asked Randy to supervise the transportation of the Mitsubishi Evo loaded with the Cicada back to their trailer, parked behind the racing pit, while she, Bobby, and Niles finished their notes from the test. While the Cicada had outperformed her early projections, there was still a lot of potential for improvement based on what they had observed. They were also brainstorming ways to tweak the drivetrain design that could create more speed.

"I can look at other generators. There were a few in the catalog that could work," Niles suggested. He had been assigned to build a mechanism that converts methanol gas power to the electrical power stored on high-capacity lithium-ion batteries.

"But they were heavier, right?" Alex recalled. "I don't know if we can afford the extra weight."

"We could if we made the combustion engine smaller," Bobby proposed. "We only need enough gas to recharge the battery for ten to fifteen minutes when the batteries run low."

"Or maybe we try various configurations in the drivetrain to maximize power output and save weight elsewhere," Alex threw in.

"Like on the body of the Evo?" asked Bobby.

"Yeah," she confirmed. "Let's assume that what-ever we add to the mechanics can be saved else-where."

The three looked at each other, brains working.

"Hey, guys," Randy interrupted as he ran up to them. "The car's packed."

"Randy, you did some work with carbon fiber panels in your last job, right?" Alex asked him.

"CF? Yeah. It's amazing stuff but insanely expensive," he replied.

"We might need to add weight to the power unit to get more speed. Could we do that by replacing parts of the body with CF?" she quizzed.

"Sure," confirmed Randy, crossing his arms across his rounded chest. "But it'll shoot your budget to shit."

Alex let out a deep breath and looked at the ground.

"Okay, let's head back to the shop and get everything in the system." She started walking back to the pit stop area and her team followed. "Then we'll run some models to improve the power-to-weight ratio."

They loaded everything into the truck cabin and trailer, then headed back into the city. While Bobby drove and Randy rode shotgun, Alex sat in the backseat of the truck with Niles. They had gone to the University of Waterloo together, and he was the first person she had hired last year for the Cicada project.

"So, what do you think?" she asked, studying his expression. "Am I in over my head?"

Niles opened his mouth a few times, clearly trying to find the right words.

"It's ambitious, Alex," he finally replied. "When you revealed the final design this morning, with all the pieces we've been working on put together, I have to admit, I was skeptical. A series design hybrid hasn't ever seriously been considered in passenger cars, never mind for racing. The typical electric motor just doesn't generate enough sustainable power."

"I know," she conceded. "Which is why I started

from scratch. Nothing on the market was going to work, right?"

"Exactly. It's your motor that makes it work, Alex," finished Niles. "So, no. You're not in over your head. Even if we don't get to the Sea-to-Sky Highway race with this design, you've already had a huge accomplishment. There's nothing more to prove."

She let out a big sigh before giving her friend a grateful smile.

"Thanks, Niles. I know it was awkward for you guys to be in the dark for so long. But it was essential before we filed the patent," Alex explained. "Marco was really worried about the motor design ending up in the wrong hands. We still are."

Nile waved his hand dismissively.

"You guys were very clear about the situation from the get-go. I don't know about the others, but I've been too busy building the regenerative braking system and diagnostic controls to really worry about anything else."

"Good. That makes me feel better. But I'm really glad to have you guys in the know so I can pick your brains."

"That's all we're worth to you? Brain-picking?" Niles shot back with a big laugh. "In that case, I might be overpaid."

Alex playfully punched him in the shoulder.

CHAPTER 5

Alex and her team arrived back at the Magnus building shortly after two o'clock in the afternoon. Once the damaged race car was securely parked back inside the shop, ready for the required repairs, they went to get lunch. As promised, Norma had ordered pizza from a local bistro and had the now lukewarm pies laid out in the largest conference room, across from Alex's office. Half the food was already gone, presumably eaten by the other mechanics.

The Cicada team grabbed slices of cheesy pizza laden with a variety of traditional toppings. Alex placed two pepperoni wedges on her paper plate, then ate them while making notes on her iPad. The other engineers were talking about the damage to the Mitsubishi, listing the body repairs need to the backend.

"It's almost two thirty," stated Alex after her lunch was finished. "Are you guys good with what we need to do with all the files related to the

Cicada? I promised Markie that they would be all cleaned up by the end of the day."

Niles, Bobby, and Randy nodded, still working their way through the food.

"I've already set up folders for each of your projects, so just store everything you need on the portal. Delete everything else," she continued. "Then tomorrow, we can start tweaking the powertrain for the Cicada in the Mitsubishi."

"What about the body damage?" Bobby asked. "We'll need to get the repairs on the schedule with Dale's team so the car is ready for testing. Do you want me to talk to him?"

Dale Winters managed the Magnus auto shop and the team of eight mechanics. They were really good at doing any basic work on the racing cars when needed.

"Sure, that would be great," Alex agreed as she pushed back her chair to stand up, grabbing her cell phone, iPad, and a diet cola from the table. "I'm going to be with the security guy for a little bit. But send me a message if you need me."

The guys waved her off fondly, their mouths still full.

Alex walked down the hall to the small meeting room near Marco's office where Lucas Johnson had set up shop. The door was open and she could hear the low, smooth pitch of his voice as she approached. There was a tingle in her stomach that caught her by surprise, causing her to pause outside the entrance for a few seconds. She took a deep breath and straightened her back, thinking well-worn work overalls weren't exactly what she had fantasized wearing if she ever saw him again.

"I won't bite."

Lucas was now standing in the doorway with that charming smile on his lips and a teasing twinkle in his eyes. His cell phone was held up near his ear. He pressed what she assumed was the mute button and he went back to his conversation without missing a beat. Alex clenched her teeth with annoyance as she followed him into the room and closed the door behind her.

"I'll meet Ned, Lance, and Michael at the airport tomorrow," he stated into the phone, but his eyes were watching her every move. "Let's leave Raymond on his current assignments. I can complete the system update."

Alex unlocked her cell phone and scrolled through e-mails, but her attention was unwillingly fixed on Lucas. He walked two paces along the back wall, behind the round conference table, then back two paces. She scrolled through the same list of messages again.

"'K, call me if you need anything."

Lucas put the phone on the table next to his laptop, and there was a small pause before she looked up. He wasn't exactly smiling, but his eyes still seemed to be making fun of her. It made her stomach clench again.

"So, Alexandria Cotts, why don't you have a seat."

He pulled out the chair next to where she was standing, then sat in the one beside it. Alex wanted to refuse, but couldn't find a justifiable reason. That only made her feel petty, and even more annoyed. She sat down in the chair offered, working to keep a neutral expression.

"So, is it Alex or just Lex?" he finally asked.

Of course Alex knew the question would eventually come but was still caught unprepared for how uncomfortable it made her.

"Alex," she stated simply.

One of his eyebrows quirked up.

"Alex," he repeated, as though testing it out. "Are you familiar with Fortis and our work for Magnus over the last nine months?"

His professional focus was both confusing and a relief. She put her things on the table and sat back.

"You installed our new computer network, right?" Alex summarized.

Lucas looked amused by her statement, though she could not imagine what was so funny.

"Yes, we did. But we've also monitored and administered it," he added. "That's how we discovered the attempt to access files last week."

She nodded, recalling her meeting with Marco on Friday afternoon.

"So, how can I help you?" Alex asked, getting impatient.

"What's your relationship with Adam North?"

His tone was still smooth and his posture relaxed, yet Alex felt an accusation in the question. She sat forward, with her arms crossed on the table.

"What do you mean, my relationship? We brought Adam on to provide the new battery technology for the Cicada," she explained, sounding a little more defensive that she intended.

"How were you introduced to him?"

"Why?" she shot back, knowing there was more to the questions than idle curiosity.

He didn't immediately respond as he looked back at her with an unreadable expression. Alex deliberately raised her brows to remind him she was waiting for his response. He smiled, as though her attitude amused him. She tried not to glower back.

"Marco hired Fortis to protect the new technology you've been developing," he stated simply. "Until your new engine was built, we focused on the intellectual assets. The ideas, design schematics, and related notes. Anything that could be stolen and used by one of your competitors."

"I know that," Alex interjected. "But what does that have to do with Adam?"

"My team confirmed that the network intrusion we detected last week was done through North's computer."

"What? That can't be true. Why would Adam try to access our network?" she objected. "You must be mistaken. How do you know that?"

That look of tolerant amusement was back on his face.

"We know it for a fact," he replied calmly and simply. "But I didn't say that North did it. Someone used his computer for the encrypted access to your file-sharing server and planted a bug, or Trojan horse program on the Magnus system. We detected it and shut it down."

"So Adam had nothing to do with it?" she confirmed, feeling relieved. His work was too vital to the success of the Cicada design for Alex to imagine not trusting his motives.

"No. We're fairly certain he was unaware of what

happened. But someone knew enough about his work with you and Magnus, then took the time and effort to hack his system. With some sophistication, I might add," explained Lucas. "Which is why I need to understand your relationship with North. How were you introduced to him and his technology?"

Alex looked down at her fingers, resenting the necessity to reveal details about her personal life to this frustratingly attractive man who was practically a stranger.

"I first met him a couple of years ago, at a racing event. We were introduced by a friend," she explained.

"A friend?"

Alex swallowed.

"Yes, Jean Renaud."

"You're friends with Jean Renaud?" Lucas asked sitting a little higher in his chair. "French Indy car driver, Renaud?"

She shrugged.

"The racing world is small."

"Go on," he urged.

"Adam was a research professor of physics at the University of Illinois. We talked a bit at the event, and he told me a little about his work with high-capacity lithium-ion battery power," Alex told him. "After some research, it got me thinking about car applications, like in a hybrid or electric engine. So, I arranged to meet Adam again at another event last year and asked him to design a battery for the Cicada."

Lucas just listened intently, brushing an index finger slowly over his silky-looking lips. He made no attempt to make notes. Alex wanted to shift uncomfortably in her chair, but she resisted. The physical effect he had on her was very distracting.

"How do Renaud and North know each other?" he finally asked.

"I'm not sure," she replied honestly. "But Adam is a big Indy car fan, so I assume they met in the industry."

Lucas nodded, as though getting the details he needed.

"Lex, I need you to tell me what exactly your Cicada is," he stated firmly. "From what I know about hybrid vehicle technology, what I saw today on the track was pretty incredible."

Alex felt a swell of pride at his words, though she was certain he intended it as a statement of fact, not as a compliment.

"It's Alex," she pointed out.

He shrugged.

"The Cicada," he repeated.

She sighed loudly, resenting his high-handedness.

"It's a hybrid design, just more simple than currently used by the big car manufactures," she explained. "There is a small gas-powered engine that's used only for battery charging, while the electric motor powers the wheels."

"Show me," Lucas instructed, pointing to the large dry-erase board mounted on the far wall of the room.

"All right."

Alex stood up and grabbed a black erasable marker from the small container mounted to the wall. At the whiteboard, she drew a simple diagram of the drivetrain mechanism behind her design.

"Almost all successful hybrids use both the gas and electric motors to run the car, switching as needed when the electric battery runs out," she explained. "But that's because the electric batteries are so heavy, and have limited range per charge. The best on the market can go four hundred, maybe five hundred miles, max, then need hours to charge. So dual-powered drivetrains are a good compromise, providing a longer driving range than pure electric cars, and more fuel efficiency than gas cars.

"But their batteries are still heavy and expensive, and speed is limited, right?" she continued.

"So, what's different with yours?" he asked.

"The high-capacity battery attached to the series design," she told him simply. "Adam's rechargeable battery is smaller, lighter, and more durable than anything used in cars today. My electric motor is more powerful than almost all in production, providing consistent speed in flat and hilly terrain. Together, they have the torque and horsepower typically found in high-performance engines, with long-range capacity per charge. Just based on what we did today, I think we could eventually get zero-to-sixty in under three seconds, with top speeds north of two hundred miles an hour."

Alex wrote out the numbers on the whiteboard and circled each passionately.

"And that's just the racing application," she added, tossing the marker on the table. "With the right configuration, my computer models project that you could drive coast to coast at a hundred miles an hour on a single tank of gas and never need a plug-in recharge."

"How?" Lucas asked, now leaning forward with his elbows on his knees and his hands clasped loosely between his knees.

"Once the gas-combustion engine is ignited by the battery, its only function is to charge the battery, for ten to fifteen minutes every five to six hundred miles. With the right-size gas tank, a car could easily do four thousand miles."

He looked at her rough sketch and the circled numbers for well over a minute. Alex sat back down about thirty seconds into his silent contemplation. The impact of her statement seemed to fill the air with thick tension.

"Who else knows all of this?" Lucas finally asked, pinning her with a sharp, assessing stare. There was no trace of his casual flirtatiousness.

"Marco, of course. And my team is now helping me with the final calibrations," she stated.

"How much does North know?"

"Adam knows that Magnus makes racing components, and that I'm trying out electric motor designs," she explained. "He's also aware that we're planning to launch it at the Sea-to-Sky Highway race. But I haven't told him anything else."

"Why not?"

"Marco and I decided not to tell anyone else about the potential for broader use in passenger cars, not even our investors. We've also only told them about the racing applications."

"Well, someone knows something. And it seems that they're going out of their way to steal it," he stated in a deceptively soft tone. "Any suggestions?"

"No, I don't have any. I mean, I've been concerned about something like this from the moment

I gave Marco my proposal. And I've been racking my brain since Friday trying to think of anyone else who could know what we've been working on. I just don't know."

Lucas stood up and walked the few steps over to the room door, where he planted himself in a wide stance and crossed his arms across his chest. Alex knew she wasn't going to like the direction of the conversation. She stood also.

"What does North get out of this deal? Why sell his design to you versus a company with deeper pockets? No offense to Magnus, of course."

"Adam is a professor. His focus has been solely publishing his research to academia. I had to really encourage him to build us a power pack and sell us the patent, and we paid him a good amount for it," Alex explained. "In his nondisclosure agreement, he's then able to publish the results of the battery performance of the Cicada three months after its official launch."

"What would happen if he broke the NDA?"

"We would sue him for damages. It would be millions, and would ruin his reputation."

Lucas nodded.

"What about your team?" he asked.

"What about them?" she shot back obstinately, planting her hands on her hips.

He stared back at her hard, letting her know he wasn't buying her sudden obtuseness.

"Could they have leaked information somehow?" Lucas finally added, still pinning her with his unwavering stare.

"No," Alex replied firmly and unflinchingly.

He lowered his arms to plant them on his hips.

"Alex, I know it's hard to look at the people you work with every day suspiciously," Lucas added softly. "But I need you to be completely objective here. Are there any risks among your other engineers?"

His tone felt patronizing and hit all of her buttons. She could not hold back a snarky response.

"What exactly makes you think I'm not being objective?" She took a step forward.

She waved her hands in front of him. He raised that annoying brow again.

"Is it my height?" Alex demanded.

"Alex—"

"Ahh," she cut in dramatically, snapping her fingers. "I know! It's the breasts, isn't it?"

"That's—"

She ignored his exasperated sigh.

"These damn boobs! Always interrupting my rational thoughts. Forcing me to get all emotional and incapable of logical reasoning," continued Alex in a tone dripping with sarcasm, stepping even closer to him until they were only an arm's length apart.

The mounds of flesh referenced were bound and secured behind a heavy-duty sports bra, and well hidden in the baggy, heavy cotton overalls, but she noted with satisfaction that his gaze fixed on them like they were naked. Until she forcefully crossed her arms in front of her chest, and Lucas raised his eyes again to meet hers. Finally, there was something more than calm amusement in his dark brown depths.

"They are very distracting, but I'm sure you manage just fine, Lex," he retorted in a bland voice. "Now, just answer the question. Or have you forgotten it already?"

Alex glared and clenched her jaw hard as she stepped right up beside him, until her side was almost brushing his. He towered her by a good ten inches, but she refused to be bullied by his size and pretty-boy charm.

"There is no risk that someone on my team could have leaked information. They didn't know anything of value until this morning. All they knew is that we were working on a hybrid to win at Sea-to-Sky Highway," she snapped in clipped words. "And my name is Alex."

Done with him, Alex made for the conference room door in long, firm strides, but was stopped abruptly by a firm grip on her upper arm. She gasped in surprise and spun around in reflex to attack him with her free arm, but Lucas swiftly and easily caught that one as well. He pulled her up to him until their bodies were almost flush and his head was bent low next to hers.

"Lex suits you much better," he whispered into her ear before abruptly letting her go.

She shot him a final, scathing glare then marched out of the room.

CHAPTER 6

Lance, Ned, and Michael arrived at the Toronto Island Airport on Tuesday morning. They had hitched a ride on a cargo flight, needing room for several large aluminum cases with the equipment required for the Magnus job. Lucas met them on the tarmac with a large black SUV that he had rented last night, and ferried over from the city.

The men greeted him with wide grins and hand slaps.

"Raymond looked pretty disappointed that he wasn't coming along," Ned stated as they worked to load up the back of the truck with their cases. "I think he's bored out of his mind on Sam's bodyguard job."

"Yeah," Michael piped in. "The client's daughter is a real piece of work. She's barely eighteen and all over Sam like a cheap suit. Maybe Ray's worried that once she finally gives up on Sam, she'll set her sights on him."

The guys all laughed. Raymond was a brilliant tech wizard and decent as an agent in the field, but he was a classic introvert and not at all equipped to deal with an aggressive crush-obsessed adolescent girl.

"Poor guy," Lucas sympathized. "He's probably having nightmares about it."

"Or maybe his disappointment has more to do with what he's missing out on here, huh, Luc," Ned speculated. "Based on the pics in the case folder you sent last night, Alex Cotts is pretty easy on the eyes. Maybe they had some kind of connection when he was here in Toronto last fall."

"Nope. Cotts was out of town when Raymond set up their network security," replied Lucas in an easy voice. "And she's definitely more than our Raymond could handle."

The other three men raised eyebrows and looked at each other speculatively.

"Sounds like a handful," scoffed Michael.

"And then some," Lucas muttered, more to himself than anyone else. "I'll fill you guys in on the drive to the auto shop."

They quickly finished loading up the truck.

"What about customs and our weapons?" Lance asked once they were all seated and Lucas was driving away from the runway.

"All taken care of," Lucas told them. "Fortis is a registered private security and investigation firm in all ten provinces and three territories, and a specialized contractor to the Canadian government. I arranged your clearance in advance."

"Nice!" Michael replied. "I guess Secret Service contacts are still useful."

"Occasionally," chuckled Lucas.

The ferry ride and drive into downtown Toronto took them around thirty minutes. Lucas used some of that time to review the key facts about Magnus and their Cicada engine that he had provided in the case folder. It was a few minutes to ten o'clock in the morning when Lucas drove the large SUV around to the rear side of the Magnus Motorsports auto shop. He reversed into the open spot closest to the large open garage bay, parking close to the sleek gray Porsche with matte black rims and hot red brake calipers.

"We have a room that we can set up as our control center, so let's get unpacked," he told the team. "I want a plan confirmed by twelve hundred hours."

A couple of Magnus mechanics stepped outside from the shop floor with coffee cups and packs of cigarettes just as the four big men filed out of the SUV. All the agents were dressed in black with full-size handguns clipped into shoulder holsters worn over their shirts. The mechanics froze with looks of alarm on their faces.

"Morning," Lucas said smoothly with a nod as he strode by them toward the garage bay at the center of the building, carrying two of the equipment cases. Lance and Ned followed in a single line, similarly loaded up, with Michael in the rear carrying the last case, with only their personal luggage left behind in the trunk.

Lucas could feel almost a dozen eyes following him and his men as they walked through the shop floor to the entrance to Magnus's offices. One pair of eyes in particular felt so hot that it might singe his flesh. But he resisted the pull to look back at Alex as she stood with the other racing engineers in the right side of the shop. He had been much too distracted by her already over the last day and a half as it was.

The Fortis team was entering the small conference room given to Lucas just as Norma and Marco came through the doors to the showroom at the front of the building. Their client and his assistant stopped short, with very similar expressions of alarm as everyone else in the building.

"Marco, Norma, this is the Fortis team that will be on the ground for you," Lucas stated in an easy, casual voice that was at odds with the armed presence now lined up behind him inside the small room. "Lance and Ned will provide security detail, and Michael will work with me on the investigation."

Each of the other agents nodded when their names were mentioned, even as they began opening the large cases to unpack the contents.

"You're wearing guns," Norma stated as though she couldn't quite understand what was going on.

"Are those legal? Are you allowed to wear them?" added Marco, pointing at the weapon Lucas had not been wearing yesterday.

"I assure you, all our weapons are licensed and very legal," Lucas told them both in the same calm voice.

"Is this necessary?" Alex demanded as she marched up the hall with indignation written all over her face. Lucas couldn't help but notice how cute she looked, all agitated. "You can't just walk around strapped to the teeth."

Lucas tried to keep his lips still to suppress a grin.

"It is and we can," he replied briefly.

Her mouth hung open, as though his explanation meant nothing.

"Who are you people, anyway? It's not Texas, you know. This is Canada!"

"I know where I am, Cotts, but thanks for the reminder," he shot back quietly before turning to Marco and his assistant. "Marco, I'll need ninety minutes with my men to get situated. Can I provide you a review of our plan by, say, one o'clock?"

"Sure, that's fine," Marco told him, swallowing tightly.

"I will be there also," Alex demanded, practically vibrating with frustration.

"As you'd like," he told her politely before he walked into the meeting room leaving the door open.

"Did you know anything about this, Markie?" he heard her asking her boss from a short distance down the hall. Marco's response was too quiet for Lucas to hear as they walked away.

"You weren't kidding," Michael quipped, barely looking up from his task of setting up a high-capacity computer system at the far end of the conference room table. "She's definitely a handful."

The other men snickered, but Lucas ignored them. He was too busy trying to figure out how to get rid of the energy and anticipation that swept down his back every time that damn woman was anywhere near his vicinity. Sure, she was cute, and those golden eyes were captivating, but he usually preferred his women with dispositions more like his own: light-hearted and easygoing. Alexandria

Cotts was proving to be as easygoing as a territorial panther.

The Fortis men worked in silence to set up all the equipment they had brought with them for the assignment, then stacked the empty aluminum boxes along the back wall, out of their way. There were two powerful, dual-core computers connected to an ultra-high-speed router with an untraceable, ricocheting IP address. They also had a storage and backup server stack, configured with a new Fortis security encryption algorithm designed by Lucas. The last couple of boxes had the latest in digital laser technology surveillance equipment, and locked cases with extra handguns and ammunition, just in case.

"Okay, we'll work in two teams," Lucas stated to Lance, Ned, and Michael as he stood in front of a large map of the Magnus building with schematics posted on the wall of the room. "Building security will be in twelve-hour shifts, six to six each day. Lance, you take days; Ned, you take nights with their regular security guard, Oliver."

Lance and Ned nodded.

"You'll follow the our standard security pattern, so each of you will rotate your surveillance position in thirty minute intervals, altered by seven minutes every four hours, reset on a five-day cycle. We'll do a full sweep to make sure there are no bugs or listening devices planted. Then we'll wire up the building with external and internal surveillance cameras, using sensors at night," Lucas continued, circling the connection points on the building map. "Michael, you'll be monitoring everyone who comes within a mile of the building, using my facial-mapping search engine. Anyone we can't identify through social media will be tagged as a potential threat. I will focus on trying to find out who's funding our friend Pratt, and monitoring the network for any new intrusion attempts. Questions?"

There was a moment of silence as Lucas looked to confirm that everyone was clear on the instructions, though he knew it would be. It was a pretty basic plan.

"Hopefully, this will be the easiest assignment we've had in a couple of years, and we're just over-dressed for the party," he finally added.

"But you don't think so," responded Ned. It was a statement, not a question.

The two men had met during their time in the Financial Crimes division of the United States Secret Service. While Ned was a special agent assigned to investigative work, Lucas worked as a systems security consultant for protection against financial crimes. They had seen enough similar patterns during their careers to know when something noteworthy was in the works.

"No, I don't," Lucas finally confirmed. "Someone wants this Cicada technology, and they are too invested already to just walk away. Now, the only way to get the information they want is right here is this building. I'd rather figure out who it is before they show up at our doorstep to try to take it."

Lucas walked over to one of the two computers on the table and pulled up pictures of two men.

"We have two targets to start our investigation," he stated, clicking on the image of a tall, slender, ruddy-skinned man wearing a gray cardigan and blue plaid shirt, carrying a messenger bag strapped across his chest. "Adam North, thirty-five-year-old associate professor of physics at the University of Illinois, Chicago. He designed the battery for the Cicada engine. Since our visit to Chicago last week, we confirmed he was unaware of Pratt's hack into his computer. We also know that Pratt pretended to be a student at the university to gain access.

"What we don't know is how Pratt and whoever is funding him knew what North was working on for Magnus. He's married, no children, and lives a pretty routine life from what we've seen so far."

"Who's the second guy?" Michael asked, since the details about North were already in the case file they read during the trip to Toronto.

Lucas pulled up the second image of a smaller man with wavy black hair, blues eyes, tanned skin and a boyish smile. The shoulder of his racing suit was visible in the picture, with various logos covering the front.

"Is that Jean Renaud, the race car driver?" Ned guessed, leaning forward to be sure.

"One and the same," Lucas confirmed. "Twenty-nine years old, French-born Indy Car driver, winner of the Daytona 500 two year ago. Cotts confirmed yesterday that she was introduced to North through Renaud at a racing event, also two years ago."

Lucas clicked on another file on the computer desktop and another series of pictures came up of a couple in various kinds of public displays of affection. The most intimate was a very deep kiss at a winner's podium while Jean Renaud held up a large trophy.

"What Alex hadn't mentioned was that she and Renaud had dated for over a year," he added, zooming in on the face of the Magnus lead engineer in the arms of the race car driver. In the picture, she looked sexy and glamorous.

"You think Renaud has something to do with all this?" Lance asked.

"That's the first thing we have to find out," Lucas replied softly. "Based on what I found last night, I'd say they stopped seeing each other sometime last fall."

"So, Cotts shares her design ideas with her boyfriend who's in the racing industry, then he sells her out when they break up?" suggested Michael.

"I've seen far worse from an ex-lover," replied Lucas. "And it gives us motive and opportunity. Renaud knows cars. If both Cotts and North told him about their individual work, he would definitely see the bigger potential, and he has the sponsors and contacts in the industry who would pay big for the information. If we can connect Pratt and Renaud to the same contact, we'll know the threat."

"Sound like a plan," Michael summarized, slapping his hand on the table.

The other agents voiced similar confirmations.

"Good. I'm meeting with Marco and Alex now, then we'll get the perimeter hooked up after lunch."

"Alex?" Ned questioned with raised brows.

Lucas cringed inside, suddenly aware of his unintended slip.

"Cotts," he growled back, ignoring a knowing light in his friend's eyes and telling himself that

Ned could speculate about insignificant things all he wanted, it didn't mean anything.

Lucas walked into Marco's office through the open door a few moments later and found Alex alone in there, leaning against the back window and looking outside. Her mass of jet-black dreadlocks was pulled back into a high ponytail at the crown of her head, revealing the striking contours of her cheeks and jawline. She looked incredibly young and fragile, swallowed up the shapelessness of her gray overalls.

"Sorry, I came to see if Marco was available for an update," he stated once she finally noticed his presence.

Her shoulders straightened and her full lips flattened with annoyance.

"He's just finishing with a customer," she stated stiffly.

"Okay, let him know I'm available whenever he is," Lucas told her, then turned to leave.

"Wait," she demanded as she strode across Marco's office. "You didn't answer my question. Who are you people? How does a network security consultant get to walk around on the streets all strapped with guns?"

Alex stopped with her arms crossed defensively across her chest and her hip cocked to one side. Lucas decided to draw on his natural, persuasive charm in an attempt to disarm her. Getting the job done would be a lot easier with her cooperation. And he wouldn't mind reacquainting with the sexy, playful Alex he had met on Sunday night.

"Systems security is just part of what we do," he

explained smoothly. "Fortis specializes in all aspects of asset security, protection, and recovery. Our agents are the best trained in the world in our field."

"Trained how? For what?"

Lucas walked out of the room into the hall between the offices and gestured for Alex to follow him. She hesitated for a moment, then went along. He stopped in front of the newly constructed Fortis control center so that she could see each of the three men inside as they worked on their individual tasks.

"We recruited Michael out of the FBI two years ago," he stated, pointing to the youngest of the three men. "He was the best in his class in investigative science at the academy, then spent four years in the field working kidnap and hostage cases.

"The big guy with blond hair is Lance Campbell, former Army Ranger, specialist in close contact combat. I'm not sure if he's ever even fired a gun outside of training," Lucas told her with a smile. "The last guy is Ned Bushby. He and I met ten years ago in the Secret Service. He was a special agent in the fraud and cybercrime division."

He watched Alex looking over the men speculatively before she finally looked up at him.

"And you?" she finally asked. "You were a Secret Service agent, too?"

"Definitely not!" he replied with a sharp laugh. "Way too many rules for me. I was a consultant to the various government agencies for a few years, including the Secret Service. My training was more cerebral than theirs. But don't worry, I picked up a few physical skills along the way."

There was a hint of a smile on her lips, but they were interrupted before he could have enough time to enjoy it.

"Sorry to keep you waiting," Marco stated as he walked toward his office. "I just had a couple of customer issues to deal with."

"No worries," Lucas replied as he and Alex joined Marco, each taking a seat in one of the chairs in front of his desk. "It hasn't been long. My men are now working on getting your building set up with our full security program. We'll be ready to implement for tonight."

"Okay, okay," Marco said, nodding. "That's good."

"It's everything I had outlined in my proposal from last week," continued Lucas, making sure to direct his attention to both Alex and Marco. "Twenty-four-hour manned security outside, in addition to your night security guard inside. We're adding digital surveillance around the outside of the building, with motion sensors for after hours."

"What about the weapons?" Marco asked. "You didn't mention those in your recommendations."

"No, I didn't. But that was before I understood the potential risks to your assets," Lucas stated calmly. "Right now, they are just a precaution. My team will wear them at all times. It's not negotiable. But they will be concealed outside of the offices and shop floor, so your customers will not be aware that we're armed."

Marco looked as though he was about to argue the fact, but then he sighed and relaxed.

"Okay, I suppose that will be fine," he finally conceded.

"Good."

"What about the guys?" Alex asked, sitting forward in her chair. "They're pretty freaked out about a team of armed men lurking around. We have to tell them something, Markie."

"I'm happy to meet with your employees to explain our presence. Depending on how much you want them to know, of course," Lucas suggested.

Marco nodded, accepting the offer.

"I'm sure we can set a quick staff meeting this afternoon."

They were interrupted by a beep and vibration from Lucas's phone, held in the breast pocket of his shirt. He immediately pulled it out to read the message, then stood up.

"Excuse me, I have to make a call. But go ahead and set up a time for me to talk to your people later."

He strode out of the room while calling the direct line to one of his employees at the Fortis headquarters on speed dial.

"What do you have, Laura?"

"I finally have something useful from that spy software you left on Pratt's computer on Friday. From the instant message he's just opened, it looks like he's about to get cut off by his sponsors," said Laura Speedman, one of several operations analysts in the Alexandria, Virginia office who worked on special research and investigative projects. "They're using a free dating site to communicate and I can't get a lock on the other user. If we're going to find out anything useful from Pratt, it's now or never."

"How much time do we have?" Lucas asked as he walked into the on-site control center.

"Less than twenty-four hours. He's confirmed a meeting for eleven o'clock tomorrow morning, central time; twelve o'clock eastern."

"Where?"

"Not communicated yet."

"Okay, keep me updated. We need to be there for that meeting."

CHAPTER 7

Through Tuesday afternoon, the Fortis team implemented their plans. While Lucas set up the upgraded server equipment and implemented even more strict data storage protocols, Lance, Ned, and Michael swept the property for any hidden bugs and installed the new surveillance equipment.

At three o'clock, Alex and Marco gathered all of the Magnus employees on an open area on the shop floor so that Marco and Lucas could introduce them to the Fortis team.

"Guys, I'm sure you all notice the small security team that arrived this morning," Marco said to kick off the brief meeting. "They're with a company called Fortis, and I've hired them to provide some extra security as we prepare for the summer racing season. I'll let the Fortis team tell you more."

Marco looked over at Lucas and nodded, which was Lucas's cue to begin. "Hi, everyone, I'm Lucas Johnson. This is Michael, Lance, and Ned," he stated in an even, casual tone, pointing to each man as they each nodded in turn to the small audience. "As Marco said, we're here to provide on-site security for the building and equipment, and will in no way interfere with your work. I know there is some concern about the fact that we are armed, something we understand is unusual for you to see. It is a precautionary measure, but standard for the services we provide, and they will be concealed in front of your customers. But I can assure you that you have no need to worry. We are all licensed and well-trained marksmen. Within a couple of days, you won't notice we are here.

"Any questions?" he asked, but the twenty people just looked around at each other. "All right, then. If you do think of something, don't hesitate to let me or one of the agents know."

The small gathering quickly dissipated as everyone returned to their jobs, until only Lucas, Marco, and Alex remained.

"Thanks for that," Marco said, looking much more relaxed than he did a few hours earlier. "At least now, they can stop speculating about the situation and get back to work."

"No problem at all," replied Lucas pleasantly. "Was that the reaction you were expecting?"

He directed the question to Alex, since she had been the most concerned about the other employees.

"They were a little quieter than I expected, but I'm sure they'll eventually speak up if they want to know anything more," she admitted.

Lucas smiled easily down at her, noting that her

body language was far less guarded than in their previous encounters.

"While I have you both here, I have an update that you should be aware of," Lucas told them. "We have a lead on whoever tried to get into your network. I'm taking Lance with me tonight to check it out. We'll be gone for about twenty-four hours."

"What did you find out?" Marco asked, looking hopeful and alarmed at the same time.

"Nothing specific yet, but I'll know more by to-morrow," explained Lucas, unwilling to share too much until he had some concrete information. "Michael and Ned will stay here and we'll start our security detail as planned. But here is my personal cell phone number so that you can reach me if needed."

He took two of the Fortis business cards out of his pocket and handed one to each of them.

"Okay. Well, I hope you find something useful," said Marco with a sigh. "I'd feel much more excited about this project if we didn't have to worry about who's trying to steal it. Excuse me."

Just then, Marco's cell phone started ringing. Lucas and Alex watched him walk out of the shop floor to take the call, then they looked at each other. There was an awkward pause.

"I'm sure you're very busy, so I'll leave you to it," Lucas finally told her.

"Wait," she stated as he turned and was walking away, then she fell in step beside him. "I'm going to get a cup of coffee, if you have a minute."

It sounded like she was inviting him to go with her, but it was so unexpected that Lucas hesitated to follow her. Until she looked back over her shoulder, now from a couple of steps ahead of him. He then walked behind her in silence until they reached a small kitchen. It was stocked with a fresh pot of coffee, a rack of white coffee mugs, sugar packets, and stir sticks.

"Do you want one?" she asked as she poured the rich, fragrant coffee into a cup.

"Sure," Lucas accepted graciously, then watched patiently as she poured a second cup.

"How do you take it?"

Alex opened the compact fridge built in under the counter and took out a carton of half-and-half milk.

"Cream and sugar, thanks."

She added the ingredients, than handed him his drink.

"I want to apologize for my behavior since you arrived," she finally stated after they had both taken a couple of large sips. "I'm not usually so uptight."

Lucas only listened, not willing to test the statement.

"But I guess this whole situation has just caught me off guard," she continued, her eyes fixed on the black contents of her cup. "I just can't believe that there is such a threat to the company. I feel responsible."

The last statement was made just above a whisper.

"You're not responsible for any of this, Alex," Lucas immediately replied.

"Of course I am," she insisted. "I'm the one who decided to push the boundaries, work outside of the box. And look where it's gotten us. What if I can't even deliver on the forecast? Then all this will be for nothing."

She swept her hand in his general direction, clearly referring to the presence of his team.

"My dad always said that I better learn my limits or I'd wind up in a situation I couldn't handle."

"I don't know. You seem to be handling yourself just fine," he countered, trying to erase the forlorn look on her face.

"Yeah? Well, it must be these designer power suits I wear every day," retorted Alex, but it was laced with humor. "Anyway, I just wanted you to know that I appreciate your work for us and I'll cooperate any way I can."

"All right then," Lucas stated softly. "Why don't you tell me about your relationship with Jean Renaud?"

She blinked a little, but otherwise didn't react, which told Lucas that she wasn't surprised that he knew.

"What do you want to know?"

"Are you guys still seeing each other?"

"No. We ended our relationship last September. We spoke a few times before Christmas, but I haven't seen him since," she replied simply, then took a long drink of her coffee.

"Was the breakup amicable?"

She looked at him steadily for a few seconds, and Lucas could see her brain working through the deep brown pools of her eyes.

"You want to know if he might have something to do with this whole thing? That if things ended badly between us, then maybe he's behind the leak of information?"

She didn't miss much, Lucas thought to himself, a little impressed.

"It's a plausible theory," he replied with a shrug.

"But not a viable one," she countered. "Jean and I never discussed my work. I don't think he even knew what I did for Magnus, to be honest."

"How is that possible?"

It was her turn to shrug.

"We met at an industry event, and he just assumed I was a racing fan like every other woman who wanted to meet him."

"And you never told him different?" asked Lucas, trying to understand her thinking. "How long were you guys together?"

"About a year and a half. It never came up. What difference would it make?" Alex countered. "We met, we had a connection that led to a thing for a while. That's it."

She turned to the sink and began washing out her now-empty mug.

"You didn't want him to know that you're an automotive engineer," he finally stated.

"Why wouldn't I?" she attempted to dismiss, but her back was still to him.

"I don't know. That's what I'm trying to figure out."

"Well, you're wasting your time," she stated with a tolerant smile when she turned back to face him. "Jean has nothing to do with any of this. We had a long distance thing until it wasn't convenient anymore. No messy breakup, no hurt feelings. He didn't even know that I had connected with Adam."

Lucas nodded in understanding.

"Thanks for clearing that up."

"Glad I could help." There was another pause where they both just looked at each other.

"Well, I have to get back to work," she finally stated. "Good luck with that lead you have."

"Thanks," replied Lucas as he watched her walk away.

A couple of hours later, he and Lance were on a commercial flight to Chicago with a plan to catch Timothy Pratt connecting with whomever was sponsoring his attempt to hack the Magnus computer system. Laura had confirmed the location of the meet at a deli in the southern end of the city, about two miles from Pratt's apartment. Lucas designed a plan for a small team to have eyes and ears on whom Pratt spoke to and what information was passed on.

When Lucas and Lance arrived at a small budget hotel facing Pratt's apartment, it was almost eight thirty, and the third member of their tactical team was already checked into their room.

"Ice," Lucas called out in welcome to Evan DaCosta. "When did you arrive?"

"About an hour ago," Evan replied as he shook hands with each of the men. The nickname "Ice" was a remnant from his former career as a field agent in the Protective Services division of the Central Intelligence Agency.

Lucas and Lance dropped their overnight bags on the ground.

"Anything to report?" asked Lucas.

"Nope. Pratt's at home, watching television," Evan confirmed, pointing to the long-range binoculars mounted on a tripod in front of the window. "The place is still a mess, but he's packed up some of his personal things."

Lucas walked across the room and took a look through the binocular viewfinder. Their subject was standing in the kitchen talking on his cell phone.

"Any more intel from the computer or cell phone activity?" continued Lucas.

"Nope, nothing new," replied Evan. "He talked to a small number of people in Maryland including his family and a couple of friends from college and his Best Buy job. No additional message on the dating site to the contact."

"Well, hopefully we'll get a solid piece of intel tomorrow to identify who's trying to steal the Magnus technology," Lucas concluded.

"Yeah, well, every one of the big car manufacturers have similar research and development projects on the go. So it will be interesting to see how they'll respond once the Magnus hybrid is officially revealed," Lucas pondered. "There is certainly incentive for one of them to steal it if they can."

"Let's hope it's one of the manufacturers," Lance added as he stood between the two other men with his arms crossed across his chest. "Just with the fuel efficiency projected, the impact to gas consumption is massive. Like, industry-changing massive. So we better hope it's just one of the car companies that knows about this. Because an oil company won't just want to steal it, they'd want to bury it, and anyone who can recreate it."

The three men looked at each other. Lance had just stated exactly what Lucas and his partners had been thinking. "All right, let's grab some grub," Lucas stated to cut the tension. "I'm starving."

"I'll go pick up some food from that restaurant we passed down the block," offered Lance. "What do you guys want?"

Lucas and Evan both ordered steak, done rare with whatever came on the side.

"How's Nia doing?" Lucas asked once Lance had left.

Nia James was Evan's girlfriend, a burgeoning singer-songwriter who had just relocated from Boston to live with Evan in Alexandria.

Evan smiled, looking very satisfied with life.

"Nia's good," he said simply. He wasn't the most talkative guy. "She's going to Detroit this weekend. One of her cousins is getting married this summer, and Nia's helping with some of the planning."

"Really?" Lucas asked, surprised. "I thought she wasn't very close to her family."

Evan had met Nia last year during a mission in Boston to recover millions of dollars in rare jewels that were stolen from the auction house where she worked at the time.

"She wasn't until her mom got sick and Nia went to visit her last fall. They've been communicating more ever since."

"That's good, right?"

"Yeah," Evan agreed. "Nia was pretty cautious at first, uncertain of what the relationship would be like. But now, she seems calmer, less guarded. It's a good thing."

Lance returned a short time later with their meals.

"Hey, do either of you know a good house-cleaning service," Lucas asked while they ate dinner.

Lance shook his head.

"Nia fired mine once she moved in, preferring to do it herself," Evan explained. "Why?"

"I have a woman who's supposed to clean the house for me while I'm traveling, but she's been pretty flaky over the last couple of months," replied Lucas with annoyance. "She's through a service. I'll just call them and get someone else."

"Why don't you hire a house sitter when you're gone," suggested Lance. "That's what I do."

"I would if I had dogs, like you," Lucas agreed. "But my neighbors do a good job keeping an eye on things. I just need the plants watered once a week."

"Maybe my mom's housekeeper, Agnes, will know someone," added Evan.

"It's not urgent, but let me know," Lucas told him.

The men finished eating, then began a meticulous prep of the weapons and equipment needed for their mission in the morning. Without knowing whom Pratt was meeting, they were prepared for anything. Their subject remained quiet in his apartment.

Wednesday morning, Lucas was up by five o'clock and out the door for a long run. It was an opportunity to map out the route from Pratt's apartment to the meeting coordinates, and the vicinity around it. When he got back to the hotel room with coffee and bagels, he, Evan, and Lance finalized their strategy to spy on the meet. At ten o'clock, one hour before the scheduled meet, Lance and Lucas left the room, armed with several of their favorite concealed weapons. Lance headed to the deli, where he would be seated fifteen minutes before eleven o'clock and he'd order a late breakfast. He would get access to an empty ketchup bottle, to add a small listening device. Then when Pratt was seated, either alone or with whomever he was meeting, Lance would simply ask for their fuller bottle of ketchup, leaving the empty wired one behind.

Lucas took the rental car that Evan had picked up the day before, and parked in a spot on the street across from the deli where he could have eyes on the entrance and everything nearby. Evan stayed at the hotel until Pratt left his apartment, then would follow the target to the meet, dressed as a jogger wearing a hoodie, and with his pistol tucked into a back belt holster. All three of them had wireless earpieces, connected to Laura at the Fortis headquarters.

Everything went like clockwork until Pratt was seated at a booth in the deli.

"All looks good inside, Lance?" asked Laura at ten minutes after eleven o'clock.

"Yup. Pratt's starting to get a little anxious, but it's quiet in here," Lance told them in whispered tones.

"I see a suspect about to enter," Lucas announced from his vantage point in the car across the street. "Slender guy, brown hair. That jacket looks a little thicker than needed for the temperature today."

"I got him," Lance confirmed a few seconds later. "He's just sat down beside Pratt. I'm going to plant the bug."

The team waited, listening to Lance's movements for a few seconds.

"Shit! Something's wrong!" muttered Lance. "Pratt's body just jerked forward. I think he's been shot and our guy's on the move!"

"I got him," Evan stated from his position two stores down from the restaurant.

"I'm with you," Lucas added as he threw aside the binoculars and jumped out of the car.

The shooter was walking swiftly away from the scene, cautious of his surroundings but trying to look inconspicuous. Lucas and Evan looked at each other, with a silent plan to get close enough to the suspect without tipping him.

"The suspect is armed, with a silencer," Lance stated through the earpiece. "Pratt's been shot in the side. He's bleeding out pretty fast."

"I've called an ambulance, Lance," Laura told him. "Can he talk? Has he said anything?"

Lucas listened to chatter but his focus was on their suspect. For sure, there was a getaway car parked somewhere nearby. Lucas and Evan had to take him down before then, or they would lose him. Both men picked up their speed, until Evan was just a couple of people behind him, and Lucas was almost parallel on the opposite side of the street. Suddenly, their target looked backward and spotted Evan, paused for a second, then started running. Lucas and Evan immediately burst into full sprints.

"He's made Ice, and he's now running down West Taylor Street," Lucas told Lance and Laura. "Ice's almost on him. They've just turned right on South Loomis."

Lucas cut across the street, dodging traffic and ignoring the blare of horns from annoyed drivers. He kept his eyes fixed on the shooter whom Evan had just reached about a block up, grabbing the man by the jacket and shoving him face first into the brick wall of a store.

"Who are you working for?" Lucas heard Evan demand.

The suspect grunted, shoving his elbow into Evan's stomach. They started grappling, with Evan trying to restrain his arms and the assailant trying to break free in order to reach his gun.

Lucas ran up on them within a few seconds, then skidded to a halt as tires squealed from farther up the street.

"Ice, I think we have company," he announced loudly.

It was a black sedan with Illinois plates and only a driver inside, and it was coming up on them fast. Lucas saw the arm coming out of the driver's window, but was already prepared for what he knew was coming. He was running for cover in a store doorway, with his gun drawn and pointed at the right side of the front windshield.

"Gun," he yelled at Evan, and squeezed off two shots before ducking for cover.

Four bullets splintered the bricks near his head. More gunshots went off nearby.

"Shit!" Evan muttered into his earpiece, followed by heavy breathing and more scuffling.

Lucas quickly leaned forward, firing two more shots into the windshield. He could see Evan rolling to a safe spot behind a parked car, but their suspect was now free and scrambling to the door of the sedan. Lucas took aim at him, then felt the burning pain of a bullet as it sliced through the flesh at the top of his right shoulder. He clenched his teeth and fired at the target. First shot. The car was pulling away, tires squealing. Second shot. The suspect had a gun pointed out the passenger window aimed right at his chest. Third shot. Lucas felt the heat of the shooter's bullet as it whizzed past him, hitting the brick behind him. He also heard Evan beside him, also shooting a series of bullets back at the getaway car, now speeding down South Loomis Street.

CHAPTER 8

"Hey, Alex."

It was eight thirty on Thursday morning, and Alex had been working over an hour already. She looked up to find Marco standing at the doorway of her office.

"Hey, Markie," she replied with a smile. "What's up?"

"I spoke to Lucas last night," he started, but she could tell by the look on his face that it wasn't good news. "His lead didn't pan out yesterday. They weren't able to find out who tried to hack our system."

Alex let out a big sigh. She had tried not to get her hopes up, but it was still very disappointing news.

"Okay. Thanks for letting me know," she told him.

But instead of walking away, Marco hesitated then walked farther into her office.

"There is something else," he stated, clearly uncomfortable with what he needed to tell her.

"What, Markie?" Alex demanded. "What's going on?"

She stood up and walked over to her boss.

"Nothing, nothing . . ." He cleared his throat and shoved his hands in his pants pocket. "It's just that Lucas is recommending a security detail for you."

"What? Why?" she demanded.

"He's doing some work with his team right now, but I'm sure he'll explain more when he's free," Marco explained.

"Markie, this is ridiculous!" she insisted. "Why would I need a bodyguard?"

"Alex, the design is in your head as much as it is in the computer or installed in the Evo. You're the only one who understands why it works, end to end. You know that," he detailed with a sigh. "So, Lucas considers you one of the assets."

"I'm a person, not an asset!" countered Alex. "I can't be treated like an engine part. This whole thing is completely out of control, now. I know we have to be cautious and protect the Cicada design. I get that, I do. But armed security? Now a personal bodyguard for me? Come on!"

Marco shrugged with his hands up in the air, suggesting he had nothing to say.

"I know it seems as though things have gotten really serious really fast, but there's just too much at stake not to take precautions, Alex," he finally told her. "You know what this technology could mean for the car industry. For you, for this company. We have to do whatever it takes to protect it until the launch."

"Of course I agree with that, Marco," Alex replied with a sigh. "But I don't think we should just follow this Fortis company blindly, doing whatever they tell us to do without question. I mean, what do we even know about them anyway?"

"Alex, they've come very highly recommended. From what I've been told, they get the job done," Marco told her.

"I'm sure they do. But at what cost? How do you know they aren't just exaggerating the threat to pad their bill?"

"Oh come on, Alex," he scoffed.

"What? It happens. These military types always use fear to push their agenda," Alex shot back, with her arms planted on her hips.

"Okay, you've been watching too much television," chuckled Marco. "But in case you're serious, I can assure you that they have no agenda other than completing their job. And they're job is to secure and protect the Cicada until we officially launch it in June. They don't get paid until then, and then they only bill for the work required to complete the job."

Alex thought through what her boss was telling her, and felt some of her indignation melting away.

"That's an interesting arrangement. How did you negotiate that?" she finally asked, grudgingly.

"I didn't. That's their standard contract," he clarified. "They do whatever is needed to deliver, then only bill for what was required. So if all of this extra security isn't necessary in the end, they don't get paid for it."

Alex looked at the floor.

"So, Alex, if they say you need protection, I'm going to assume it's necessary."

She nodded, now starting to feel a little silly about her outburst.

"Fine, okay," she finally conceded.

"Hey." She looked up at the man whom she considered a very good friend. "It's not a big deal. They obviously know what they're doing, so I'm sure you won't even notice their presence."

Alex nodded, even managed a smile.

"I have a couple of meetings booked in the east end of the city, so I'll be gone most of the day," Marco added. "Call me if you need to."

She nodded again. He left the office and Alex went back to work.

The next couple of hours went by slowly while she tried to focus on the very tedious computer configuration and virtual tuning of the Cicada drivetrain. Niles, Randy, and Bobby were all tweaking their own components and had been sending her the various specs they had sourced or customized to create the perfect power-to-weight ratio. They planned to put together a modified design by Monday, ready for road testing next week when the body repairs to the race car were completed.

There wasn't any time for brooding about Lucas Johnson and his new edict. To be fair, Alex had to admit that the two Fortis agents, Michael and Ned, who had started the security detail yesterday were pretty invisible. She had caught a glimpse of them a couple of times, but with blazers on to conceal their guns, Alex barely took note of them. And there was really no sign of the extra surveillance cameras that she knew had been installed. So, after a little bit of retrospect, maybe her personal security wouldn't be as invasive as Alex had initially feared.

Knowing that Lucas was back from his trip and planning to meet with her was a whole other cause for concern. Something about his tall good looks and boyish charm was messing with her hormones and disturbing her sleep. And the memory of that hot, sizzling kiss between strangers only made it worse. Just last night, Alex had dreamed about him. It was nothing specific she could remember in the morning, but he was the first thing she thought about when she awoke with her body humming with arousal.

Her thoughts were interrupted by a call on her desk phone.

"Alex Cotts," she answered after the second ring.

"Hey, Alex, it's Frank at DS Distributors," said the voice over the line.

"Hi, Frank, what's up?"

"Do you remember that power converter you were looking for last month? The one that's on back order?"

Alex sat up straighter. It was a part for the Cicada that could be more effective than the one she was currently using.

"Sure, I remember it. Do you have one?"

"Yup, it just came in. But there's another customer who's looking for it, too, but he can't get it until tomorrow at the earliest," Frank told her. "If you can pick it up today, it's yours."

Alex looked at the time on her laptop. It was twenty minutes to eleven o'clock.

"Okay, I should be there by noon," she committed, quickly calculating how long the drive uptown would take.

"Good, see you then."

Alex hung up the phone, then checked her schedule. She had a meeting at one o'clock with their event management consultant to finalize the schedule and logistics for the Sea-to-Sky race. And it would take about forty minutes to drive up into Frank's warehouse in the northwest end of the city in midday traffic. There was plenty of time, if Alex left within the next thirty minutes.

The only hiccup was Lucas. He wanted to speak with her about the personal security.

Alex tapped her fingers on the desk, trying to think about what to do. Finally, she decided to give Lucas until eleven o'clock to meet with her. If he didn't show up by then, Alex would take a quick trip to get the converter and be back in less than two hours. Chances were, Lucas wouldn't even know she had left.

She went back to work and the next fifteen minutes ticked by slowly. There was no sign of Lucas.

At five minutes to eleven, Alex locked her computer then peeled off her overalls. She had on slim black jeans and a white T-shirt underneath, so she added the light blue jacket she had worn to work, then grabbed her purse and left her office. In the hallway, she paused from a niggling sense of uncertainty about her decision. Instead of heading through to the shop floor and out to the parking lot, Alex walked a few doors down to the office used by the Fortis agents. The door was open but the room was empty.

She stood there for a few minutes, but no one came by. Finally, concerned that she was running out of time, Alex left the building for the drive uptown through the city. Trying to relax about the decision, she turned the music up loud in her Porsche and enjoyed the ride. Thankfully, traffic was pretty light on the route, and Alex was on her way back to the office within an hour. She was making such good time that it seemed like a good idea to stop for an errand. Shawn's wedding was on Saturday, and this might be the only opportunity to pick up a card and withdraw some cash as a gift.

It was only twenty minutes to one o'clock when she pulled into the Magnus Motorsports parking lot feeling pretty good about her efficient use of time. Alex was about to step out of the low-riding body of her car when a big black truck sped into the parking spot right beside her, its brakes squealing in protest at the abrupt stop. Annoyed by the aggressive driving, she grabbed the boxed power converter and her purse, then stepped out of the Porsche. And right into a solid wall of black cotton.

"Lucas," Alex gasped once she had determined who was blocking her path.

"Your office, now," he demanded in a soft, low voice.

Something about the dark look in his eyes and the hard line of his jaw suggested he expected her to follow his command without question. But that wasn't in Alex's nature. She was about to object to his high-handed manner, when Lucas stepped even closer to her, completely invading her personal space. Alex gasped with annoyance, but instinctively backed up a bit. He approached again, bending so their faces were more leveled.

"Now," he growled.

Mindful that some of the other employees might be in earshot, Alex swallowed back sharp words of protest and instead turned on her heels and walked into the shop floor, head held high. But once they were in the privacy of her office, she fully intended to give him a piece of her mind.

The walk through the building seemed to take forever. Though Alex could feel the formidable presence of Lucas against her back the whole way, his steps were so silent that she couldn't help checking over her shoulder on occasion, hoping he had wandered off. But of course, he remained right behind her, matching her two strides to one, his face devoid of any expression other than determination.

Finally, they reached the door to her office. Alex swung it open and walked across the room to lay her purse on the box on her desk, and to put some space between them. The silence was so uncomfortable, she felt the need to say something.

"I tried to find you before I left," she finally stated, watching him warily and trying to seem unaffected by his obvious annoyance with her.

He closed the door quietly behind him, then followed her path without pause.

"You have my phone number, Alex," he growled.

"You should have called me, or sent a text," he replied, in his usual smooth tone.

"Okay, I get it. But I just needed to pick up a part—"

"Alex, I know where you were," Lucas cut in, continuing across the room toward her in a slow, deliberate pace until Alex felt like prey. "I was right behind you for most of your trip."

Her first thought was to stand her ground, refuse to back down or show fear. But then he was behind her desk and in her face.

"What are you doing?" she demanded, trying to control her breathing while backing up. "Stop it."

Lucas kept coming, forcing Alex to reverse until her back hit the wall. He planted his hands on either side of her face and leaned in close, looking deep into her eyes, now wide with surprise and apprehension. Without a single touch from him, she was trapped, unable to move, and every part of her body felt the power of his presence.

"Lucas," she stammered, her brain struggling to find something more coherent to say.

"Alex," he mocked. "You will not do that again, do you understand?"

She swallowed, finding her mouth dry and her throat very tight.

"Do what exactly?" she questioned breathlessly.

If possible, his dark stare became even more intense.

"Don't pretend ignorance. You were told you'd have personal protection going forward," Lucas stated in a silky, smooth voice. "Which means you will not go anywhere outside of this building alone."

He leaned even closer until his body was a breath away from hers. His skin smelled faintly of bath soap and testosterone. Alex swallowed again.

"Do you understand me?" he demanded. "From now on, you don't go anywhere without me or one of my men."

The last sentence was whispered into her ear and sent a shiver down her spine. Her heart was beating hard and fast in her chest, as indignation mixed with physical awakening. Alex heard his words, understood what he was saying, but could only anticipate his touch and think about what he might do next.

"Am I clear, Alex?"

His lips brushed the rim of her ear, and Alex had to hold back a breathy sigh.

"Alex!" he insisted, surely knowing the effect he was having on her and using it to his advantage.

"Yes," she finally whispered, now feeling light-headed from the heat between their bodies.

Lucas let out a sigh and lifted his head back a bit as his gaze roamed over her face. Alex felt the warm brush of it on her skin. Until their eyes met again. It was obvious that he was still annoyed with her, but something more intense was reflected in his pupils. There was budding awareness, very similar to the sensation that was pooling low in her stomach.

He paused for several moments, and she waited for him to do something, anything. The anticipation for whatever it might be kept her frozen against the wall, framed within his body. Alex finally took a deep breath, and her breasts almost brushed against the hard plane of his torso. Lucas looked down between them, at her nipples now tight and pointed through her thin T-shirt and jacket. Then his eyes raked over her face again, lingering on her lips.

"Lex," he whispered roughly, sounding as wound up as she felt.

One of his fingers brushed the curve of her cheek, and Alex closed her eyes, willing him to touch her again. It was insane! They were in her office, in the middle of the day and all she wanted was for this man to kiss her.

After a long silent pause, she finally opened her eyes to find Lucas staring down at her intently. Then he slowly leaned forward.

CHAPTER 9

Lucas covered his mouth with hers in a deep kiss, delving into the wet cavity of her mouth. Alex immediately responded by entwining her tongue with his with equal urgency. Delicious sensation rippled through his body, twisting his gut and weakening his knees. God, he had been wanting this for days, and to finally taste her lips again was setting him on fire.

"Lucas," Alex gasped, sounding as hot and eager as he was.

With open mouths, they licked, sucked, swirled, and devoured each other. The sound of their breathing was ragged and labored as the heat between them flared out of control. She ran her hands over the back of his head and down to his shoulders, clutching at their broad strength as though to hold her upright.

The incessant throbbing from the fresh gunshot wound along the top of his shoulder seemed to have disappeared.

Lucas tried to hold back from touching her, to

get a grip on his desires, to remember where they were—in her office, while he was on the job. But her taste was too sweet to resist. He pulled her into his arms, melting their bodies together tight through the torso. He ran his big hands down the length of her back. Damn, she felt amazing. All soft curves and lean lines. And her smell. Amber and brown sugar. Lucas squeezed the mounds of her ass, and his erection swelled to new lengths.

"Lucas," purred Alex against his mouth. Her hips rotated against him in agitation.

"Yeah," he muttered, incapable of anything more intelligible.

He needed more. Just a little more. The touch of her naked skin, the feel of her silky flesh. Then he'd stop, put on the brakes, get some air. Remember she was an asset under his protection . . .

"Touch me, Lucas. Please . . ."

His brain stopped. White-hot desire coursed through his veins, destroying his better judgment. He took her face into one hand, dragging his thumb over her mouth. With the other hand, he deftly undid the fly of her jeans and pulled down the heavy material. Alex gasped. Lucas swept his finger between her thighs, under the edge of her panties. Her skin was soft, the folds slick with arousal. She licked one of his fingers near her mouth with a torturous wet tongue. He thrust his middle finger into her tight sheath, chanting her name in a breathless whisper.

Somewhere in the background, an alarm was ringing.

Lucas sighed, trying to hold on to the feel of Alex, wet and quivering in his arms. The ringing became insistent and louder, signaling morning and destroying the delicious dream. Eyes still closed, he turned off the alarm on his watch, then lay there for several minutes to regulate his breathing. Finally, he rubbed the palm of his hands over his eyes and swung his feet onto the floor to sit up. It was six o'clock, Friday morning, and he had been stretched out on the couch in the living room of Alex's town house.

The tense confrontation in her office had happened the day before. There was a moment of madness when he had been so drawn to her that Lucas had actually moved forward to taste her lips. But his discipline and professionalism finally kicked in, and he walked out the room. But leaving her standing there, smelling so good and vibrating with the same sexually charged energy that was flowing through him, had been harder than Lucas wanted to admit.

Jesus, that dream had felt so real, so vivid. It was everything he had wanted and craved while up against her in her office, yesterday afternoon. In that moment, while frustration and anger were still driving him, Lucas had almost lost his cool and crossed the line. Thank God he'd gotten it together enough to walk away from her at that point. Judging by the dream he just had, if Lucas hadn't walked away, it was difficult to know just how far he would have let things escalate. It was a sobering thought.

But that didn't change the fact that he had been seriously tempted. Or that he still wanted her.

Lucas stretched, then winced. The torn flesh on the top of his shoulder was bandaged and sore. It was a good reminder of how quickly this mission had changed from a simple network security administration job to a dangerous, high-stakes protective situation in less than a week. By the time the Fortis team had flown out of Chicago, Timothy Pratt was dead, Lucas was shot, and their only lead was a stolen car, eventually found ditched outside the city a few hours later. Not even Pratt's laptop, which was recovered, or a full search of his apartment produced anything new or useful, except further confirmation that whoever was after Magnus information was well equipped and well funded, and they were not going to stop their attempts to take what they wanted. Fortis had to assume what they wanted could include the Cicada engine, the design, and potentially anyone who knew how to build it: namely Alexandria Cotts.

He had used the flight back to Toronto to call Marco Passante and provide an update on their progress, without too much alarming detail. Lucas had also advised his client that their analysis suggested Alex could also be at risk, and should have personal protection going forward. Unfortunately, Alex had not taken the direction as literally as it had been intended. Michael had seen her drive off the property during his surveillance review, and advised Lucas right away. Lucas was in the server room testing a new encryption algorithm when he got the call. Within minutes, he was in the black truck, trailing her sports car as she headed into the north end of the city.

Even though he had eyes on her for the full trip, including the pit stop to the drugstore, Lucas had been furious at her reckless behavior. The murder of Timothy Pratt and the gunfight after were very fresh in his mind. So to see their most valuable asset alone and out of his immediate reach on a stupid errand for over an hour was beyond frustrating. By the time they returned to the auto shop, Lucas was more heated than he rarely ever got. It was the only explanation for his behavior in her office, up against the wall.

It hadn't taken long after he had walked away from Alex to realize that he had overreacted, and to see her perspective. While he and the team were preparing for a threat they were certain was coming, Alex and Marco couldn't really know what that meant. Lucas had seen it many times through his career and since starting Fortis almost six years ago. The idea of a threat against Magnus and the Cicada was abstract and undefined. Hopefully, Alex and Marco would never experience concrete evidence of that threat, but Lucas knew with almost absolute certainty it was wishful thinking.

Though he had managed to avoid Alex for a few hours after the incident, Lucas had sent her a message later in the afternoon to confirm he would directly provide her protection outside of the office. He took a small overnight bag and drove home with her. They hadn't spoken much for the rest of the evening, other than exchanging information that Lucas needed to do his job.

Now, Lucas stood up, rolled his wounded shoulder again, then quietly walked through the first floor of Alex's town house and up the stairs to the main bathroom on the second floor to take a shower and get dressed. Back downstairs twenty minutes later, he found a large French press on the kitchen counter. He turned on the gas stove and filled up the whistling kettle before heading through the house to do a full security check.

The three-floor, three-bedroom town house was the end unit of a new complex built about five years ago. While the walls were still builder's white, the rooms were decorated with cozy and colorful furniture and fabrics. Lucas started on the bottom floor, checking each potential point to ensure the silent alarms he had installed last night were still working and undisturbed. On the second floor, there was a spare bedroom used for storage and exercise equipment. When he reached the top floor, the two bedroom doors for Alex and her cousin Noelle were still closed. He inspected the laundry room and closets, then went back into the kitchen to check in on his coffee.

Lucas was pouring hot water over ground beans in the French press when he heard footsteps coming down the stairs. He turned to find Noelle Cotts walking toward him in pink hospital scrubs. She had the same look of curiosity and concern on her face as she did the night before when he had introduced himself.

"Morning," Lucas stated softly. "Coffee?"

Her eyes shot up in surprise.

"Ah, sure."

"It'll be ready in a couple of minutes."

She nodded warily as she entered the kitchen. Lucas walked out of the room and across the living area to give her some space. He picked up his cell phone from the counter on the way and began reading through the various e-mails and messages that had come in through the night, knowing that if anything urgent had happened, someone from the team would have called him.

"So, what exactly are you protecting Alex from?" Noelle finally asked from behind him.

Lucas turned to answer just as Alex came down the stairs. His eyes met Alex's briefly. She was wearing gray, stretchy workout pants and a basic black V-neck T-shirt.

"It's just a precaution at this point," he replied with a calm smile.

"I told you, Noelle. It's nothing," added Alex as she joined her cousin in the kitchen. "My boss is a little paranoid, that's all."

Noelle didn't appear at all assured. She looked Lucas up and down as though assessing his tall, hard body and seeing the lethal capabilities.

"A precaution against what, exactly?" asked Noelle, removing cream from the refrigerator.

"Nothing specific," Alex insisted, sounding dismissive.

"Seems a little intrusive for nothing specific, don't you think?" noted Noelle. "You said you're not launching the new product until June, right? So, you're going to have a bodyguard following you everywhere until then?"

Alex looked at Lucas briefly.

"Alex's coverage will only be for as long as needed," Lucas added, walking closer to Noelle and turning on the charm. "But I assure you, I will be as invisible as possible. Within a couple of days, you won't even notice that I'm here."

His smooth tone and warm smile seemed to make a dent. Noelle's shoulders relaxed a bit and she smiled back. Alex rolled her eyes from where she stood behind her cousin, then turned to the counter.

"Coffee? Nice! Did you want a cup?" Alex asked, opening the cupboard where the cups and mugs were stored.

The question was directed to Lucas.

"Thanks," he replied politely. "With cream and sugar, please."

Alex took down two coffee cups out of the cupboard and filled them both with the rich, dark java. Noelle put her coffee in a travel mug. There were a few moments of silence while the drinks were being made and Alex handed Lucas his drink.

"What about tonight, Alex? Are you still staying with Shawn?"

Since the incident yesterday, the Magnus account file had been updated to include a brief summary of each employee's immediate family and known relationships. From that, Lucas knew Alex had three brothers and a father living in the city or surrounding area. None of them was named Shawn. There was also no evidence of a boyfriend with that name.

Lucas raised a curious brow, looking at Alex over the rim of his cup. She shrugged at her cousin, but didn't seem at all uncomfortable about the question.

"Apparently, he goes where I go," she replied dryly before taking a drink of her coffee.

"The wedding, too?" added Noelle. "That's going to be interesting."

Alex flicked a glance at Lucas then back to the floor. Noelle looked back and forth between the other two.

"I have to get going or I'll be late for the clinic," continued Noelle. "Let me know what the plan is for tonight?"

"Sure," Alex replied with a quick smile. "I'll call you later this afternoon."

Noelle gave Lucas a small wave and left the room. Alex and Lucas continued drinking their coffee in silence until they heard the front door close. He looked at his watch. It was just after seven o'clock. Enough time for the necessary conversation about logistics that he had deliberately but unwisely skipped the night before.

Alex seemed to read his thoughts. She put her empty cup in the dishwasher, then sat down at one of the stools in front of the kitchen counter.

"So, how exactly does this work?" she asked calmly. "I've never had a bodyguard before."

"Well, it's pretty simple. You just need to tell me what your plans are a day or two in advance, and we'll work out the details," Lucas explained, taking a few steps closer to where she was sitting. "Let's start with your schedule for today."

He took a relaxed stance in front of her, legs wide and arms crossed against his chest. Lucas caught Alex's eyes brush over the bulge of his biceps before she looked to the floor. He wanted to grin with satisfaction, but controlled his expression. The last thing either of them needed was a reminder of the chemistry that seemed easily sparked whenever they were in very close proximity.

"Usually, I'm just at the shop late, then home. But I have a bridal shower to go to tonight. At the Metropolitan, actually," she explained evenly. "The wedding is tomorrow morning also, if you're still staying there."

"We have a couple of rooms booked there," he confirmed. "And who is this person, Shawn, you're staying with tonight?"

He watched her carefully.

"Shawn Hampton is the groom for the wedding," she clarified. "He's my best friend, and I'll be his 'best man' for the ceremony"

She used air quotes at the term.

"Or maybe it's best woman . . ." Alex pondered, clearly amused by the unconventional concept. "Anyway, since the wedding party is staying at the hotel for the night, Shawn and I decided to share a room."

Lucas nodded, stringing together various facts.

"That's why you were there on Sunday?"

"Yeah. It was the bachelor party," Alex confirmed.

"All right. I'll accompany you to the shower, we'll stay in my room for the night, then I'll go with you to the wedding," Lucas confirmed. "What time is the shower?"

"Seven o'clock."

"Okay. Probably best for you to take everything you need with you now, then we'll go straight there after you finish work. Send me an e-mail with all the details and I'll make arrangements to get access to rooms in the hotel early to ensure they are secure."

Alex stared back at him, obviously confounded by his plan.

"What do you mean, access the rooms early? Why would you need to do that?"

"It's just a pre—"

"I know, a precaution," she interrupted, standing up and closing the distance between them. "You've said that already, it's starting to sound more and more like bullshit."

Lucas clenched his teeth, but kept his face neutral and his stance relaxed.

"I'm not a pop star, Lucas! I'm an engineer. There are no crazy stalker fans hiding in hotel rooms dying to get access to me," Alex surmised, crossing her arms also in a much more assertive fashion. "So unless you're going to tell me exactly what's going on, there is no way I'm going to let you go all Secret Service on me."

For one moment, Lucas considered telling her about the murder of Timothy Pratt and the fresh gunshot wound in his shoulder, closed with eight stitches. But he dismissed it just as quickly. While he needed her cooperation, he didn't want her to be unnecessarily afraid.

"Why don't you just let me do my job," he replied with a small grin and a slightly patronizing tone that he knew would annoy her enough to be distracting. "Just send me the details for tonight and tomorrow and I'll take care of things on my end."

She shot daggers at him, but didn't reply. He took it as reluctant agreement.

"Now, get your things together," Lucas added, looking pointedly at his watch.. "I'd like to be at Magnus by eight o'clock."

For a few seconds, he was certain Alex was going to argue with his direction. But she surprised him by walking away without another word.

CHAPTER 10

"Look on the bright side, Shawn. You can have the bathroom to yourself all morning. I know how long it takes to get your hair to sit just right," Alex teased her best friend over the phone.

She was standing in front of the bathroom mirror in Lucas's hotel suite on the top floor of the Metropolitan Hotel. It was almost six thirty and they had stopped there so she could drop off her things and change her clothes before going to the shower for Kate Nguyen, Shawn's bride-to-be, in another room. Lucas was waiting for her in the room, and Alex could hear the faint rumbles of his voice suggesting he was also on a call. She redirected her attention to her own tricky conversation as she explained to Shawn why she needed to stay with her new bodyguard tonight rather than in his room.

"It's just weird, that's all, Lex," Shawn replied. "I know you've always said your prototype engine is completely different than anything made today, but I didn't think it was dangerous. Are you sure you know what you're doing?"

Alex sighed. Shawn was a successful real estate agent and a pretty simple guy except for his expensive taste. He made good money selling high-value properties, and worked as little as possible to do it. Alex knew that he never really understood her drive to work sixty-plus hours per week designing new car components that may or may not work marginally better than ones that already existed.

"It's really no big deal, Shawn. Honestly. Someone tried to hack our system and steal my work, and these security guys my boss hired have gone a little over the top. So, I'll have a tail for a few days until it blows ever," she dismissed, sounding much more carefree about it than she actually felt. "Anyway, I'll stop by after Kate's shower and we'll hang out for a bit so you won't be lonely."

Shawn snorted and Alex laughed.

"Adrian and I are going out to eat nearby. I'll send you a text when I'm back," he told her.

"Do me a favor, Shawn? Don't tell Adrian about all this yet, okay?" she asked.

"Sure. But how are you going to explain your shadow tomorrow?"

"I'll tell him before the wedding," Alex promised.

"Yeah, sure," Shawn finally agreed. "See you later."

"Bye."

Alex hung up her cell phone and placed it on the marble bathroom counter. She sighed again, something she seemed to be doing a lot lately. This whole bodyguard thing was a huge pain in the neck. Explaining it to Noelle and Shawn was annoying enough. Tomorrow, she'd have to convince her father and three domineering brothers why they shouldn't be alarmed about an ex–Secret Service consultant shadowing her indefinitely.

Alex looked into the mirror to finish brushing on a light layer of mascara and eyeliner, then a sheer pink lip gloss. She had changed out of her work clothes into dark blue skinny jeans and a soft, blush pink cashmere tunic. Her thick curtain of dreadlocks was now hanging loose in spirals around her shoulders from the twists she had pinned her hair into over night. Alex toyed with the strands around her face until they fell in her desired pattern, then stepped out of the bathroom carrying her other clothes and purse.

Lucas was on the phone, standing in the living area in front of a deep sofa on the left side of the large room, next to the full wall of windows. He barely looked up as she walked in. Alex quickly folded her work clothes and put them into her large tote bag, on the floor next to a wide, king-size bed to the right of the bathroom door. Her outfit for the wedding was already hanging in the closet next to the room door.

"All set?" Lucas finally asked, walking toward her.

She nodded as he passed her, then took a deep breath and followed behind him.

The next couple of hours went by fairly painlessly. Kate had booked a small meeting room on the third floor of the hotel. It was a typical shower event with about twenty-five of her female friends and family eating and drinking between silly games to win small prizes. Alex and Lucas arrived a few minutes before Kate, while two of her friends and the hotel staff were still setting things up. Lucas casually did his now-familiar inspection around the room, while Alex introduced herself and offered to help out the two women. While they definitely noticed Lucas, occasionally looking him over with speculative glances, they didn't comment about his presence, not even after he took a watchful position in the back corner of the room near the bar table.

Once the party was in full swing, Alex had to admit that Lucas did a good job of blending into the background. In his black shirt and black cotton pants, he easily passed for one of the hotel staff. Of those women that did take note of his sentry-like presence, Alex suspected they were too busy appreciating how good he looked to care why he was there. He was that kind of male specimen.

"Everything okay?" Noelle asked about an hour into the shower, between even more competitive quizzes about the bride and groom. Noelle looked over at Lucas and back at Alex, clearly still concerned about what was going on.

Alex nodded and smiled.

"It's fine, Noelle. Please don't worry, okay?" she pleaded.

Noelle sighed.

"If you say so. But you'd tell me if you were in any serious trouble, right?"

"Yes, of course I would," Alex promised.

Noelle nodded, appearing to be satisfied for the moment.

"What are you going to tell Uncle Hubert?" her cousin asked after a few minutes, reminding Alex of the dilemma still unsolved.

She bit her lip and looked at the ground. Noelle groaned, reading her very clearly.

"You're not going to tell him or your brothers, are you?" guessed Noelle with a groan.

"Noelle, you know what they're like. They'll start freaking out no matter how much I try to explain things. And I don't want to ruin Shawn's wedding with the commotion," Alex explained her reasoning. "Lucas will probably only follow me around for a few days before he realizes it's completely unnecessary, so why stress them out over nothing?"

Noelle had that disapproving look on her face that Alex saw fairly regularly.

"If I need the protection for more than a week, or if anything more serious happens, I'll tell them. I promise," she finally swore.

Her cousin was still not happy about it, but her face softened a bit. Maybe the real possibility of four Cotts men dragging Alex away from the wedding to hide her somewhere under lock and key made her see reason.

"Okay. But how are you going to explain him?"

Noelle pointed a thumb over her shoulder at Lucas, who seemed capable of standing forever without moving.

"My date?" suggested Alex.

They both looked over at him and back at each other.

"Will he go along with it?"

"He will once he sees the Cotts men and I explain the alternative."

The two women grinned at each other then walked over to the bar to get a glass of wine.

Alex and Lucas stayed at the shower until just after nine o'clock.

"I'm going to hang out with Shawn for an hour or so," she stated once they were in the hallway walking toward the elevator. "He's in room eleven twenty-two."

Lucas didn't reply but did press the button for the eleventh floor when they got into the elevator.

"Aren't you going to ask about Shawn and me?" she finally questioned as the elevator slowly climbed upward.

Lucas shrugged.

"Ask about what?"

"Our friendship. Me sharing a hotel room with him the night before his wedding. Most people find it very unusual for a man and woman to be best friends with no benefits," she stated, watching his reaction.

He was pretty straight-faced.

"It's not my place to question," he finally replied in the easy tone that was so attractive and annoying at the same time. "I'm sure it's possible. But I don't think his fiancée is as open-minded."

His lips twisted into a teasing smile.

Alex let out a sharp laugh at his understatement. Kate Nguyen absolutely did not think such friendships were possible, and wasn't very good at hiding her resentment about how close Alex and Shawn were.

"Yes, well. That's old news," she told him with a dismissive wave of her hand. "I'm not going anywhere, so she'll have to get used to me eventually."

"How long have they been together?" he asked when the elevator door opened.

Alex grinned.

"Almost four years." He raised a brow. "She's a little stubborn and Shawn's way too tolerant. I, for one, couldn't give a rat's ass what she thinks, as long as she doesn't make his life miserable about it."

They reached Shawn's room door, but Alex stopped Lucas with a touch on his shoulder before he could knock.

"Listen, about tomorrow," she began, feeling awkward about what she was going to propose. "Can we just act like you're my date for the wedding instead of my bodyguard?"

He looked down at her speculatively.

"Why?"

Alex cleared her throat.

"It's my dad. And my brothers," she stated, wrinkling her nose. "They can be a little protective and hard to reason with. I'd rather not get them all worked up over this security thing if we don't have to."

He continued to look down at her face, brows lowered in thought.

"Trust me, Lucas. It will make your job a lot easier if you don't have to deal with them."

Finally, he nodded.

"Okay, it's a plan."

She let out a deep breath.

"Good. I've already asked Noelle not to say anything, and I'm sure Shawn will agree also."

He nodded and then knocked on the door.

"Thank you," Alex told him sincerely.

Lucas smiled back at her, his eyes softer than

usual. Shawn opened the door, wearing basketball shorts and a T-shirt.

"Hey, Lex, you made it," stated her best friend loudly with a board grin.

He was a handsome man, almost five feet ten inches tall, with dark blond hair and hazel-brown eyes. His tanned face was a little flushed.

"Someone's been having his own party," she laughed back.

It was pretty obvious that he had enjoyed a few drinks through the evening.

"Don't worry, I saved some for you," Shawn replied before he spotted Lucas off to the side of the doorway. "You must be the muscle."

Alex laughed and Lucas had that stoic, patient look on his face.

"Lucas, meet Shawn Hampton," Alex stated.

"Come in, grab a drink! Relax for a while," Shawn invited, a little louder than needed as he turned back into his room.

She laughed again, then whispered dramatically to Lucas as they both followed.

"You can't fault him for dulling his senses with alcohol. He's tying himself to that insecure sourpuss tomorrow, and it's almost too late to back out."

"Help yourselves to beer," Shawn told them as he flopped back on one of the beds and grabbed his own half-empty bottle from the nightstand. "Should we order some food? Are you hungry?"

Alex took a chilled bottle of beer out of the twelve-pack on the television credenza. There were now only six remaining, with four empties lined together beside the box. Shawn was usually just a casual drinker, having one or two whenever they went out. Alex could count the times he got more than just a little tipsy. So she could tell a little intervention was needed tonight, or he was going to be a mess in the morning.

"I ate at the shower," she replied, sitting on the bed beside him. "Didn't you go out for dinner with Adrian?"

"Yeah, I'm good," Shawn confirmed, taking another big gulp of beer.

"Lucas, are you hungry?" Alex asked, looking over at him as he walked around the space to do a discreet security inspection.

"I'll eat something later," he replied from a spot between the bathroom and front door.

"You okay, Shawn? You're drunk," she stated, looking back at her friend as he lay across the bed with his eyes closed.

"Isn't that what a man's supposed to do the night before his wedding," Shawn questioned with a goofy smile. Thank God he was a happy drunk.

"I have no idea," Alex said with a laugh.

She shoved him over then lay down beside him.

"I'm fine, Lex. Just chilling," he eventually added, sounding sleepy. "How was Kate at the shower?"

"She was good," Alex told him in a neutral voice.

The tension between the two women closest to him was something she and Shawn didn't discuss. Not since the first year or so of his new relationship when Kate could not seem to fathom that Shawn's best friend was a girl.

"Good," he sighed in a low, rumbly voice.

"Tomorrow is going to be great, Lex. I can't wait to marry her."

Alex patted his shoulder reassuringly and took the bottle of beer out of his hand to place it back on the side table. Despite how immature Kate often behaved, it was great to see Shawn so dedicated and in love. Alex only hoped it would last and their marriage would go the distance.

"'K, I'll leave you to get some sleep," she whispered to him when it was clear that he was almost completely out of commission. "I'll be back in the morning."

"Bye, Lex," he mumbled.

Alex stood up from the bed and smiled down at him indulgently. He really did look happily in love, even as he started snoring. As though she felt his gaze, Alex glanced up to find Lucas watching her blankly, still rooted in the spot next to the front door.

"All set?" he asked.

She nodded, giving Shawn a final glance.

With her still unopened beer in hand, Alex followed Lucas back up to his top-floor suite. It was still early, only minutes to ten o'clock. Now that all her obligations were over, Alex suddenly felt awkward and uncomfortable. Ever since the incident in her office, she had tried hard to dismiss it as a crazy moment of weakness with no significant meaning, to her or Lucas. Sure, he was extremely attractive, probably to any woman with a pulse. Trapped so close to him, while he looked down at her so intense and demanding, would naturally cause her heart to race and hormones to spiral out of control.

That's all it was. Anything else would be incredibly inconvenient and just plain stupid. Alex had spent the last day and a half running that dialogue in her mind, willing her body and wayward thoughts to cooperate with her rational mind. Even now, while looking through her bag on the floor to pull out nightclothes, Alex tried to look casual and unaffected. Like this wasn't the same hotel room that she had seriously contemplated hooking up with Lucas in less than a week ago for some much needed stress release.

"I'm going to order room service," he told her from where he was now sitting, at the desk in the living room area with his laptop open. "Do want anything?"

Alex straightened up holding an oversize T-shirt, loose cotton shorts, and her toiletry bag.

"No, thank you."

She quickly went into the bathroom with her things and took a long hot shower. It helped her relax and put the situation in perspective. It also allowed Alex to come to a fairly simple realization. Lucas Johnson was a very sexy man who was now in close proximity for a limited amount of time. Rather than ignoring her attraction to him, it would be far more productive to embrace the opportunity for a bit of meaningless, satisfying sexual gratification.

If she questioned her new way of thinking, it was strongly reinforced the moment Alex stepped out of the bathroom again. At some point in the last thirty minutes, Lucas had removed his black shirt, revealing a white, ribbed cotton undershirt stretched tautly over his tight, rippled torso. He was talking on his cell phone but seemed to pause for a few moments once he saw her. His eyes trailed up her body slowly from her toes to hover somewhere around her lips.

"I have to go," he finally stated into the phone before ending his call.

Alex wondered if she was so transparent that he could see everything she wanted written clearly on her face. Lucas placed the phone on the desk next to him and started walking toward her at a pace that felt like dramatic slow motion. His chest muscles rippled with every step, his arms were strong and cut. His shoulders were lean and broad, marred only by a small square of white gauze taped over the right deltoid. Her heart rate increased in anticipation for what was to come once he reached her. She bit her bottom lip, and his jaw clenched.

"Be careful what you ask for, Alex," he stated, stopping beside her close enough to speak low near her ear, making it clear that her physical attraction to him had been well communicated. "You might get more than you can handle."

Then he continued past her, brushing her hip with his fingers and leaving a light wake of his male scent behind. Alex closed her eyes and let out a deep breath. From behind, she heard Lucas open the door to let someone in. It was a hotel attendant delivering his room service meal.

Alex pressed the heels of her hands into her eye sockets and wished the floor could swallow her up.

Instead, she pulled back the sheets of the bed and crawled under them. Too bad she hadn't drunk more alcohol through the evening. Then perhaps she could have been too inebriated to remember the last five minutes.

CHAPTER 11

It felt like forever before Alex fell asleep. Lucas ate his burger in the living room while watching television, and tried hard not to look over at her small form curled up at the far end of the king-size bed, completely buried under the bedding. He worked on his laptop for another couple of hours, crawling through all the data they had taken from Timothy Pratt's computer, trying to uncover any useful intel. At about one o'clock in the morning, he stretched out on the large sofa to try to get a good night's rest. His Beretta pistol was tucked under a seat cushion within easy reach.

In the morning, he was up by six o'clock. Alex was now spread out on her stomach in the middle of the bed, hugging one of the down-filled pillows and with the sheets twisted around her hips. He walked past her to the bathroom, resisting the urge to smile at the adorable image. The last thing he needed right now was to encourage this insane attraction to her.

The rest of the morning went as planned. Lucas

checked in with the team on-site at Magnus, and
all was quiet. Alex was up and in the shower before
nine o'clock. He ordered a coffee and a few pastries for her, oatmeal for himself. They alternated
eating and getting dressed in the bathroom with
very few words exchanged. At about ten o'clock,
Lucas escorted her back to Shawn Hampton's
room, then to the site of the ceremony in a banquet hall forty-five minutes later. Lucas found no
sign of any hidden threats or suspicious behavior.

He took a spot standing at the back of the small
banquet hall where he could monitor all people
and activity. His gun was secure in a shoulder
holster under his jacket, and a knife was strapped
to his ankle as a backup. It was a small, intimate
wedding with about forty people, which made it
much easier for him to control. Most of the guests
were on the bride's side, with only twelve for the
groom, not including Alex. It was soon very obvious that half of Shawn's guests were Alex's family.
Three big, young guys sat up front, with an older
man at the end. All four shared one or more facial
features with Alex. Noelle was one row back with
her boyfriend and another three guys who seemed
to be from the same group of friends and each
had a date. In contrast, Kate's supporters were a
mix of family members of Filipino heritage of all
ages and a handful of female friends.

The ceremony started at eleven o'clock sharp.
While all the guests watched the maid of honor
then the bride walk down the makeshift aisle with
emotional excitement, Lucas was focused on Alex.
She was standing at the front of the room next to
Shawn and the officiator, wearing a navy blue

pantsuit matching the groom's. But it was anything but masculine. The jacket and pants were slim-fitting and well-tailored to fit her body, wrapping every curve and limb perfectly. She wore high, sparkly sandals on her feet, and a bit of jewelry around her neck and in her ears. Her hair fell in spirals around her face and she looked sexy a hell.

It was a simple and brief ceremony. The guests were then ushered outside into the hallway to congratulate the newlyweds and take pictures, while the hotel staff set up the room for a sit-down lunch. Lucas stayed close behind Alex to ensure she was in arm's reach, and tried to look more like a date than protective detail. Eventually, Alex casually introduced him to her father and brothers as a "friend," garnering a few raised brows. Lucas remembered the youngest of the brothers, Alex's twin, Adrian, from the group at the hotel restaurant last Sunday. Adrian seemed to remember Lucas also, staring him down in an effort to look menacing. Lucas ignored him.

A light three-course lunch was served in the banquet room, and the atmosphere was casual and festive as soft music played in the background. Alex seemed relaxed and happy surrounded by family and friends. She laughed freely with everyone, exchanged teasing barbs with her brothers, and talked intently with her father. She and Kate even shared an awkward embrace that seemed genuine and heartfelt.

Occasionally, her eyes met his and clung for a few moments. Lucas wondered to what extent she knew the physical effect she had on him. Her gaze was bold and intense, yet not readable enough for

Lucas to know exactly what she was thinking about him, his words last night, and the attraction between them. He could only hope that she would heed his warning and refrain from looking at him with such blatant sexual invitation again.

Soon enough, the bride was tossing the bouquet, caught by Noelle, and the groom was escorting her out of the hotel to a limo to start their two-week honeymoon in Costa Rica. Alex joined the remaining group in a round of farewell hugs and kisses. Her father and brothers shook Lucas's hand, and Adrian seemed to have relaxed a little bit.

By three o'clock, only Noelle and her boyfriend, Nicholas Carter, were still in the hotel lobby.

"Are you heading back home now?" Alex asked her cousin.

"Not right away," Noelle replied. "Nick has a couple of errands to do before he drops me off. What about you? Will you be home later?"

Alex glanced at Lucas quickly.

"Yeah, I'll be home."

"'K, see you later," stated Noelle.

"See ya, Lex," Nicholas added, elbowing Alex on the shoulder like a buddy.

"Yeah. We're still on for the strip club next weekend, right?" she asked him with a face that looked serious.

"Nick!" Noelle demanded, glaring at her boyfriend.

He rolled his eyes and tried to punch Alex, but she easily stepped back out of his reach.

"She's just bugging you, Noelle. I told you, I'm not going to the club with the guys anymore."

His protests and Noelle's agitated questions continued as they walked through the lobby to the front entrance. Alex laughed out loud, clearly pleased with her efforts. Until she turned to find Lucas standing patiently behind her. Her smile faded, but the sparkle of mischief lingered in her eyes.

She turned and started walking to the elevators, her high heels clicking loudly on the marble tiled floors. Lucas fell in step beside her. Their silence continued through the ride up to the top floor and into his hotel room. He walked ahead of her to the far end of the room to start packing up his laptop and other supplies.

"Once you're all packed up, I'd like to stop by Magnus before we . . ."

Lucas stopped midsentence as he turned to see Alex toss her suit jacket on the chair in front of the desk. She was now in the center of the room wearing a thin white camisole with a white lacy bra completely visible underneath. Her fingers reached for the button at the waist of her pants.

"What are you doing?" he demanded.

She tossed her head to the side, and a mass of curly locs tumbled seductively around her shoulders.

"I'm changing into something more comfortable," she replied as though it was a perfectly natural thing to do in front of him.

Lucas clenched his jaw hard, perfectly aware that she was baiting him.

"Perhaps you should do that in the bathroom," he suggested as politely as he could.

She shrugged and lowered the zipper. The sound seemed unnaturally loud to his ears.

"I'm good. Unless I'm making you uncomfortable, Lucas."

Alex held his gaze as she wiggled the pants over her hips until the fabric fell to her ankles. Then she walked out of them, still in those sparkly sandals, one step closer to him in just her underwear.

"Alex, stop this," he grumbled, clenching his fists tight.

"Stop what exactly?" she whispered, leaning forward slightly as though waiting for an answer.

Lucas knew she was pushing for a reaction, proof that the image of her wearing next to nothing, displaying delicious curves and coppery skin was making his blood boil. He forced himself to hold still, breathe deep, and not fall for it. That attempt lasted seconds.

"What exactly do you want?" he asked, allowing his eyes to freely travel over her body.

Maybe if he called her bluff, she'd see that he shouldn't be teased. She walked closer and his nostril flared.

"I want you to know that I don't respond well to threats," she replied softly, sweetly. "And I like a challenge."

She reached out to touch the front of his jacket, but Lucas grabbed her wrist in midair before she could reach him.

"And I don't play games," he snapped back, frustrated by how much she tempted him.

"Neither do I." She tugged hard and he let go of her. "But maybe that's more than you can handle."

Alex turned away from him, but Lucas could not

stop his reaction. He reached out with one arm around her waist and pulled her back to him with his hand flat against her stomach. She let out a puff of breath as her back slammed into his torso. He felt a heady sense of dark satisfaction. But if he intended to teach her a lesson, it backfired. With her body molded against his, that sweet round ass was perfectly nestled against his groin, completely sabotaging his ability to think clearly. He breathed in deep, surrounding his senses with her intoxicating amber scent.

Shit, she was making him crazy.

He took a few more deep breaths trying to get a handle on his ranging desires. Then, any chance Lucas had to resist the temptation in his hands was eliminated when Alex reached high with her right arm and ran her hand over his head. Lucas looked down at the luscious round breasts pushed high, with puckered nipples teasing him through the sheer fabric covering them. Every valid and coherent objection or concern was quickly overridden by pure carnal need.

Lucas pressed his lips to the elegant line of her neck and cupped her breasts with his large hands. They were the perfect handful of soft plump flesh. He squeezed them, loving the sound her breathless groan. Their hard tips pressed against his palms. He scraped his teeth along her neck, then bit the sensitive flesh. Alex shivered, arching her back, and rubbed achingly along the length of his now pulsing erection. Almost all of the blood in his body was now pooled in his lower limbs, making Lucas feel powerful and weak at the same time. Whatever was left was pounding his ears.

He needed more of her.

"Is this what you want?" he demanded roughly as he slid one hand down her stomach and under the lace of her panties.

His fingers ran over inches of smooth, silky skin then a rim of soft fur along the valley of her lips. Alex gasped. Her hips rotated, telling him almost everything he wanted to know and needed to hear.

"Yes," she gasped, digging her fingers into his scalp and adding dangerous fuel to his raging arousal.

Lucas slid his fingers deeper between her thighs, dragging them within the seam of her core. She was slick and moist, just as he'd imagined. He circled the swollen bud with a light teasing brush, and Alex gasped deeply. He dipped the tip of his middle finger into her hot well. So perfectly snug. All he could think about was how incredible it would feel to slide into her, slowly, deeply.

He was throbbing so hard it hurt.

"Jesus, Alex," he muttered, losing the little fragile restraint he had left.

He pulled her a few steps over to the low television credenza then turned her around to face him. While unbuttoning his shirt, Lucas looked down at the incredibly sexy image she made. Bright, glittering eyes and flushed cheeks. Full pink lips, open and inviting. He wanted to kiss her, devour that mouth to remind himself how sweet and intoxicating she was. Intoxicating enough to easily get lost in. He resisted.

"Don't move," he demanded, keeping his eyes locked on hers.

Alex nodded. After he quickly shrugged off his

jacket, Lucas carefully unclipped his Beretta from the shoulder holster and placed it safely on the surface beside them. He then reached over to his small duffel bag sitting open beside the television and pulled out a condom. She bit her bottom lip, but stayed put.

Lucas undid his pants and pushed down his sport briefs with one hand, then tore open the packet with his teeth. He almost groaned with arrogant satisfaction as Alex looked down at the thick thrust of his arousal and watched him roll on the thin protection. When she looked back up, her eyes were even brighter, reflecting the heavy arousal that he felt. The only sound in the room was of their rough, shallow breathing.

"Lean back," Lucas instructed, taking her by the hip so she was sitting on the edge of the wood surface. He slowly, deliberately spread her legs and bent her knees. She was now reclined on her elbows, hands splayed open with the palms down, watching his every move. Lucas yanked aside the damp crotch of her panties to uncover her delicate folds. With his hand cupping her ass, he slid hard and deep into her tight sheath.

Alex groaned low and deep, her eyes closed and her head falling back. With a firm grip to hold her still, he stroked into her again, savoring the intense feel of her snug, wet grip. It was the most incredible feeling. Eyes squeezed tight, jaw clenched hard, Lucas stroked into her again deeper, rougher. All of his senses seemed completely focused into the sweet spot where his rigid length slid perfectly into her soft flesh, over and over. All too quickly, he fell into a frenzied rhythm that was driving him to the

edge of completion. Damn, he wanted it so bad.
Needed to relieve the maddening tension that was
creeping up his legs, clawing at his back, hard and
fast. Too fast, too uncontrolled.

Sweat was now trickling down his back. Lucas
took a breath, opened his eyes in the struggle for
a small amount of control. With his heart beating
like a wild drum in his ears, he looked down at the
woman who was able to destroy his willpower and
self-control without even a touch. Her eyes still
closed, full breasts bouncing, she gasped with delight with his every stroke. The juices of her arousal
glistened on her lower lips.

She was so incredibly sexy that Lucas felt mes-
merized, enraptured. The need to come was now
tempered with the desire to savor her arousal, watch
it build until she climaxed tightly around his cock.

As though feeling the heat of his eyes, Alex raised
her lids and met his gaze. Everything suddenly got
hotter, more intimate and feverish. Lucas felt his
heart jump and slowed his rhythm in surprise. Then
he watched with anticipation as she shifted her
weight to one side, using her now free hand to slide
down her torso and over her clit. She began a slow
rub in small circles, her body vibrating from the
added stimulation.

He didn't know which of them groaned louder.

"Harder," she whispered.

Lucas had been watching her so intently that he
was now almost standing still. With her prompt,
he took a new firm grip of her ass and let loose
with long deep stokes. Alex was tighter now, hotter,
gripping his length within a body that seemed to
be designed just for him. She bit her bottom lip,

whimpered like a sensuous cat, then started to come with shallow thrusts of her hips. It was the most beautiful thing Lucas had ever experienced.

Within a minute, he was rushing back to that place at the edge of climax, with no ability to restrain the force. The tight grip of a shattering orgasm slammed through his body, stealing his breath and wiping his mind clear. He didn't hear the deep, throaty moans he emitted or the way he whispered her name as the last wave of pleasure rippled down his back.

As the world started to come back into focus, Lucas was still rock-hard and encased in silky warmth. Alex was flat on her back, breathing deep with her legs limp and hanging over the edge of the credenza. Her eyes were closed and she looked spent. He wanted to grin with satisfaction. Instead, he leaned over her body to rest his forehead on the delicate curve of her neck. His heartbeat was quickly returning to normal.

"This wasn't a good idea," Lucas growled in a tone far rougher than he intended.

"It felt pretty good to me," Alex countered, her dry tone laced with amusement.

Lucas gave a sharp laugh mixed with a throaty groan. "Pretty good" didn't begin to describe it. His erection was now down to a controllable state.

"Come on, let's get you cleaned up," he stated, straightening again to finally withdraw from the cradle of her body.

He gently righted her lace panties, helped her sit up, then lifted her off the surface from around the waist. They stood close in a loose embrace for a few moments. Lucas used a finger to lift her chin. Her hair and face looked deliciously mussed.

"Go take a shower," he suggested softly, feeling an unexpected affection. "We'll get going whenever you're ready."

Alex nodded, then sauntered off into the bathroom. Lucas took a deep breath, while removing the used condom and using tissues from the desk to do a quick cleanup. He was straightening his clothes when his phone beeped repeatedly, indicating an urgent call from Fortis.

"What's happening?" he demanded when he answered.

Immediately, Lucas heard the sound of emergency sirens in the background.

"There's been a fire in the auto shop," Michael stated in serious voice. "The motor's been completely destroyed."

CHAPTER 12

Alex spent an inordinate amount of time under the hot spray of the shower. She felt fantastic. While her heart rate was back to normal, the memory of the experience alone made her body feel flushed with exhilaration. Like after she had gone ziplining, or whitewater rafting, or rode a ridiculously fast roller coaster.

She smiled to herself, letting the water pound on her back long after the luxurious bubbles from the spa-quality bath gel had rinsed away. But eventually, she turned off the water and stepped out of the shower to towel off. There was only so long she could put off facing Lucas again.

That was one of the problems with casual, toe-curling sex with a business associate. Once the moment was over, no matter how good it was—and it was beyond good—you had to maintain a professional relationship. Alex wasn't certain if Lucas fell into that category. They didn't really work together, and she wasn't exactly his client. But, for however long he was going to be in town working for Magnus, things between them needed to be un-complicated, un-distracting.

In her sex-induced fog, Alex hadn't brought any extra clothes with her into the bathroom. But her toiletry bag was still on the counter from that morning. She generously applied face and body lotions, then wrapped herself in one of the over-size bathrobes hanging on the back of the door. It still took her a few moments to ready herself for her next encounter with Lucas.

Would he be the easygoing, flirty man she had first met in the hotel restaurant? Or the man who had returned from his trip during the week: intense, controlling, and unreadable? Which would she prefer? Alex looked at herself in the mirror, wondering why it was the latter version of Lucas Johnson that had prompted her to drop her pants. Literally.

Eventually, she opened the door and walked back into the large hotel room. Whatever she had antic-ipated, it wasn't to find Lucas with Lance, one of the other Fortis men, huddled in front of Lucas's laptop, intently watching a video. They both turned to look at her, twin expressions of fierce determi-nation on their faces. Alex pulled the edges of the robe a little closer at the neck, and walked hesitantly toward them. Something was obviously wrong, and she was immediately filled with apprehension.

Lance looked down, but Lucas's eyes never wavered from hers.

"What?" she finally demanded.

"There's been a fire," Lucas stated. "In the auto shop."

Alex's heart started beating frantically.

"What? What happened? Did anyone get hurt?" she fired back, staring back and forth between the two men.

"No," Lance confirmed. "Looks like it started sometime after about two thirty when the mechanics had locked up and gone home."

"How is that possible?" she questioned, feeling some relief. "Things don't catch on fire on their own. What happened?"

"Alex," Lucas began, his jaw hard and his hand shoved into the front pockets of his slacks. "The fire was in the race car. The one with the Cicada."

She looked back at him, eyes wide and unblinking while her brain tried to register his words.

"From what we can tell, your motor has been destroyed," he finished.

"Wait!" she shouted, waving her hands back and forth as though to stop any other words. "That doesn't make any sense! How does a motor catch on fire by itself? Was Dale's team doing some of the repairs to the body panels? Did someone screw up with the blowtorch? They're supposed to drain the ethanol fuel first—!"

"Alex," Lucas stated firmly, stepping close to her. "There was no one working on the car. The shop was already closed when it happened."

His expression was stoic, but his eyes were soft with compassion.

"Then . . . how?" she questioned. "I don't understand."

"Lucas, we have the team set up," said Lance from where he stood in front of the couch.

Lucas turned from her to walk over to where

the other agent was standing. She followed them, crossing her arms at her chest. They had connected a laptop computer to the flat-screen television to show a video image. Alex could see it was from the inside of the Magnus shop, and probably from one of the new surveillance camera feeds. The scene was chaotic, with a fire crew still working on the charred, smoking metal shell of what used to be a high-performance race car.

Heart beating with a mix of shock and dread, Alex covered her mouth with both hands while her eyes remained wide and fixed on the television.

"Ned," Lucas stated into the speaker of his cell phone lying on the console table. "Show us the footage you mentioned, from before the shop closed."

"Yup," said the voice through the phone. "The time stamp is one forty-two. You'll see two men talking to one of the mechanics near the yellow Ferrari. Then one of them walks away casually and stoops down to look inside the passenger window of the Mitsubishi."

Lucas, Lance, and Alex watched the scene play out as Ned described. Both men leaned forward. Alex didn't understand what they were looking for or what it would have to do with a fire that started at least a couple of hours later, according to what Lucas had told her.

"Replay it again," instructed Lucas. "Pause it there."

As requested, the pixilated surveillance video was frozen at the point that one of the men had lowered himself behind the race car, appearing to check out the inside.

"Alex," Lucas stated in a soft voice. "What car parts would be located where that guy is positioned?"

She looked back at him, her brain sluggish with shock.

"What mechanics would that guy be able reach from that spot?" he repeated patiently. "The gas line, maybe the batteries for the electric motor?"

"No, neither," she whispered, then cleared her throat. "That's all at the rear of the car. He's in front of the passenger door, so he could reach the tire, the rotor brakes, and calipers through the rims."

"What else?" Lucas probed, looking back at her intently. "Anything underneath the car?"

"There's the electrical wiring, connecting the motor to the control modules," Alex immediately confirmed. "But the conduit runs through the center of the floor. I'm not sure he could reach it from the position he's in. I think he'd have to be lower. But the brake line is closer. It extends from the front axle, along the right side of the floor, about three inches in from the frame."

"The brake fluid," muttered Lance, as though it made sense. "He punctured the line to create a slow leak."

The two men looked at each other.

"Ned, did you hear that?" Lucas asked louder. "Go back to the live feed and get Michael to check for a combustible near where the unknown suspect was bent down."

"You got it, boss," Ned answered. "The fire marshal has just arrived, so it's good timing."

The image on the television switched back to the

current activity in the shop. It was less chaotic, with only a couple of firemen who were packing up the hose and other equipment. Alex watched as a Fortis agent, Michael, walked into camera view, followed closely by a shorter man in a bright canary yellow uniform and helmet. They stopped beside the wet, blackened body of the car and started to look around with flashlights at the area Ned had specified.

"What are they trying to find?" Alex finally asked after a few moments.

"Chlorine," replied Lucas with his focus fixed on the television and the slow, meticulous search underway. Michael and the fire marshal were both bent low, inspecting everything within a small radius of the car, factoring in trajectory from the hard water pressure of the fire hose.

"Lucas, Mr. Passante has arrived," Ned interrupted from the speakerphone. "I gave him a full update over the phone before I called you."

Alex watched her boss jog across the shop floor then come to an abrupt stop a few feet away from the car with both hands clasped on top of his head. He looked down at the sodden floor, then back at the destroyed race car. She could practically feel his horror and disbelief since it must echo her own.

"Let him know we'll have a debriefing with him as soon as the marshal's finished the inspection," Lucas instructed to Ned.

About five minutes later, the fire marshal pointed his flashlight into a spot between a pile of miscellaneous automotive parts lined against the wall next to the Mitsubishi. Then, he pulled out a container and tweezers from his jacket to carefully collect whatever he had found. Michael quickly joined him to look at the particles. The Fortis agent took out his cell phone and dialed a contact. Lucas's phone rang with a second caller, and he conferenced Michael into the discussion with Ned.

"What is it?" Lucas asked, still watching the live feed.

"Scraps from some sort of fabric" Michael immediately replied. "There are scorch marks under the car, right where the unknown suspect had stopped, so the fire marshal thinks the fragments are part of the accelerant, maybe a bag or something it was contained in."

"Was it chlorine?" Lance asked.

"We can't be sure until the marshal's office tests everything and inspects the car," Michael explained. "But I'd say it's pretty likely. My guess is that they punctured the brake line with a small hole, creating a slow dripping leak. Then, if he placed chlorine disks under the drip, it would set up a time delay for an explosive fire. The right combination could buy a couple of hours, easy. Add another combustible fluid, like gasoline or ethanol, and the fire would burn long enough to ignite the car."

"Oh my God!" Alex groaned.

It wasn't an accident or carelessness. The Fortis agents believe someone had walked into Magnus and deliberately set the Mitsubishi on fire, completely destroying the Cicada motor inside.

"Boys, we need to reevaluate our plan for this

mission. I'm going to get Sam and Evan on the line to look at our options. Michael, let Marco know we'll meet with him in thirty minutes," Lucas instructed. "In the meantime, let's provide the fire department with everything they need, except the footage of our suspects. We need to identify and locate them first. Ned, can you get Raymond working on it with the facial-mapping program?"

"You got it, boss," Ned replied before both agents disconnected their phone lines.

"Alex, why don't you go and get dressed?" Lucas suggested in a quiet voice.

She looked back at him, then down at the white robe. Was it only a few minutes since she had stepped out of the shower, still feeling the afterglow of their intimacy?

Alex nodded, finding her throat too clogged to speak. As she walked across the hotel room, she heard her cell phone ringing from the inside of her purse that lay on the bed. She took the mobile out and found Marco's number on the video call display.

"Where are you?" he asked right away. "Are you okay?"

"Yeah," Alex replied in a whisper. "I'm still at the hotel, with Lucas Johnson and one of his agents."

"Shit, Alex! They've destroyed the car," he groaned with defeat. "It's gone."

Alex pressed the heel of one palm into her eyes, wishing this was just a nightmare and she'd wake up soon.

"I know," she finally stated. "I can't believe it, Marco. We need to be in Vancouver in six weeks to start the track trials. That's not enough time to rebuild it."

"Alex, there's no rebuilding, not for the Sea-to-Sky race. It's gone," he repeated. "Completely destroyed. Even if you could rebuild the components, we still wouldn't have a battery. You said it was a one-of-kind prototype that took Adam North months to make—"

"But—"

"It's over, Alex. We're done," Marco continued talking over her.

"Marco, listen to me," she insisted, raising her voice. "It's not over. I have the battery."

There was a long pause.

"What? What do you mean?" he demanded.

Alex looked over at Lucas and Lance who were working quickly and efficiently to set something up with the laptop.

"One second," she added, then grabbed her travel bag and slipped into the bathroom, closing the door behind her.

"Marco?" she asked.

"Yeah, I'm still here," he confirmed, sounding impatient. "What do you mean you have the battery? Where?"

"I had picked up a new power converter on Thursday, so I took Adam's battery out of the Evo to connect them and create test models," Alex explained, her heart pounding harder and harder. "It's still in my office, locked in my drawer."

"Holy shit, Alex!" There was another long pause. "Does anyone else know that?"

Alex looked down at the marble bath tiles,

thinking of everything that had happened over the last couple of days.

"I don't think so," she finally replied with a deep sigh. "I didn't tell anyone. The guys were researching modifications to the other components, but we weren't planning on implementing them until the repairs were done to the Evo."

"Okay. Okay. I'm meeting with Fortis in a few minutes. Maybe we can figure something out."

"I don't know, Marco. Even with the battery, we still only have six weeks. I don't know if I can do it."

"Don't worry about it for now. Let's see what Lucas and his team recommend, then we'll figure out what to do. Okay?" Marco assured her.

Alex nodded, biting her lip with apprehension, forgetting that he couldn't see her through the phone.

"Alex?"

"Okay," she finally replied.

They hung up the call, and Alex looked into the bathroom mirror as she tried to stay calm.

CHAPTER 13

In under five minutes, Lucas had both his Fortis partners on a three-way video call. At three fifteen on Saturday afternoon, Evan DaCosta and Samuel Mackenzie both were at home. Lucas quickly gave them a summary of the new developments on the Magnus Motorsports mission.

"How bad is the property damage?" asked Samuel with a deep, rich voice and a cultured Scottish accent.

"The fire alarm went off pretty quickly. Ned attacked it with an industrial-size fire extinguisher within two to three minutes after that to contain it. So far, other than superficial water and smoke damage to the area, looks like only the race car was damaged."

"Brake fluid and chlorine," Evan mused. "Pretty low-tech, household stuff, Lucas. High school chemistry one-oh-one."

"Exactly," Lucas agreed. "Based on the surveillance video, these guys walked in as customers, no evidence that they were carrying anything suspicious. Whatever they used was small and easily concealable. Based on what Michael and the marshal found, I'd say it was a few pucks of generic pool chorine, coupled with a highly flammable liquid to ensure it spread fast enough to do the damage needed."

Sam blew out a deep breath. As a former British Secret Service MI5 agent for over ten years, he had a lot of experience with all forms of creative threats.

"This changes the mission significantly, Lucas," concluded Sam. "Whoever's behind all this isn't just trying to steal the design and technology, they want to shut down the Magnus project altogether."

Lucas and Evan nodded.

"And their behavior is escalating in their attempt to do that," Evan added.

Lucas glanced over at Lance who was standing beside him, looking just as serious as the rest of them.

"To what end, though?" Lucas finally asked, though it was a question reflected on all their faces. "Are they trying to stop Magnus from being first to market by stealing the tech for their own future release? Or bury it completely?"

Evan sat forward in his chair from the living room of his apartment in Alexandria.

"Based on Raymond's research on the big car manufacturers, they all have electric or hybrid models on the market now. And there's dozens of concept models making the car show rounds this year that promise results similar to what Alex Cotts has designed," Evan argued. "So, this isn't like the Avro Arrow in 1959. Shutting down the Magnus project isn't going to hinder the advancement of electric car technology in any significant way."

"That's assuming it's one of the oil companies behind this, right?" Sam threw in. "They ultimately have the most to lose."

"I looked through Raymond's file last night," Lucas explained. "And I wouldn't rule out oil and gas. None of the designs solve the cost problem. All of the car companies still use battery technology that is expansive and motors that lack real power. Which means that electric and hybrid cars are really only targeting the eco-conscious Prius buyer, at least for another three to five years."

"Or the rich one-percenters that can afford both an Aston Martin and a Tesla," Sam added dryly.

Lucas chuckled. And since Evan owned both cars, though the Tesla was really for his girlfriend, Nia, he gave the Scotsman the middle finger in protest.

"You should try entering the twenty-first century Mac. Maybe upgrade that boat you drive into something more responsible," Evan shot back.

"It's a Jaguar XKR-S, my friend. There is no other upgrade," Sam replied sardonically, showing a rare flash of teeth in a big smile.

"Okay, boys, settle down," interrupted Lucas, though he appreciated the moment of levity from the serious situation they were facing with Magnus and Alex Cotts.

"Maybe we're thinking about this too big," stated Lance.

"How so?" Evan asked.

The ex-Ranger stepped closer to the computer screen.

"Once we saw the setup in Chicago with Pratt, we assumed big-budget backing. Which logically led to us thinking major players, right? Then we learned more about the Cicada design and the impact to automotive engineering far beyond the racing industry. So, again we expanded the pool of industries and companies who could be responsible," Lance summarized. "If we limit the scope to North America, there's the big three car manufacturers, assuming we don't include Tesla. Then the top five or six gas companies."

He counted them off with his fingers.

"But that all assumes that someone found out the full capabilities of Cotts's design. We have no proof that happened," continued Lance. "Maybe this whole thing is just your everyday, run-of-the-mill small company competition."

The other three men thought for a moment in silence.

"It's a good point, Lance," Lucas finally agreed. "So, let's review the facts that we know. One: Magnus Motorsports is registered for the Vancouver race in June, like they have been for the last three years. Their three investors think they will launch a new hybrid engine and none know it's actually electric-powered. Two: Someone knew Adam North was working with Cotts, and they also would know that he's a physicist with a specialization in battery technology. Three: Timothy Pratt got access to North's computer at the university, then used his access to the Magnus file-sharing server to plant a Trojan horse. Four: Pratt was payrolled, then killed in Chicago when he failed to get access to the Magnus network. Five: Thirty-six hours later, the Cicada engine is cleverly destroyed by arson inside the Magnus auto shop.

"Have I missed anything in the sequence of events?" he finished, looking at each of the other men.

"No, that about covers it," replied Evan.

"Yup, that's it. Until we can identify the two men who set the fire today," Lance added. "We got nothing on the goons that attacked us in Chicago."

"And the copy of Pratt's computer didn't provide any clues about how much these guys know of North's battery technology or the Cicada design," Lucas confirmed. "We only know for sure that they want information from the Magnus network and to destroy the prototype. There are no facts to tell us who or why. So, to Lance's point, this could all be personal, or another small racing company trying to knock out the competition."

"We know a couple more things," Sam inserted. "They didn't do it all for shits and giggles. Someone had invested a bit of time and money into this endeavor. So they have access to funds, and contacts in the U.S. and Canada to get things done without getting their own hands dirty."

The four men were silent in contemplation for a few moments.

"Okay, let's outline our go-forward plan," Lucas finally stated. "Until we know more and can determine who we're dealing with and what their ultimate objective is, we need to take every precaution. While we could assume that whoever is behind this whole thing has accomplished their goal today by destroying the engine, my instincts tell me that's not the case."

"It's not all destroyed."

The comment came from a silky feminine voice. Lucas and Lance turned to Alex who was now standing next to the bed, dressed in loose blue jeans and a black T-shirt with sneakers. With her arms wrapped around her waist, she looked young and vulnerable.

"Alex, please join us," Lucas told her, then waited until she was in visual range to do introductions. "Alexandria Cotts, meet Evan DaCosta and Samuel Mackenzie, the other managing partners in Fortis."

She gave them both a casual hand wave and a tight smile.

"Nice to meet you, Ms. Cotts," Evan replied with a nod. "Did we hear you correctly? Your engine wasn't destroyed by the fire?"

"Not all of it," she stated, looking between the two men. "Everything that was still in the car is probably irreparable. But I had removed the rechargeable batteries on Friday."

"The ones Adam North customized for you?" Lucas clarified.

Alex nodded.

"I was creating test models on the computer for a new part I picked up on Thursday, so I took it out. It's now locked in my office."

"Lance, call Michael to confirm there has been no attempt to access any other part of the

Magnus building, particularly Alex's office," Lucas instructed.

Lance walked to the other side of the room while dialing out on his cell phone.

"I already told Marco, but no one else would know that," Alex explained. "So, I think I can re-build my motor and the full drivetrain. The battery is the only thing that is irreplaceable."

"Passante still plans to launch in June?" Evan questioned. "Is that feasible?"

"I'm not sure, to be honest. But I have to try," she stated with determination.

"All right then," said Sam with a sparkle of what looked like admiration in his eyes.

Lance returned as he hung up his call.

"Michael and Ned have done a full reconnais-sance," he confirmed. "No other signs of intru-sion."

Lucas folded his arms across his chest and widened his stance as he spoke to his partners.

"If that is the objective, to allow Alex to rebuild the asset, then we'll have to implement Omega protocol for the next six weeks."

"Agreed," stated Sam, and the other two men nodded in accord.

"What does that mean?" Alex asked.

Lucas hesitated, knowing she wasn't going to like it.

"I'll explain when we meet with Marco," he told her briefly.

Alex looked as though she was about to protest, but he turned away to discourage more questions.

"Lance, is the Magnus building secure yet?" he asked instead.

"The fire department is packing up now, so we'll have complete containment in about fifteen minutes."

"Okay, let Michael and Ned know we'll be there at four o'clock to meet with Mr. Passante," instructed Lucas. "Sam, Evan, send me the best options for an extraction and a safe site based on all the variables. We'll work out the other logistics tonight."

He disconnected the video call then turned to face Alex. She looked even more worried than before.

"What are you planning?" she asked right away.

"We're only looking at options right now. Our recommendations will depend on our meeting with Marco, and what he decides to do. Then, my job is to provide the required asset protection," explained Lucas. "Why don't you finish packing your things? We'll be leaving here in five minutes."

Alex sighed deeply, but walked away to do as he instructed. While he continued to pack up the laptop and his other things with efficient practice, Lucas struggled to contain his displeasure at the new developments at Magnus. Two men had simply walked onto their client site and successfully implemented a plan to destroy the motor prototype. Which means he had underestimated the protective support required. That was unacceptable and could not happen again. He knew all too well that there were more than machines and schematics as stake. There were people. There was Alex.

Lucas took a deep breath and put a firm halt to the direction of his thoughts. That moment between them earlier was an unexplainable act of madness, and best forgotten. It certainly could not happen again.

"Do you really think we need the Omega protocol," Lance asked, interrupting Lucas's thoughts.

"We don't know anything about the threat, except that it keeps escalating," replied Lucas in a low voice. "If Cotts is going to rebuild her motor, the only way to assure protection is to completely contain the environment and tighten the restrictions on all information and access."

"Makes sense," Lance replied. "But I don't know how you're going to convince Cotts of that."

"If that's the plan, then she won't have a choice."

They left the room shortly after, with Alex sandwiched between the two men as they walked through the hotel and out to the car parked on the street. They drove with Lance in their rented truck around the block to Magnus with no sign of any threats, then parked at the back entrance. All signs of the fire department were now gone, and Ned was outside waiting for them.

"The marshal left a few minutes ago, but he provided his contact information for follow-up," Ned stated as they all walked quickly into the building. "He found a tiny puncture in the brake fluid line of the car, just as we suspected. Raymond's got a hit on one of the perpetrators. He's sending us the file, and we think we've tracked their car to the west end of the city."

"Good," Lucas stated. "I want a plan confirmed by tonight, so we need all the answers we can get."

Marco Passante was standing in his office, talking on his cell phone while pacing back and forth in front of his desk. He looked up at the group gathered in the hallway.

"I'm on with our insurance broker," he muttered, then went back to pacing.

"Alex, why don't you wait in your office while my team gets set up for the debriefing," Lucas suggested while the Fortis men entered the meeting room they had set up as a control center.

"No," she stated, following them all in and taking a stubborn stance next to the table. "I want to know what's going on."

Lucas stopped in front of her with a look that should make grown men back down, but Alex just lifted her chin higher and boldly glared back.

"Lucas, I have Raymond's report," Michael stated from a seat in front of one of the computers.

"Put it up on the other monitor," Lucas instructed with a final hard stare at Alex before he turned to stand with the other men.

Several pictures tiled onto the screen in front of him. The first was a still shot from the surveillance footage before the fire, showing two men talking to one of the mechanics. The next was a second, closer image of the guy who created a distraction while his partner had sabotaged the Mitsubishi race car. Several other pictures showed the same man in social media postings.

"This is Oleg Petrov, thirty-eight years old, and

a Toronto resident," Michael stated based on the report provided. "He works as a supervisor for a company called Bold Management that owns a few properties around the city. No criminal record in Canada or the U.S."

"What do we know about this Bold Management?" Lucas asked. "Does it have any ties to the automotive or racing industry?"

"None that we can find. But their properties are leased to a couple of bars and a restaurant, so Petrov may be freelancing for someone in his network."

"Raymond said he located the car the two had used earlier," Ned stated. "Did he send anything?"

"Yeah," Michael confirmed as he pulled up more pictures. "Based on the timing of the surveillance video, I managed to get an image of the front fender of the car we think they were driving. It's a black, four-door sedan."

"It's a Ford Fusion; 2010 or 2011," Alex stated easily.

Michael showed another clearer picture of a black car at a traffic light with two men in the front seats, time-stamped at 2:55 in the afternoon, about five minutes after they would had left the auto shop.

"Here they are headed toward the westbound entrance to the highway. This view provides a clear picture of the license plate. Then we located the same car parked about fifteen miles away, behind one of the Bold properties; a bar called Red Inferno." The last image was a still picture from some sort of digital surveillance, with a time stamp of only twenty minutes earlier. "Raymond is watching the area and will let us know if there is any additional activity."

"We need to get eyes on this Petrov character," noted Lucas. "No doubt, he's going to communicate with whomever hired him, and if we're lucky, it will be in person. And let's identify the second perpetrator. Whoever came up with the plan and put together the incendiary may have knowledge of cars, and we need to know the connection."

Marco Passante walked into the room at that point, looking harassed and disheveled. Lucas turned to their client, prepared for the difficult conversation to follow.

CHAPTER 14

Alex knew that she wasn't going to like the plan Lucas Johnson recommended for how to safely rebuild the Cicada engine, but she couldn't have imagined what came next.

Once Marco joined the meeting, Lucas took a few minutes to get him up to speed on everything the Fortis team had uncovered since the fire.

"We'll move in to set up surveillance on Petrov after this meeting in order to uncover who hired him and his partner to destroy the engine," concluded Lucas. "The best way to protect your assets is to understand the threat, about which we've had very little information to this point."

Marco ran his hand through his hair creating an even more unruly mess.

"Okay," he replied with a sigh. "The police called earlier. They'll be here in the morning to take a full report. What should I tell them?"

"Just the facts for now. We need some room to do a more covert investigation. If the police go after Petrov, he and whoever hired him will just get spooked. Then we'll lose our best opportunity to get more information."

"Okay," Marco agreed.

"Now, Alex has told us about the battery North had provided," Lucas continued in an even tone. "Will you be rebuilding the engine with the intent to launch it in Vancouver for the June race?"

Marco looked at Alex, as though still struggling with the decision. She could tell that he was torn by the desire to successfully achieve their goal, and the concern of the clear danger they were in.

"Yes," Alex stated clearly, stepping forward. "We have to try."

"Alex, I don't know if it is a good idea," Marco replied facing her. "Maybe we should wait, let things die down a little. We can always do the Sea-to-Sky race with one of our other engines."

"No, Markie," she insisted. "We've worked too hard on this to just let them stop us. You know something like this is all about timing. If we don't do it now, we could easily lose the advantage of being first to market."

"They just set fire to the shop, Alex. Someone wants to shut us down, and they're not shy about it. What do you think they'll do if we continue working on it? We don't know how far they are willing to go. Someone could get hurt. It's not worth it," argued Marco with his hands buried in his pockets and his shoulders slumped in defeat.

"They don't have to know," countered Alex. "Whoever did this thinks they've shut us down because the Cicada engine was in there. So I'll rebuild it on my own. No one will know about it until we're launching at the race. Then it will be too late."

"I don't know—"

"You know I'm going to do it anyway," she stated with her hand planted on her hips. "I am not walking away from two years of work just because of a bully. So there's no point in arguing about it."

Marco's shoulder lowered even more, as he recognized her inability to budge once she'd set her mind on something.

"Okay, fine. But you have to promise to do whatever Lucas and his team decide is necessary to keep you safe," her boss stipulated. "Promise, Alex."

Though Alex hated being forced to compromise, she was smart enough to see that it was in her best interest.

"I promise," she replied with a cheeky grin.

Marco let out a deep sigh then turned back to the four men who had been waiting patiently through their debate.

"We're going to rebuild the Cicada, still aiming for the June launch," he finally confirmed.

Alex watched as Lucas nodded then stepped forward while the other three Fortis agents seemed to line up behind him.

"Based on the escalating attacks over the last week and our lack of information about the motive behind them, we need to secure Alex and the assets in a safe, impenetrable environment," Lucas stated, stoically.

"What does that mean?" Marco asked, while Alex was thinking about the conversation back at the hotel and the protocol Lucas had referenced.

"We'll put Alex in a safe location unknown to

anyone but my team, where she can rebuild the motor."

"What?" Alex demanded, certain she had heard wrong. "Where?"

Lucas looked back at her with his brows raised.

"It only works if no one knows where you're going, including you," he replied in a tone that was a little more condescending than she would have liked.

"Okay," Marco replied.

"Markie! No!" she shot back. "I'm not going to be locked away for six weeks. That's crazy!"

"Alex, you just agreed to whatever security plan Fortis recommended. This is it," Marco reminded her. "And it makes sense. Right now, if they want to destroy the Cicada, they'll be going after you. All the information is in your head just as much as the specs stored on our computer network. So there is no debate here. Either they take you somewhere safe, or I'm shutting down the whole thing."

Alex looked into the eyes of her boss and friend, and read his resolve loud and clear. He was not going to back down. So either she would have to hide away for weeks or give up on her dream. As much as Alex hated to admit it, it was an easy decision.

"Fine," she eventually muttered.

"All right, boys, we're implementing Omega protocol," Lucas stated, turning back to his team. "Michael and Lance, you'll stay here to provide ongoing security and continue any local investigation. Ned and I will go with the assets."

Michael continued working on the computer

while the other two men took out their cell phones and started working through information.

"Lex, we'll need a list of everything you need to rebuild your engine," Lucas continued as he turned back to her and Marco. "Start with the most immediate. We can continue to get supplies shipped to us as you need them."

"What about the stuff here? Should I be packing them up?" she asked, her heart racing at the size of the task. "And should I check out the car to see if there is anything salvageable?"

But Lucas was already shaking his head.

"We're not taking anything with us from here. Everyone needs to believe that the engine was destroyed and the projects is dead. Including the shop employees. So everything stays here except the rechargeable battery."

Alex didn't know what to say. Her brain was suddenly frozen from the overwhelming amount of details that would need to be planned and executed. Was this even possible? Had she let her stubborn pride and determination drive her too far?

"Lex." She looked up at Lucas as he said her name gently, the beautiful face softened with support. "It's going to be fine. You'll have the whole Fortis team at your disposal. Just step back and list out everything you need to make it happen. I'll take care of everything else."

She let out a deep breath she hadn't realized she was holding.

"Okay. Okay." Alex felt calmer after each utterance.

Lucas nodded and gave a hint of that sexy smile. "You'll have the next three to four hours. Then we'll take you home so you can pack a bag and get a little sleep," he added. "Lance, Ned, I need a drink. Let's check out that bar in the west end, and see how our new friend Petrov is doing."

Alex watched the Fortis team get ready to leave, her mouth agape. Ned unlocked and opened a large, silver trunk by the back wall, which seemed to have an endless supply of small weaponry. Each of the three men added a second gun to what they already wore, plus a few other bits of metal concealed under their clothes. A few minutes later, they filed out of the room, looking fierce and formidable.

"Wait," Alex called as she started following them out into the hallway. "I can't just take off for weeks without an explanation. What do I tell my cousin, my brothers?"

"Use your imagination," Lucas replied over his shoulder. "After all the hard work and stress you've been under, I'm sure you need a long vacation. Choose somewhere tranquil or exotic."

Then he and the other two agents were gone out the back entrance through the shop.

"How about a yoga retreat in Thailand?"

Alex looked back at Michael to see if he was serious.

"I don't do yoga."

"Then you're going to learn. It's great for stress management," the agent stated, barely looking up from whatever he was reviewing on the computer.

"What about Europe?" Marco added. "Start in France, then travel to Italy and Spain. That would eat up a few weeks for sure."

"Sightseeing by myself?" It did have some appeal, Alex thought.

"Sure, why not?" stated Marco. "No one who knows you will think twice about it, trust me. You are a bit of a loner, you know."

It was true, it wasn't the first time she had taken off alone for a last-minute trip. Never for more than a weekend or a few days, but then again, she never had her biggest accomplishment destroyed by arson before.

"Okay, Europe it is," she finally agreed. "I guess I should go start working on that list of parts and supplies."

Michael stood up and walked over to her with a card in his hand.

"Here is a secure e-mail address you should use to send us your requirements. Use it for anything related to the rebuild going forward," he outlined. "Then once you've told people where you're going, we'll create a full online experience to back it up."

Alex didn't really know what that meant, but took the card. She walked slowly down the hall to her office at the other end, feeling the heavy weight of her decision and the task ahead on her shoulders.

"Are you okay?" Marco asked as he followed her into the room.

Alex let out a deep, long breath followed by a humorless laugh.

"Jesus, Markie, I just can't wrap my brain around this craziness," she finally admitted. "It's just a car motor. I mean, I know it's different from anything out there on the market right now. And sure, it has great potential. But it's still just a motor and a drivetrain, and we're such a small shop. Why would anyone want to go through all this trouble to destroy it?"

She buried her head in her hands out of sheer frustration.

"What am I doing? Why did I pursue this?" she continued. "I'm about to disappear for weeks to rebuild this stupid thing. Why? To prove that I can? That I'm as good as or better than a male engineer?"

"Alex," Marco tried to interrupt, using a tone meant to calm her down.

"God, my dad was right. I really am that person, aren't I? Always reaching for something outside of my grasp, taking more risks that I should," she muttered. "What's wrong with me?"

"Alex, there's nothing wrong with you," Marco interjected, standing in front of her to offer a comforting presence. "You're smart and ambitious. Those are good things and you shouldn't need to hide them. From anyone. And if you want to rebuild the Cicada despite all the challenges, then that makes you brave, too."

Alex looked up at him with watery, red eyes, really wanting to believe the wonderful things he was saying.

"Is it worth it, though? The time? The cost? You've hired a band of frigging gun-toting mercenaries!"

Marco grinned.

"They are not mercenaries, they are security specialists. The best in their field, from what I've been told."

"Fine, gun-toting security specialists."

He laughed. She felt marginally better.

"Seriously though, Alex. You don't have to do this," he continued. "Like I said earlier, we'll just reinvest in one of the other combustion engines for the June race."

"What about the investors? They're expecting a new hybrid to be launched, and they're already getting antsy for more details," she protested.

"Let me worry about the investors. We've been conservative with our cost, so they'll all at least break even."

Alex bit her lip. He was giving her a window, a free ticket out of crazy town. She should grab it in both hands and run with it. Move on, work on other smaller projects, and get a life. That's what made sense. But Alex couldn't say the words. She looked back at Marco and just couldn't do it.

She didn't want to give up and walk away. She had set an objective, dedicated over two years toward it, and refused to allow some unknown force to stop her before the finish line. Alex wanted to see her Cicada launched into the marketplace, and be a part of revolutionizing the auto industry. And she was prepared to do whatever it took to make that happen.

"I want to rebuild it," she finally told Marco, who did not look at all surprised.

"Good," he replied with a tolerant smile. "Then let's get to work."

They spent the next two and a half hours creating a detailed list on her iPad of all parts, equipment, and supplies needed to create a small, stand-alone fabrication shop. Alex then copied the full design schematics for the electric motor, lithium-ion batteries, and all the customized and modified components that connected them.

"I'm sure I'm missing something," Alex admitted after a long pause spent just staring into space.

"Like Lucas stated, just focus on what you need to get started," Marco reminded her. "Then they can order other things as you identify them."

"I guess. But we'll be on a really tight timeline. Some of this stuff can take weeks to get if they're on back order," she reminded him.

"Something tells me Fortis can get their hands on anything required," he interjected. "So don't stress about it, Alex."

There was a knock on her open office door, and Michael was standing in the entry.

"Lucas and the team will be back here in about fifteen minutes," he announced.

"Did they get any information about who hired those guys to set the fire?" Marco asked.

"They'll provide an update when they arrive," Michael explained.

"I can't wait, unfortunately," Marco advised them. "I'm already pretty late for an engagement with one of our clients. Can you ask Lucas to give me a call with the details?"

"No problem," confirmed Michael. "Alex, how are you coming along with the list?"

She sat up and took a deep breath and looked at her watch. It was about ten minutes after seven o'clock. This was it, there was no going back.

"I think I'm done. I'll send it to the e-mail address now," she told him.

"Good. Let's also pack up the rechargeable battery," he instructed.

Alex took her keys out of her purse and unlocked the cabinet next to her desk. She took out the battery and new power converter and handed them over to the agent.

"If you want to make a few phone calls, now is a good time to do it," suggested Michael. "Then Lucas will take you home to pack for the trip."

Then he was gone, leaving Alex and Marco alone. It was time to say good-bye.

"You won't know where I am," she stated softly.

"I know, but we'll stay in touch," he replied, reassuringly. "We'll come up with some code words for the project so you can keep me updated on your progress."

Alex smirked, appreciating his effort to lighten the moment.

"Sure. I'll pretend I've discovered a new appreciation for wine, so you can ask me how I'm doing on a tour of the major wineries across southern Europe," she elaborated.

"See! You're pretty good at this," exclaimed Marco, his eyes sparkling.

There was a long pause.

"It will be fine, Alex. You're in good hands," he finally added.

Alex nodded, suddenly emotional. They hugged.

"Thank you," she whispered into his ear with one final squeeze to his shoulders.

"For what? Profiting from your genius?" Marco teased when they stepped apart.

"Whatever," she dismissed with a wave of her hand. "For believing in me, investing in my crazy ideas."

"That's the easy part. Dealing with your temperamental bossiness, and high-maintenance demands? That's what you should be grateful for."

Alex opened her mouth with outrage and slapped him on the arm. Marco laughed.

"Send me a note a soon as you can?" he finally asked.

"I will."

Then he was gone and Alex was alone. She checked her watch again. Only about ten minutes left. She walked over to her desk and took out her cell phone from her purse to make a few phone calls.

"Hi, Dad," she started when he picked up the phone. "Did you enjoy the wedding?"

"Hey, Alex. It was a really good time," he replied in his low, slow voice. "You looked really nice."

"Thanks. No comments about how weird it was for Shawn to have a girl as his best man?"

Her dad chuckled, used to her teasing him about all the things that were very untraditional about his daughter's life.

"Yeah, it's a first for me. But different times, I guess."

Alex smiled. He really was trying to let her live her life with no rules.

"Dad, I'm going to take off for a last-minute vacation," she finally stated, biting her lip in anticipation of his reaction.

"Really? Where're you going?"

"Europe, for a few weeks."

"That long, eh? Is everything okay?" he asked with some concern in his voice.

"I just need a break, that's all," Alex explained with some honesty. "That big project I've been working on? It's dead. So I'm going to enjoy some downtime."

"Dead? What happened?"

Alex paused, uncertain of how much she should reveal.

"There was a small fire at the shop, and it destroyed the prototype. And there just isn't enough time to start over."

"Oh baby, I'm sorry to hear that," her dad exclaimed. "How bad was the damage?"

"It was limited, thank God." She looked at her watch, conscious of the fact that she would have to go soon. "Anyway, Dad, I just wanted to let you know about my trip. I'm leaving tomorrow, but I'll stay in touch while I'm gone. Okay?"

"Sure, sweetheart. You deserve to relax and have some fun for once. So have a good time."

"Thanks, Dad. Love you."

"Love you too, baby."

Alex hung up with a mix of melancholy and relief. Then she made the next call.

"Adrian?"

"Hey, Lex, what's up?" replied her twin brother.

"What would you say if I took off for a few weeks? On an extended vacation?"

"Cool. Where to?"

"Europe."

"Nice," he exclaimed. "Does this have anything to do with the new boyfriend?"

"No! And he's not my boyfriend," she insisted.

"Whatever," he dismissed, clearly not hearing her. "When are you leaving?"

"Tomorrow morning."

"Wow, that fast."

"I know. It was a last-minute thing," she conceded, hoping he wouldn't ask more questions.

"Okay. Well, have fun and keep us posted on where you are," he insisted "And don't forget to bring me back something."

Alex smiled. Typical Adrian.

"I'll see what I can do."

CHAPTER 15

"Petrov hasn't left the building and the car is still parked in the back," Michael confirmed though the earpiece Lucas and the other agents were wearing.

"We haven't seen him yet, so maybe he's in the kitchen or an office in the back?" Lucas suggested.

He and Ned were sitting at the bar in the small pub in the west end of Toronto. They had arrived about fifteen minutes earlier and ordered draft beers. Lance stayed in the truck to provide eyes on the outside.

"Any sign of his partner in crime?" Michael asked.

"Negative," Ned mumbled in a low voice. "There are five men in here, including the bartender. But none fit the general description."

"Well, let's settle in, boys. See what develops in the next hour or so," Lucas instructed.

He and Ned then spent a stretch of time making small talk and nursing their drinks while remaining vigilant about their environment. The bar was in a trendy part of the city near the lakeshore among a string of boutiques and other restaurants, and the area was pretty busy on an early Saturday evening. The five patrons quickly doubled, then tripled as the dinner crowd started to trickle in. Yet none of the men who entered the establishment looked like the second man in the arson video, or the person who had hired their services.

The six o'clock news came on, broadcast on a large television behind the bar. They started with local city events, including a fire at a closed auto shop in the downtown core. The anchor read a press release from the fire marshal, putting up a picture of the Magnus Motorsports building. He noted that the cause had not yet been determined, but that the investigation was ongoing.

Lucas and Ned listened to the summary of what they already knew and watched the room for any telling response to the story. The bartender didn't pause to look up, and no one else seated at the bar or at the dining table looked particularly interested. Except an older man sitting on his own at a table in the back, nearest to the kitchen. He took out his phone and made a call while his eyes never left the television screen.

"We have some action," Ned stated quietly into his earpiece, where the other Fortis agents were connected. "Image coming."

The agent then lifted his cell phone as though responding to something on it, quickly snapped three photos, and e-mailed them to Michael.

"Got it," Michael confirmed within a few minutes. "Searching the database."

"Is this your doing?" Lucas asked Ned with a nod up to the news broadcast.

"I may have mentioned to the marshal that the public may have seen something that would be helpful to the case," Ned admitted.

They were both former Secret Service agents, and having worked many cases together over the years, employed similar methodology.

"Good move. Public confirmation that the deed was done successfully," Lucas stated.

"Hopefully, it helps remove the heat from Magnus and Cotts, and gives us some breathing room."

"Hopefully," Lucas agreed though his tone was skeptical and laden with concern.

Ned looked at him hard then touched his earpiece to put it on mute. Lucas noted the move and did the same.

"Do want to tell me what's going on with Cotts?" Ned finally asked in a low tone.

"What are you talking about?" asked Lucas, doing his best to seem unfazed.

"You called her *Lex* today," Ned replied. "Twice. We've worked together for a long time, Lucas. Protected a lot of people over the years. I've never seen you call an asset by a nickname."

Lucas took a drink of beer then carefully put down his cup. He knew exactly what Ned was referring to. He had known the moment he felt Alex's fear and apprehension in his gut and let his professional guard down.

"It's nothing," he told Ned. "I had met her briefly before arriving at Magnus, and she had introduced herself as Lex. The name just stuck, that's all."

"It's no biggie. Just curious," Ned replied, shrugging and taking a drink of his own. "She's a very attractive woman. We both know shit happens in this job."

Lucas definitely knew that. Now thirty-one years old, he'd gotten into the security-consulting business in his freshman year at MIT. Fifteen years later, he understood that an effective protective strategy for vulnerable people often meant extremely close contact in stressful, dangerous environments. That occasionally led to an artificial sense of intimacy that was hard to resist.

There was nothing in the unwritten rule book against relationships with clients or assets, as long as it didn't cloud judgment or impede the mission. While Lucas hadn't gotten physically involved with a woman during an assignment, he had seen it happen on occasion. His friend and partner Evan had met his girlfriend, Nia, just last year on his first mission with Fortis, and their relationship had survived the ordeal.

Not that Lucas was contemplating the same thing. What had happened with Alex just hours earlier was a one-time thing. He had no intention of encouraging something more between them. He preferred his relationships to be less complicated and less intense.

Thankfully, Ned didn't really require a response to his statement, and Michael's voice came through the earpiece with an update.

"We have a match to the photo you sent. His name is Frank Nunez from Chicago. Security manager for a venture capitalist company called Red Creek," Michael outlined. "No criminal record, nothing else noteworthy."

Ned and Lucas discreetly unmuted from their earpieces.

"Chicago? That can't be a coincidence," Ned muttered. "Do we have any info on his movement over the last few days?"

"Yup, looks like he arrived in Toronto Thursday afternoon," confirmed Michael. "I'll get Laura at headquarters to do a full review of all his activities since he arrived."

"What about this company, Red Creek?" Lucas asked. "Any obvious ties to the auto industry?"

"Nothing I can see immediately from their Web site or media clippings," Michael told them. "They seem more focused on buying out small to medium-size companies, then liquidating their assets and intellectual property."

"Okay, thanks, Michael. Let's see if Nunez makes contact with Petrov while he's here."

The team went on radio silence for another thirty minutes or so, but Nunez didn't appear to be in any hurry. They watched as the middle-aged man ordered another glass of wine followed by a prime rib dinner.

"I'm hitting the head," Lucas eventually announced. "I'll scope out the back area while I'm there. Let me know if anything changes with the target."

"You got it," Ned replied.

Lucas stood up from the barstool and casually walked to the right side of the pub, following the sign to the restrooms. As he walked down a narrow hall, he passed a row of autographed pictures that caused him to pause.

"Boys, I've got something," he said quietly. "They have a wall of photos, all related to car racing. There's everything from signed portraits, shots from race events, three pictures inside the bar with guys wearing racing jackets. Looks like Red Inferno has hosted events for at least one team."

"Anyone you recognize?" Michael asked.

"Not yet, except from the sponsor logos," Lucas stated as he walked along the line of twenty or so pictures. "Shit! The racetrack. There's picture from the racetrack that the Magnus race team uses for trials. I'm going to get images of each of these. There has to be something here that will connect back to who's targeting Magnus."

"Lucas, I hate to rush you, but Nunez is getting ready to move." Lucas was working his way through recording each of the framed photos. "He's paid his bill and headed toward you."

"Got it," replied Lucas, who looked down at his phone when the target entered the back hallway.

But instead of turning into the door labeled for the men's restroom, the older man brushed by Lucas and went through a door at the end of the hall labeled as private.

"Tracking him into the back of the building," Lucas whispered as he easily reached under his jacket and unlocked his pistol inside the shoulder holster.

"I'm at your back," Ned acknowledged.

"I've got eyes on the back door. All quiet on my end," confirmed Lance.

Lucas paused by the closed door Nunez had

gone through and listened for any activity. After a few seconds, he pushed it open with his left shoulder, keeping his right hand in easy reach of his gun. Through the exposed crack, he could see a passageway leading farther into the space.

"I'm going in," he notified his team, then stepped fully into the space.

It was a hall with a door on the right. From the sounds and clanging and running water, Lucas knew it led to the kitchen. In front of him was a door that led outside, and beside it, a staircase to the upper level of the building. He took the stairs two at a time, careful not to make any noise. A few steps near the top, he paused hearing voices. Lucas pressed his back to the wall and went up farther until he could see into the room.

There were three men: Nunez, Petrov, and a third whom Lucas instinctively knew was the unidentified subject who had planted the incendiary device. They were talking, but based on where they were standing in the room and the angle of the staircase, Lucas couldn't make out the words. Then there was laughter, and the sound of their voices moved closer to his position, suggesting they were headed toward the staircase. He backed down as quickly as possible, taking the fastest cover, which was the rear exit to outside.

"Ned, the targets are on the move," he whispered to the others as he quickly pulled out his gun and darted behind one of the parked cars. "There are three of them including our mystery suspect."

"I got 'em," Ned added. "Petrov and his partner

went back upstairs. Nunez is leaving through the front."

"Lance, can you make your way to the front and get the license plate?" Lucas asked. "Then let's meet back at the truck."

"You got it," the ex–Army Ranger replied.

Lucas waited a full minute before he retreated through the back parking lot and around the side of the building, then casually to their rented vehicle parked a block away.

They were driving back to their client's location within five minutes. By the time they arrived at almost seven thirty that evening, Michael had Laura, the Fortis analyst at headquarters, running search strings to assimilate all the new information uncovered. Evan and Sam had also sent the details needed to implement the Omega protocol.

"Let's see what Laura can uncover by tomorrow to confirm who exactly Nunez is working for," Lucas stated as he and Lance started packing up their things. "Then we can hand over the security footage from the fire to the Toronto police. They'll be able to round up Petrov and the other guy pretty quickly, and we can track Nunez to his boss."

"His rental car is now parked at a hotel near the airport," Michael told them from his seat behind the laptop. "Looks like he's headed back to Chicago."

"Good. That will get us to our target faster. Maybe we'll only need to tuck Cotts away for a few days before we can shut this thing down," Lucas added, then checked his watch. "I'm going to get moving to take her home. Michael, Ned, I'm going to make a digital copy of the Magnus storage server. Then I'll do a full system restore to ten days ago, prior to any updates about the Cicada testing."

"You want to bait them into another network attack?" Ned asked.

"No, just covering all our bases until we solve this," explained Lucas. "Let's not underestimate them again. If they're still after the Cicada design as well, then they'll try again and soon. If they get in, then the data will be stale."

"And we'll be here to take them down," Michael confirmed.

"That's what I'm counting on," Lucas added with a quick grin. "Ned, I'll confirm a rendezvous time later tonight."

"You got it, boss."

"Cotts should be ready to go. I have her list of requirements, and I left her to make any calls needed," Michael noted.

Lucas slung his duffel bag across his chest, and said bye to his team. He found Alex in her office, sitting on the edge of her desk and staring into space with her cell phone in her hand.

"All set?" he asked in a soft tone as though not to startle her.

Alex blinked a little and straightened up.

"Yeah," she replied in a firm voice.

As Lucas watched her put her cell phone, iPad, and a few other things in her purse, he had to admire her fortitude. Though she looked calm and resolved, he knew she must have some trepidation about what was to come.

"All set," she added as she met him in the doorway.

He looked down at her face with its strong chin and bright, sharp eyes and felt the strong urge to touch her, hold her, give her the reassurance that she must certainly need. Lucas tightened his fists from the effort to resist. Instead, he waved her in front of him.

"Did you speak with your family?" he asked as they walked out through the back of the building.

"Just my dad and Adrian," she explained. "Adrian will tell my other brothers, and I'll tell Noelle tonight. You know, she's going to think I'm taking off with you."

Lucas smiled to himself since Alex sounded more mischievous than concerned about the idea.

"Stranger things have happened. And it could work in our favor. Where did you say you were going for vacation?"

"Europe."

"Good choice. We'll create a profile to match," he told her.

"Michael said the same thing, but what exactly does that mean?"

"It means that we'll reprogram your cell phone SIM card to point to wherever we want. So anyone that's looking for your digital footprint will find you there. Any pictures you take will be coded to the right coordinates."

"Not sure how that will work. The pictures won't exactly have the Eiffel Tower in the background," she shot back sarcastically.

"Minor details," he assured her, then smiled again when she scoffed at the suggestion.

They were outside, and Lucas opened the passenger door to the truck. The area around the building was quiet and deserted.

"So, what happens now?" she asked while they drove out of the parking lot.

"We'll leave this truck at the hotel and drive your car home," he explained smoothly. "Then, you need to pack a suitcase suitable for a trip overseas for a few weeks. You'll get a good night's sleep, then we leave at dawn. But first, we'll get some dinner. Are you hungry?"

"Starving, actually."

"Let's grab something on the way, then we'll eat at your house."

They drove around the block to the hotel, then switched to her Porsche from there. Alex let him drive. They were on the highway with a few more minutes of silence.

"Did you find the guys that set the fire?"

Lucas looked over at her, speculatively. In every mission, there was a decision made on how much information should be revealed to the asset under threat. Too much could cause panic and irrational behavior, not enough might lead to reckless and uncooperative actions. Sometimes, their client made stipulations up front, but in this case, Marco Passante had already shared all aspects of the mission with Alex.

"We did," he confirmed, making the gut decision to provide full transparency, at least for now. "Hopefully, they'll lead us to whoever paid them to do it."

"That's great!" she exclaimed, clearly relieved by the news. "Sounds like I might have to cut my European tour a little short. How unfortunate."

He looked over at her profile, amused by her sense of humor, but still surprised by how well she was dealing with his situation. They made the rest of the drive to her town house in silence, stopping to order burgers from a local restaurant. Lucas parked in her driveway then carried both of the travel bags into the house while she held her purse and a paper bag with their meals.

When they got inside, her cousin Noelle was sitting in the living room watching television. Lucas gave a polite hello then took Alex's overnight bag up to her room before doing a full security sweep. He also wanted to give Alex some time to tell Noelle about her trip in private.

When he returned to the living area about ten minutes later, Alex had food set out on plates in the kitchen and she was a few bites into her burger. Noelle watched his progress across the room with suspicious and questioning eyes, but she didn't say anything. Lucas sat down beside Alex and started eating.

"Noelle doesn't believe that I'm vacationing by myself. She thinks I'm taking off with you in secret," Alex suddenly announced to break the awkward silence.

Lucas continued eating calmly.

"Did you explain to her that I'm providing security detail in Toronto? My job ends when you leave tomorrow," he finally replied in an even, casual tone.

"I did indeed, but she watches too many old movies." She flashed him a big smile with her eyes sparkling mischief. "Apparently, it's obvious that I've fallen for your pretty charms, and you're whisking me off to take advantage of my unfortunate situation at work. Her words, not mine."

Lucas wanted to laugh, but he didn't take the bait. She really enjoyed stirring things up. He just finished his burger in one more bite while looking back at her stoically.

"See, Noelle? Mr. Johnson is paid strictly to provide protection. He has absolutely no interest in taking advantage of me."

Lucas still held her gaze, refusing to back down from what they both knew was the truth. He had wanted her the moment she had sat down in front of him in the restaurant, and certainly still did. The chemistry between them was vibrating at a low frequency that was impossible to ignore. But that did not mean he meant to act on it again.

"I'm going to pack," Alex finally stated before heading off up to her bedroom.

Apparently, Noelle was too embarrassed by her cousin's outburst to stick around, which left Lucas to himself to read through all the details and logistics sent to him by his partners.

Fortis had secured a large housekeeping cottage on Skaneateles Lake in upstate New York. The area was quiet in the spring, which made it easier to secure, but close enough to Auburn and Syracuse in order to get supplies or receive shipments. The property also had a large shed that would be converted to a workshop for Alex to work on the engine.

Lance and Ned would pick him and Alex up at six o'clock in the morning for the drive to the Island Airport. From here, Ned would pilot a small, leased seaplane to their destination. The cottage was fully stocked, and the housekeeping services would include the delivery of groceries and other basic supplies. They only had to bring their bags.

Lucas sent Ned and Lance a quick note to confirm their plans for the morning, then went back to work reviewing the portfolio Michael had pulled together on what they knew about Nunez, Petrov, and the third man. At ten o'clock, he went upstairs to check on Alex and suggest she get some sleep.

CHAPTER 16

Alex had managed to get about five hours' rest. Packing had proven to be more challenging than she had anticipated. It started out simple, with a few piles of jeans, yoga pants, T-shirts, and a couple of hoodies suitable for work. Then it hit her. She might end up away with Lucas for the next five, maybe six weeks. Should she bring anything a little more feminine? Maybe a casual dress, at least one pair of nice shoes. A blouse. That decision took a long time. Even asking herself the question forced Alex to think about why. And about what happened in the hotel room.

Eventually, she figured it was better to be safe than sorry, adding a few items suitable for something other than working.

Sunday morning, Alex was up by five thirty to take a long shower and pack up her toiletries. The skies were a clear blue, the morning air was still chilly in late April. She dressed in comfortable cotton twill pants and a light sweater. Noelle had said good-bye the night before, so Alex crept downstairs without waking her. Lucas was waiting by the front entrance, wearing all black and looking serious. There were a few polite words of hello before he loaded her things into the large black truck parked out front. She tied up her sneakers and took a short trench coat out of the closet, then grabbed her purse.

"All set?" Lucas asked when there was nothing left to do but leave.

"Ready as I'll ever be," she replied in a tone that was much lighter than she was feeling. "Do I get to call shotgun?"

His lips quirked.

"We have a short ride. You'll be fine in the backseat."

Alex shrugged and followed him into the car where Lance was in the driver's seat and Ned was beside him. Lucas opened the rear passenger door and helped her into the spacious interior. Then he walked around the side to sit beside her.

"We're driving to the Island Airport," he told her after Lance started up the car. "Then we're taking a small plane into Upstate New York. We'll get you some coffee and a bite to eat before we take off."

"You might have mentioned that earlier," Alex protested. "You're lucky I thought to bring my passport as part of this elaborate ruse."

"Don't worry, it's not needed. We've already provided the required travel documentation to U.S. Immigration," he explained.

"Wow, okay," she breathed. What world did these people live in where that was possible? "Can you tell me more about where we're going now, or am I still on a 'need to know' basis?"

"I will tell you whatever you want to know, Alex," he replied patiently. "As long as you remember that you cannot reveal anything to anyone that doesn't align with your cover of being on vacation overseas. That includes Marco."

"I understand," she conceded.

"Good."

Lucas then proceeded to tell her about the cottage they would stay in for as long as needed. Alex was excited to hear that there was a work shed on the property that was solely for her use, and relieved to know that all of her supplies were already on their way. Though how that was accomplished so quickly was beyond her comprehension.

The rest of the trip went by quickly. As promised, Alex was able to get a hot fresh cup of coffee and a toasted bagel in the airport. Then, they were on a flight into New York State in a small eight-seater amphibian plane piloted by Ned. It took off on the tarmac, then landed smoothly on a beautiful, still lake about fifty minutes later. She felt more and more like Alice in Wonderland every minute.

Lucas helped her exit the plane and onto the long, wooden dock with a boat tethered on the other side. From there, steep wooden steps led up a hill to a modern home on the landing. The large windows along the back of the house reflected the blue skies and sparkling sunlight. The men were busy unloading the bags and other cargo, so Alex made her way up to the house, looking around at the lush, manicured landscaping that surrounded the property. The work shed was a modest structure about the size of the double garage and situated in the back corner of the lot, almost at water's edge.

As much as she wanted to explore, Alex hesitated to go farther into the property, suddenly concerned that she was alone and exposed. She looked behind her, relieved to see both men approaching from the steps.

"Come inside and get settled," Lucas instructed as he walked past her carrying her suitcase and his smaller bag. "Then we'll look around a bit."

She let out a deep breath and followed his path. As they reached the house, Alex immediately noticed the extensive network of tiny mounted security cameras that moved to track their approach to a side door. Lucas entered a code into a security pad and the door unlocked. He pushed it open farther to allow her entry first into a wide mudroom with coat hooks, storage cupboards, and laundry machines. From there, she walked into the crisp, white kitchen with big windows. It opened to a great room with high vaulted ceilings and a wall of glass to showcase the wonderful backyard and lake view. There was a sitting area in front of a fireplace and a wall-mounted television to one side, then a long harvest table surrounded by eight deep upholstered chairs on the other.

It was a very cozy home.

"The bedrooms are through here," Lucas told her as he continued toward a small hallway on the opposite side of the kitchen and off the living area. "There are four. Ned and I will take the first two rooms. You can have the one at the back. There's a second bathroom there for you."

They passed a few doors until he pushed into the last one at the end. It was a good-sized room with a queen bed, dresser, and night tables. Lucas put down her suitcase near the closet.

"Let's meet in about half an hour or so. I'd like to go over the security protocols as soon as possible."

Alex nodded, and he left the room. She let out a deep breath and looked around again. If she ignored the surreal events of the last week, this place could feel like a relaxing vacation rental. It made her want to lie back on the bed and dream of long spa visits and leisurely shopping excursions. Or at least that's what Noelle and Aunt Nadine would suggest. Alex's dream would have her sitting on a comfy chair in a coffee shop reading through articles on automotive design and new technology. But hardly worthy of a getaway to a decked out lakefront cottage.

And she wasn't here to relax.

With another sigh, Alex unpacked her things, starting in the bathroom connected to her bedroom. About forty minutes later, she returned to the living area to find Lucas and have that talk. He was sitting at the dining table where he had set up a laptop and several other pieces of network equipment.

"Would you like some coffee? Anything to eat?" he asked, sensing her presence while still focused on his task. "There's a fresh pot brewed."

"Yeah, sure," Alex replied, walking over to the kitchen.

A quick look around revealed mugs and sugar in the cupboard, and a new box of cream in the fridge. There was a bowl of fresh fruit on the counter as well. She made a cup of coffee, and grabbed a small bunch of grapes.

"Ned has gone into Syracuse to pick up some of the things we've ordered for you," Lucas explained when she was seated at the end of the table. "Another large shipment will be delivered here tomorrow."

"That's great. I need to get started right away if I have any chance of meeting our timelines," she replied, sipping at the hot, rich drink.

"Like I said, just let us know what you need and we'll get it delivered. But, I need you to follow my instructions to the letter," he stipulated with his gaze now fixed steadily on her. "We've already discussed the communication protocols. And I've configured your work e-mails to be routed through an IP address in France. You're supposed to be on an overseas flight right now, so I've also made sure that any network activity on your devices will be delayed until you would have landed in France. But I'll need your cell phone to complete the adjustments.

"Will anyone be expecting you to post pictures or status updates on social media? Your online profiles are pretty sparse."

"No, not really. I haven't had time to be very active over the last couple of years," she admitted.

"Good, that makes it easier. But we will keep a file of photos that you can access if anyone expects one and would be suspicious otherwise," he explained. "Now, let's discuss your security while here. You will have free use of the property, but do not go onto the street or down to the docks without either Ned or me with you. Always make sure the door is closed behind you when you leave or enter the house or the shed. I will provide you with the entrance codes for both."

Alex nodded. It sounded a little constricting but she understood the rationale.

"Do not use or answer the land line phone. It's strictly for outgoing emergency calls. Do not answer any of the doors, ever. And keep your cell phone with you at all times, even in the bathroom. If there is a situation that requires lockdown, we will send you a text message with only the word 'red.' Wherever you are, lock yourself in and do not leave until we call you or send a text message with the word 'blue.' Do you understand?"

"Yes," she replied automatically, her appetite for coffee and fruit having completely disappeared.

"This is just a precaution, Alex," he added in a much softer tone. "This house and the grounds are very well wired to ensure no one comes close without advanced warning. So, it's very unlikely that we'll need to use any of those tactics. But in the unlikely event that something does happen, it's incredibly important that you follow my instruction to the letter."

"Okay, I get it," she whispered back, remembering the force of his displeasure after she had left the shop on Thursday without telling him. "What if I want to go for a walk, or if I need something at the store?"

"Just tell us and one of us will go with you."

That all didn't sound so bad, Alex thought to herself. Chances are, she'd be too busy for excursions. And taking one with Ned didn't seem very appealing. One with Lucas was even less so, for very different reasons.

"There's one more thing that we need to address."

Alex felt her stomach drop a little. His tone, and the fact that he had walked away from her to stare out at the back windows at the view, told her it was going to be something awkward.

"What happened yesterday should not happen again," he stated.

Her stomach dropped further. Hearing him say the words felt worse than Alex expected, even though she had already told herself the same thing.

But, why did he get to decide to draw the line after being the one to pursue her first? Sure, he didn't know who she was at the time, but that didn't change the physical attraction that was between them. It was a little insulting for him to make that decision now.

"What exactly are you referring to?" she asked, as her stubborn streak refused to let him off that easy. "The wedding? The fire? It was a busy day."

She tossed a plump grape into her mouth, though it tasted sour on her tongue.

There was a heavy pause. Usually, Alex took guilty pleasure in moments like these. When she needed to show someone that she was a force to be reckoned with, that she wouldn't take the polite way out by avoiding a confrontation like all the other sweet, likeable girls often did. Alexandria Cotts had never developed that particular feminine characteristic. In a houseful of testosterone-flooded men, a sweet girl would have been eaten alive.

But now, while she sat straight and waited for

Lucas's response, Alex wished she knew how to back down a little. Her assertiveness was about as endearing to men as her superior knowledge of car mechanics. Lucas turned to face her in a more relaxed stance than she expected.

"I'm referring to you, lying back on the dresser in my hotel room wearing underwear and pretty sandals. Does that jog your memory?"

Alex felt the heat rise in her body until her cheeks felt flushed. It should have been with embarrassment or shame, but it wasn't. It was the warm flutter of growing desire. She plucked another grape and slowly placed it her mouth. This one was a little sweeter.

"It sounds familiar. But I'm sure it will happen again," she murmured after swallowing. "I think it's my favorite position."

"Alex," he muttered, and it sounded like a warning.

"Don't worry, Lucas. It won't be with you."

Feeling victorious, she stood up, intending to turn sharply on her heel and make a regal exit. But he stopped her in her tracks, blocking her path by moving with lithe speed that shouldn't have been possible for a man his size. Alex stepped back, bumping the table with her hip and wondering how she was again trapped by the mere presence of this man.

"That was clever," he said softly, looking down at her with sparkling eyes.

"I thought so," she quipped back, never knowing when to quit.

They stood like that for several seconds, and she didn't dare move. The soft warmth that had ignited in her body was now intensified by the masculine scent of his aftershave. And suddenly, all they could think about was being laid back on the wooden credenza and feeling the hard thrust of his thick penetration.

"Stop doing that," he growled.

She licked her lips, enjoying this duel immensely. "Stop what?"

His nose flared and he leaned a little closer.

"Let me give you a little advice, Alex. Don't ever play poker," whispered Lucas, his warm breath brushing her cheek. "Everything you're thinking is written clearly in your eyes."

Then his lips were on hers, hot and intense, stroking deep. Jesus, it felt good. Alex knew she should remember his words, the feel of his rejection, more than once. She had made her point, proved that he felt the same attraction she did, despite his arrogant suggestions otherwise. Now was the perfect time to feed him some of his own medicine.

Alex meant to push him away, step out of his reach. But then his hands fell onto her hips and brought her up against the long, lean length of his body. Whatever she intended to do was overpowered by delicious sensual pleasure.

It was just a kiss, yet Alex was quickly drowning in it. His lips sucked and stroked over hers, his tongue probing in her depths and entwining hers. Everything about his touch suggested aggressive and tightly managed control, over himself, her, and the situation. It was intoxicating, beguiling her into surrendering herself over to him, letting him do whatever he wanted to with her body with the promise of a heart-stopping sexual high as the reward. Like yesterday. In that moment, while one of his hands swept up her back and the other grasped the back of her head, Alex was ready to give in to it.

Lucas kissed her harder, wetter. She reciprocated, entangling her tongue with his, then sweeping it over his bottom lip. He groaned deep and low, but pulled back slowly until only their lips hovered close, and their breaths mingled in between. The seconds stretched long, their heavy breathing echoed loudly within the spacious room.

Alex felt so hot, so primed waiting for what was to come next, until she opened her eyes and looked up into his face. His eyes were still closed, but his jaw was clenched hard and his lips twisted into a scornful sneer. It hit her like a bucket of ice water.

"Maybe," she silkily whispered while rising onto the balls of her feet to bring her lips closer to his ear, "you should be more concerned with keeping your hands off me and your dick in your pants."

She shoved at his chest, then finally walked away as gracefully as possible.

CHAPTER 17

Lucas stood looking out at the water long after Alex had walked out and his blood had cooled. What the hell was wrong with him? Why was he letting this woman goad him into behaving like a total jackass? What was it about her that had him constantly on the edge? Irresistibly drawn to her fiery energy and delicious taste, even while knowing it could lead to disaster.

Was he just horny? It had been some time since he'd been in a steady relationship with regular intimacy. Over seven months, with only a handful of onetime hookups since. But that wasn't unusual for him. The last few years of his life had been dominated by his career and getting Fortis off the ground. Relationships had not been a priority. Which was why he usually had fairly casual ones without the promise or expectation of something long-term.

But this attraction and crazy lack of control didn't feel like sexual frustration. Or curiosity. In which case, their very hot, incredibly kinky encounter yesterday would surely cure him of both. Instead, he couldn't get the image of those moments out of his head. It was annoyingly distracting. And since they were now stuck together in one house for an undetermined amount of time, Lucas kept asking himself if it was a blessing or a curse.

Logical thinking said very clearly that spending more time with Alexandria Cotts was a very cruel curse. Anything or anyone that felt as insanely good as she did could not be good for you.

Eventually, Lucas went back to work reconfiguring the Magnus server. Something Ned had suggested yesterday had sparked a new idea. Whoever Nunez was working for had used thugs in Chicago and Toronto to do the dirty work. But they'd also hired a hacker for the more sophisticated plan. Not Pratt—he was just a front. It was a black hat, skilled enough to use the right tools, and smart enough to stay in the shadows. If the Cicada design was still the target, Lucas wanted see just how skilled that hacker was.

So, he decided to set a trap by creating a virtually undetectable vulnerability deep within the original administrative code of the server box. If there was another attack on the Magnus network, he'd know what level of hacker skills they were dealing with. And if the attack was successful, the information would be useless anyway.

He was still working a couple of hours later, tweaking his code, when Ned returned. Lucas went out to help Ned move the equipment into the workshop. It was a big open space, with lots of light and an impressive collection of tools suitable for maintaining and customizing cars. It was one of the reasons Evan had recommended this location, owned by one of his former colleagues in the CIA.

"I'm going to make us some lunch," Ned stated once they were finished and were heading back to the house. "Where's Alex?"

"She's been in her room for the last few hours," Lucas replied.

"Why don't you show her the new stuff while I fire up the grill?"

They stepped into the mudroom.

"Why don't you do that? I'll take care of lunch."

"Really? And why is that?" Ned immediately asked, obviously sensing something in Lucas's tone.

"Nothing," Lucas shot back. "I went over the security protocols earlier, and she had some objections."

"To what exactly? They're all pretty reasonable, considering the circumstances."

Lucas let out a deep sigh and crossed his arms.

"It's my fault. I probably could have handled it better."

Ned started laughing as he walked toward the living room.

"What's so funny?" Lucas demanded, throwing up his arms.

"You, that's what. I've just never seen you make a wrong move with a woman. Everything you say and do usually makes them either blush or giggle," explained Ned, still chuckling.

"Yeah, well. I guess I'm not her type," Lucas muttered while passing his colleague to enter the large kitchen.

"Yeah, right," Ned scoffed. "Fine, I'll go get her.

I need to give her back the rechargeable battery anyway."

"Can you get her cell phone while you're there? I still need to set it up properly."

The kitchen was well stocked with a couple of days of fresh meat and vegetables in the fridge. Lucas grilled up some steaks and made a quick salad. While he ate at the table, Alex and Ned took their meals back out to the workshop. Dinner was much the same and created a routine for the next couple of days.

A large crate arrived by transport truck early Monday morning. Ned and Lucas supervised as the driver unpacked all the equipment and supplies. Alex used the time to set everything up the way she needed it. Then the Fortis agents left her there around midmorning, fully engrossed in the fabrication of automotive components. She only came back to the house to grab her meals and sleep at night.

The air between her and Lucas was noticeably chilly, but cordial. For the most part, she ignored him, seeking out Ned for anything needed. Lucas was fine with that at first. But by Tuesday, her subtle snubs were wearing thin. And it didn't help that Ned still found the situation very amusing.

Monday evening, Fortis had confirmation that Oleg Petrov had been arrested by the Toronto police as a key suspect in the Magnus arson. Then they got a video call from Michael on Wednesday morning that finally put the mission in the right direction.

"This is Cesar Hernandez," Michael stated as he presented a photo of a young man on one half of the computer screen while he talked to them through the other. "He's one of five partners at Red Creek, the venture capital firm that Nunez works at."

"Looks pretty young," observed Lucas.

"He is. Twenty-four years old, but his family's very wealthy. It looks like he bought into Red Creek after dropping out of college three years ago," Michael explained.

"So what's the connection between Hernandez and Magnus?"

"This."

Michael put up one of the pictures that Lucas had captured from the bar on Saturday night, showing some sort of car industry event hosted there.

"Cesar is the sole owner of Optimal Racing," Michael explained as he put up a few other pictures of cars and drivers at racing events. "Red Creek acquired Optimal as part of a buyout a couple of years back, and Hernandez bought it from the company. About five years ago, they were doing really well in stock car racing, until they had a major crash that seriously injured their driver. Looks like Hernandez has been trying to rebuild them to their former glory. But his tactics are questionable."

"How so?" Ned asked.

"There's a lawsuit pending against Optimal for patent infringement. It was filed six months ago by another custom components manufacturer."

"Does Passante know Optimal or Hernandez?" Lucas asked.

"Oh yeah," Michael quickly confirmed. "They

were big rivals before Optimal collapsed after the car crash. And Passante is well aware of the reputation Hernandez has for stealing from his competitors."

"Good work, Michael," Lucas stated. "Now we have to tighten the noose. There is no doubt Hernandez is our guy, we just need the proof. We don't have anything valuable from the Pratt situation. Did the police get anything from Petrov after his arrest on Monday?"

"We got an update today, including the identity of the accomplice. The second guy is Sergei Petrov. He and Oleg are brothers, and the company, Bold Management, is owned by their uncle, Stan Petrov," Michael outlined. "According to what they told the police, they were approached by a man and paid ten thousand dollars cash for the job. No names were exchanged, but the description they gave matches Nunez."

"Nunez might be the key," Ned suggested. "He's worked for Red Creek for almost eight years, and makes decent money. But, he has a big family to support and his financials look tight. So, I'd say he did this job with Hernandez for cash on the side. I'm thinking he has very little allegiance to the kid. Maybe we can get him to turn against Hernandez in exchange for immunity."

Lucas nodded in agreement.

"Let's make it happen. I'll check with Evan and Sam to see who's available for a trip to Chicago. Maybe Abe," he suggested.

Like Evan, Abe Smith was a CIA Protective Services operative prior to joining Fortis. By later that afternoon, he was at the corporate offices for

Red Creek Capital, meeting the head of security to discuss a very private matter. The team had the results a couple of hours later.

"We got it all," Abe reported back on a conference call with Lucas's team. "It wasn't difficult to get him to cooperate and turn on Hernandez. And it sounds like the other general partners at the firm will be happy to get rid of the punk."

"What did Nunez say?" Lucas asked.

"Pretty much what we suspected. And Hernandez paid him directly by bank transfer, and provided the cash to pay the Petrov brothers."

"Good. What about Pratt and the guys who took him out and attacked Evan and me?" probed Lucas.

"Nunez claims he didn't know anything about it. He only got involved last week to destroy the car engine, and someone at Optimal referred him to the Petrovs," Abe explained.

"Well, that has to be enough to get the FBI to bring Hernandez in for questioning. Michael, let's reach out to your contact in the morning," instructed Lucas.

"Sure thing," agreed Michael.

"Any chance they'll let Abe join the interview with Hernandez?" Lucas suggested. "I want to know what the motive is behind all of this, and everything he knows about Magnus and Alex's engine."

"I think I still have a few favors I can call on," confirmed Michael with a smirk.

"Good, I'll give Passante and Alex an update in the morning," added Lucas. "With any luck, we'll have this mission wrapped up by the end of the week."

He and Ned spend another few hours at the dining table, building out contingency plans depending on when Hernandez was arrested, and what he revealed during questioning. They took a break for Lucas to grill chicken and bake potatoes on the barbecue outside, then laid out the meal on the kitchen counter. Alex came back from the shed only to grab her meal.

"How are things going?" Lucas asked as she turned to walk away carrying her full plate, cutlery, and bottled water tucked under one arm.

Alex paused, clearly surprised by his question. The first directed to her since the incident after they had arrived on Sunday. She looked at Ned who was busy filling his plate.

"It's okay," she replied politely. "I spoke to Marco a little while ago. He said you guys think Cesar Hernandez may be responsible? That's good news."

"Could be. We'll know more tomorrow," Lucas replied cautiously.

It felt good to be on speaking terms with her, even if it was just in passing.

"Thanks for dinner," added Alex, filling in the brief silence.

"No problem."

Their eyes met briefly. That same electric charge stirred the air.

"See you guys later," she finally stated, then walked away.

Lucas watched her go, looking comfortable and industrious in loose work pants and a T-shirt. Then he found Ned glancing back and forth between him and where Alex exited into the mudroom.

"What?" demanded Lucas.

But his friend just scoffed and shook his head.

After eating and cleaning up, Ned went to do a security inspection around the property and along the dock. Lucas made a phone call he had been avoiding for a couple of days.

"Hi, Kathy," he stated when the call was answered. "I got your message."

Kathy Anderson was his next-door neighbor. Divorced, single, and in her midthirties, she lived comfortably on a sizable alimony check. She had become a friend over the last three years since Lucas had moved into his current house, and was always great about keeping an eye on his place while he traveled.

Earlier that day, Kathy had sent him an e-mail to say his cleaning lady, Prudence, who's supposed to visit twice a week, hadn't shown up since he had left.

"Hey, Lucas, how's your trip going?" she asked in her bubbly voice.

"Pretty good. How are things with you?"

"Painful and sore. I started going to a new yoga studio last week, and did a hot yoga class today for the first time. Who knew it was possible to sweat so much."

Lucas smirked. This was how all of their conversations went. Kathy treated exercise classes and shopping like others did their careers.

"Sounds interesting," he murmured. "Thanks for the heads up on my cleaning lady. But I'm not surprised. She's been a little flaky over the last few months."

"Do you want me to check in on anything? I still have your spare key," Kathy offered.

"No, that's okay. I've been meaning to call the maid service that Prudence works for and have them send me someone new. I just haven't gotten around to it yet."

"I'm not sure that's a good idea, Lucas. You shouldn't have someone going into your home if you're not here. Even if they're through a service. I've heard horrible stories about robberies and all sort of crazy things."

Lucas could hardly tell her that was the least of his concerns. His house had more than enough security to ensure no one went in or out without him knowing, and all activity inside or around it was recorded. Which is why he already knew Prudence wasn't very good at her job.

"Why don't you let my girl, Lita, work for you," Kathy continued enthusiastically. "At least until you get back. I'm sure she could use the money."

Lucas scratched the scruff on his cheek, thinking it wasn't such a bad idea. At least temporarily.

"Sure, Kathy. That would be great."

"Fantastic. I'll let her know. She's comes three times a week, so she'll just clean your house after mine and you can pay her the same."

"I don't need three days," Lucas objected. "One would be fine for now."

"Well, that's the thing," Kathy replied slowly, clearly preparing to tell him something unexpected.

"What thing?" he asked calmly.

"Lita's got another job offer that pays a little less but gives her double the hours. The only way she will stay with me is if I can offer the same," admitted Kathy. "So this will be a win-win for us, right?"

Lucas shook his head already regretting the conversation. He should have sensed from the beginning that there was a motive behind her offer.

"Fine. But I'm only committing to using her until I'm back. And that might only be another few days," he agreed.

"Thanks, Lucas, you're the best!"

He mumbled something appropriate before they ended the call.

"Everything okay?"

He turned to find Alex walking across the living room.

"Yeah, just some personal stuff," he replied. "Taking a break?"

"No. Just getting my iPad. I need to log on to the network to review some of my notes."

"That's not necessary," Lucas told her, walking over to the table to pick up a small square box. "I copied the storage server before we left, and it's all here on this portable drive. I meant to tell you on Sunday."

"Wow, that's great," she uttered, clearly surprised.

"It's wireless, so you can access it directly from your iPad. I'll send the password to your phone by text message."

She took the device from him. But any additional discussion was interrupted by the insistent beep of the alarm on Lucas's laptop, then his cell phone.

"Shit," he muttered, pulling out a chair to sit in front of the computer.

"What? What's happened?" Alex demanded.

Lucas read through the lines of programming code that scrolled up the screen. His hands flew across the keyboard as he typed in characters and responded to prompts on instinct at lightning speed.

"Lucas, what is it?" she repeated with increased concern.

"Someone's hacking into the Magnus network," he finally explained in a calm tone.

"What? I thought you said they wouldn't be able to get access unless they were in the building?" She gasped. "Are they there, in the shop?"

"Nope," Lucas confirmed, still typing at an impressive speed. "Looks like they've discovered another way in."

CHAPTER 18

The attack was fast and aggressive, immediately targeting the weakness within the administrative controls. Lucas quickly knew that the black hat on the opposing computer was far superior to Pratt. He or she wasn't using a pre-built application, or an automated tool designed to get remote access; they were actively rewriting the source code to the storage server to hijack it completely. It's exactly what Lucas would have done facing the same challenge.

The battle was intense, but over quickly since Lucas wasn't interested in dueling with his opponent. Instead, knowing the data on the storage server was an outdated copy, he just restored the box to its original factory settings, effectively wiping it clean of all information. In less than ten minutes, there was nothing left on it to hack.

Lucas sat back in his chair for a few minutes in the silence that followed, thinking through what had just happened. While he had anticipated and prepared for just such a possibility, it still surprised him how quickly it happened. With Fortis about to engage the FBI to apprehend Hernandez, the timing was also very suspicious. Maybe Fernandez somehow knew they were hot on his trail, and this was his last attempt to achieve his goal?

"What happened?" Ned asked, now standing beside Alex and looking between them.

"Hernandez just tried hacking into the Magnus system directly. I shut it down, but I don't like the timing," Lucas explained as he was calling Michael on speed dial. "I don't think we should wait until morning. Let's get the feds engaged now. Hernandez may already know we're onto him."

Michael quickly pulled some strings to get the wheels in motion, and the FBI had an arrest warrant for Cesar Hernandez within hours. He was in custody soon after midnight. Lucas and Ned grabbed a few hours of sleep, but they were up by six in the morning, waiting for an update on what Abe and the feds had uncovered in questioning Hernandez.

"I'm going for a run," Ned declared about an hour later while they still waited. "Text me when you hear something."

Lucas nodded, his attention fixed on the record of the hacker's code that he had recorded during the attack. Something about it was strange, almost familiar. But he couldn't think of how or why.

"Any news?" Alex asked as she crossed the floor from the doorway to the bedrooms in the direction of the kitchen.

He looked up, watching her progress. She always looked so energetic in the morning, as though she couldn't wait for the day to get started. Lucas stood up and walked over to join her as she poured a cup of coffee from the fresh pot he had brewed a little earlier, taking his empty mug with him.

"Hernandez was taken into custody by the FBI late last night," he confirmed, since she had finally gone to bed before eleven o'clock.

"That's amazing!" she exclaimed with a big smile over the rim of her coffee mug. "So it's over, right? It's done?"

"We need to know what he's said in his statement. But hopefully, yes," Lucas told her hesitantly.

He refilled his cup, adding cream and a little sugar from the supplies on the table.

"Why?" she asked. "We know he's responsible for destroying my prototype and trying to steal the design. What more is there?"

Lucas leaned back against the edge of the counter, captured by her animated reasoning.

"Yes, that's what it looks like. But we don't know what we don't know," he replied.

"Meaning what exactly?"

"Meaning we need to know the full scope of this whole plan. How do we know Hernandez is the only one involved? What if there are others working with him? Or someone else who planned and paid for the whole thing?"

She sighed heavily.

"Okay, I see your point."

Lucas put down his coffee and stepped closer to her.

"I know you want this over and done with. I do too. But I need to make sure it's completely safe before you go back home."

Alex looked back at him with those bright, intense

eyes. They were disappointed but accepting, and he couldn't help but admire her courage.

"Why are you doing this?" he asked, a question he had been pondering ever since the day of the fire.

"What, exactly?"

He smiled at her now familiar taunting tone.

"Why are you finishing your engine for the race?" Lucas clarified. "Why not just wait until the threat is gone?"

She snorted with a small chuckle.

"It's a little late to ask that, don't you think?"

Lucas shrugged, smiling back. Her light mood was infectious.

"I understand why Magnus Motorsports should pursue this technology, and I know timing is everything. So, my job is to keep you and the asset safe for the duration," he explained calmly. "But you're the one here, working nonstop to complete the work. And it was your decision, so I'm just curious about why."

"Does it matter?"

"Do you always answer a question with a question?"

She laughed, her eyes sparkling with amusement, causing his heartbeat to accelerate.

"Because I don't like answering questions, that's why."

"And yet you just gave me an answer, finally," he smirked, crossing his legs at the ankle.

"Well, it's a very rare thing, so don't get used to it," Alex replied with dismissive wave of her hand.

"Maybe you just need a little practice," Lucas

teased with a charming twist of his lips. "Why are you here?"

Alex studied him contemplatively, looking far deeper than just the surface of his face like she did the evening they met at the hotel restaurant. Then she looked down at the kitchen counter and placed her mug down on it.

"I don't like to quit. And I definitely don't like when someone else tries to force me to," she said quietly. "That's not a very feminine quality, I know. My dad calls it obstinate."

Lucas watched her for a long moment, surprised by the serious undertone in her voice.

"Does that happen often? People trying to stop you?"

She rolled her eyes.

"I'm a female automotive engineer. What do you think?"

"I think you have a very strange idea of what's feminine and what isn't."

Alex glanced at him with surprise in her eyes, then back at the counter. Lucas had the urge to say more, but managed to hold his tongue. She cleared her throat and turned away from him.

"Well, now that I've satisfied your curiosity, I need to get back to work," she finally stated.

"Aren't you going to eat something for breakfast?"

"Are you cooking?" she shot back over her shoulder.

"Come back in fifteen minutes if you want an omelet."

She only raised her thumb in the air as she

walked toward the side entrance and back to her workshop.

The update from Michael and Abe came later that afternoon. Lucas set up a videoconference with his team, and Evan and Sam from the Fortis headquarters.

"So Hernandez admitted to the whole thing?" Evan asked.

"He didn't have much choice after the evidence Nunez provided," Abe summarized. "He knew Magnus was going to release a new engine in June because someone approached his driver last year trying to sell him some of the technology. Hernandez turned down their offer and instead decided to shut down Magnus by stealing the whole design for his own use. When that didn't work, he had it destroyed."

"Did he say who tried to sell it to him originally?" asked Lucas. "Was it North?"

"No, he couldn't remember. Just that it was a woman during an event at a local racing club in Chicago, and that she wanted too much money for just the battery design. He figured it would be cheaper to hack into Magnus and get everything. So he hired a firm called Crow to do just that," Abe explained.

"Do we know anything about this Crow?" asked Sam.

"I've heard of them a few times over the last two to three years," Lucas told them with his arms folded. "They operate way off the grid, doing freelance work. Cyber intrusion for a fee. From what I remember, that setup in Chicago with Pratt resembles their tactics."

"Hernandez claims he only paid a retainer fee up front, the final payment was due once the intelligence was delivered. He didn't ask any questions about how the job would be executed," continued Abe.

"So, he didn't know about Pratt or his murder?" Lucas asked.

"So he claims," Abe confirmed. "Or maybe he's copping to white-collar corporate espionage to avoid a murder charge. Either way, he says he canceled the contract with Crow last weekend because it was taking too long, and instead hired Nunez to destroy the engine and eliminate Magnus from the race."

"Wait," Lucas interrupted, stepping forward. "What about the network intrusion last night? If Crow was fired last weekend, who's attacking now? And why?"

"Hernandez claims he had no idea," Abe told them.

"Lucas, do you think Crow went after the design yesterday even after their contract was cancelled?"

"I don't know. But someone did and they were really good," he mumbled. "Abe, did Hernandez say anything to indicate how much he knew about the Cicada? Did he know it was electric drive only? Or any of the other performance projections?"

"He didn't say anything specific about the technology, except that the woman talked about a battery originally, but he decided to destroy the whole engine in the end," Abe replied as he thought through the details revealed in the interview. "But now that you mention it, he seemed more curious about what the hackers would find rather than trying to get something of specific value. I got the sense that his only real objective was to beat Magnus, one way or the other."

"Whoever's going after the Magnus data wasn't just curious, they were determined," Lucas muttered. "I'd say they knew there was something very valuable stored there, beyond just beating Magnus in a race."

The men thought for a minute, and Lucas walked a couple of steps away, rubbing two fingers across his lips.

"So, what's our next move?" Ned asked finally.

"I'm going to review the information I copied from Pratt's computer again to see what I can find. He accessed Adam North's computer in order to plant the Trojan horse, so maybe he discovered more about the Cicada design than Hernandez knew," Lucas told them.

"If he did, then Crow knows about it as well. Which could explain why Pratt was eliminated in the end," Evan added.

"Until we know more, the Omega protocol needs to stay in place," Lucas concluded. "Michael, can you start looking into the woman who tried to sell the battery design last year? It has to be someone associated with North in some way. I'll give Passante and Cotts the update. Maybe they know something that can provide some answers."

They ended the meeting soon after, and Lucas went outside to speak to Alex. When he unlocked the door to the shed, it was quiet and dark inside except for the sunlight pouring through the windows facing the lake. She wasn't in there. Lucas stepped back and looked around the large backyard and toward the house. There was no sign of her. Starting to get alarmed, he took out his cell phone, ready to check the GPS location of her phone in case she had gone against the security protocols and left the property alone. Then something red caught his eye near the edge of the grass, at the wooden steps down to the docks.

As he grew closer, he saw it was Alex, sitting on the top step, looking out at the water. She glanced up with surprise as his shadow fell over her, then stood up abruptly.

"Sorry, I didn't mean to startle you," Lucas told her.

"No, that's okay. I was just thinking."

"About what?" he asked.

"Just one of the components."

She looked around, then out at the lake, almost longingly.

"Would a walk help? We can walk along the water for a bit then turn back."

Lucas thought for a moment that she was about to turn him down, and it surprised him how disappointed he would be. Talking with her earlier in the morning had been nice, and something he was looking forward to repeating.

"Sure, why not," she finally replied.

He sent Ned a brief text message with their plans, then followed her down the stairs. They walked along the boardwalk for about ten minutes in silence. At the end of April, the midday temperature was cool, but the air was still and the sun shone brightly, reflecting off the glassy lake. Alex had her hands buried in the pockets of her hooded sweatshirt, but otherwise seemed comfortable.

Another ten minutes, and they reached the park at the edge of the Skaneateles town center, with a line of quaint shops and restaurants.

"Do you think they have a Starbucks?" she asked as they walked across the grass to the sidewalk along the main street. "I would love a latte."

"Let's go take a look," Lucas suggested.

"I didn't bring my wallet, or anything."

"I think I can cover you," he teased.

There was no big-brand coffee shop, but they did find a café along the main strip that made lattes to order and had a wide selection of fresh baked breads and pastries. Alex got her latte, Lucas grabbed a sports drink and a box of pastries, which he would bring back to the house for Ned. They were walking back to the house along the boardwalk when Lucas brought up the topic of Cesar Hernandez and gave her a brief summary of the details uncovered during the FBI interrogation.

"So, you think someone other than Cesar is trying to steal the Cicada design," she said with a sigh.

"We have to consider that."

"I guess that means we're not going home yet. And here I was thinking this might be a victory celebration."

Lucas smiled down at her.

"I think I could come up with something better than a cup of coffee, if that were the case."

"Hey, I wasn't complaining. I'm a pretty cheap date."

Alex then stopped in her tracks as she threw her head back with her eyes shut tight and her teeth clenched in a grimace.

"Maybe that wasn't the best choice of words," she muttered, looking anywhere but at him.

Lucas stopped also and watched her with his arms crossed against his chest.

"Alex," he began, knowing that, though it was nice to be on cordial speaking terms, there was still an issue between them that need to be settled.

"Look, there's really no need—"

"Yes, there is," Lucas insisted gently, and she let out a loud, dramatic sigh. "I handled the situation badly and I offended you. That wasn't my intention."

"I wasn't offended. Okay, maybe a little," she quickly conceded when he raised his brows high with skepticism. "But since I came on to you, I can hardly complain, right?"

"That's not exactly how it happened."

"Yeah, I'm pretty sure it is. Unless you think I started taking off my clothes because I was too hot," she countered with heavy sarcasm.

He grinned, always surprised by her humorous candor so akin with his own temperament.

"You were. That's how I ended up with my pants around my ankles."

They both laughed for a bit over that one. Then Alex started walking again, at a slower, more aimless pace.

"You really should not tell a woman you're not

interested in her, then flirt so blatantly, pretty boy," she scolded. "She might get confused."

"I never said that," Lucas stated, stepping ahead of her to block her path. "I never said I wasn't interested in you, Alex. In fact, I'm pretty sure I said the exact opposite to that the night we met."

"Sure you did. And stop blocking my way!" she demanded, shoving at his shoulder though he barely swayed from the soft touch.

"No, Alex," he corrected. "I said what happened in the hotel shouldn't happen again, not that I didn't want it to. Or want you."

She looked up at him, clearly taken aback by his statement. Yet Lucas couldn't understand how she could get it wrong. Wasn't his attraction to her written all over his face, no matter how hard he tried to hide it? It certainly felt that way.

"Why?" she asked.

Lucas was speechless for a few seconds. Her near proximity disrupted his breathing with accurate predictability.

"Why do I want you?"

"No," she dismissed like he was slow. "Why shouldn't it happen again?"

It was his turn to start walking again. The rental house was in sight, with the seaplane docked in front. Suddenly, a movement near the plane caught his eye. Lucas stopped, reaching out his right hand to grab Alex's left arm and pull her behind him, then handed her the box of pastries. There was a man standing at the tail end, his blue jacket stark against the bright white aviation paint. Based on his height and size, it wasn't Ned.

Lucas unholstered his gun with his right hand,

placed it behind his back and out of view from anyone else who may be looking.

"Alex, see that boat we just passed? I need you to go and duck down behind it," he instructed firmly while his eyes stay fixed on the intruder. "Do not move from there until I come back for you."

He waited until he felt her back up, then heard her soft footsteps retreat. Then, Lucas strode purposefully toward the man while calling Ned on his cell phone.

"I've got him," Ned stated as soon as the call was answered.

Lucas could see his partner coming down the wooden steps from the house, two at a time.

"I'm covering Alex on the boardwalk, to the right about five houses down."

They disconnected, and Lucas watched the other agent approach the stranger with a casual walk. From this distance, the interaction between the two men looked innocuous, but Lucas remained vigilant from his position with his thumb touching the gun safety, keenly aware of the quiet, open space and Alex's vulnerable exposure.

The tense situation was over in a few minutes, as the stranger walked away, along the boardwalk in the opposite direction, then disappeared into an entrance several lots down.

CHAPTER 19

As instructed by Lucas, Alex stayed hidden behind the docked boat for several long, tense minutes before he came to get her. By then, the easy companionship they had shared throughout the walk had dissipated, replaced by the more familiar guardian/protector relationship. He silently walked her back to the shed with instructions not to leave until she received a coded text message.

It took a long while for Alex's nerves to settle down from the drama. She tried to go back to work, but found it difficult to concentrate on mechanical parts and technical specs. When her cell phone pinged, delivering the simple message of the word *blue*, she finally let out a deep breath of relief. It was now almost four o'clock in the afternoon and time to get back to work.

Hours later, Alex still found it hard to focus on reconstructing her electric motor. Her hands were busy, but her thoughts wandered back to those last few sentences of the conversation with Lucas while they were walking back from the town. The words replayed in her mind, and she remembered the heated intensity in his eyes, and the heavy pounding of her heart in response.

Lucas wanted her.

Alex had felt certain that whatever attraction he had originally felt had effectively been quelled by her less than feminine qualities. It certainly wouldn't have been the first time. Men might find her physically attractive at first, maybe even funny, until her more assertive and outspoken side eventually appeared. Or until her most unforgivable sins were revealed somehow: that all her friends were men and she knew more about cars than they did.

When she was in high school and college, there were a few guys who thought those two things were pretty hot for a girl. At first. But soon enough, after a few awkward conversations about cars where she corrected or disagreed with them, her unique appeal quickly faded into annoyance, then finally disinterest. As a quick learner, Alex decided it was just easier to only date men who knew nothing about her. Over the next few years, it was convenient and surprisingly easy to just have casual relationships, enjoy their company as the typical girl she learned to play in high school. The trick was to end it before they became too attached, asked too many questions about other parts of her life, or they wanted to meet her friends.

Lucas Johnson knew everything about Alex, including the sharp bite of her sarcastic tongue. His edict that they shouldn't be together again had bruised her ego, but like her past experience with men and relationships, it wasn't surprising. Alex had also spent the last few days trying to understand the aching disappointment that had settled in her stomach. She knew lots of strong, attractive, capable men, but Lucas and his band of agents were definitely in a league of their own. Was it the sheer masculinity of his role as her armed protector? Was it the sharp intelligence, or the way he led his team? Maybe, she thought.

Or it was much more simple and base. The sex had been heart-stopping and mind-blowing, and Alex wanted it again. Hearing Lucas state so simply that he still wanted her had only heightened that need.

It was well after nine o'clock before Alex stopped working and headed back to the house. Lucas had sent her a note a couple of hours earlier to say dinner was ready, but Alex felt too caught up in her wayward thoughts to face him just yet. Eventually, the hunger pains became too hard to ignore. When she entered the living area, he was sitting at the dining table working on the computer while Ned was on the couch watching television. They both looked up as she walked across the room to heat up her meal.

"What happened with the guy earlier?" she asked them while standing at the kitchen counter to eat.

"Nothing to worry about," Ned replied. "Just one of the neighbors checking out the plane. He was harmless."

Alex looked at Lucas, but he seemed completely focused on his work. She went back to her meal.

When finished, she washed her plate and utensils, then headed for her bedroom with a glass of water. He still did not look up.

Thinking a long, hot bath would help settle her thoughts, Alex went straight into the attached bathroom, leaving the bedroom dark. She placed her cell phone and the icy cold glass on the sink console, then turned on the tap in the deep tub. As it filled, she went back into the bedroom to undress and grab nightclothes. She pulled her dreadlocks into a high ponytail, wrapping the strands into a tight bun to keep it out of the way. As she stepped gingerly into the steaming water, Alex paused to allow each part of her skin to get accustomed to the temperature before finally lying down to submerge her body in the depth of the tub. The tension slowly seeped out of her limbs until Alex felt lazy, soothed, and eventually drowsy.

Something woke her up sometime later. Alex blinked for a moment, confused by her surroundings until she remembered where she was. She sat up quickly, looking around to figure out how long she had napped. The water was cool, and her skin felt soggy and pruned. She pulled the plug in the tub and turned on the shower spray to wash up with her favorite shower gel.

As she toweled off a short while later, Alex felt chilled and lethargic. Once dry, she drank down some room-temperature water and checked the time on her cell phone. It was almost midnight. She had slept for over an hour.

Alex was applying lotion when there was a knock on the bathroom door.

"Alex, are you okay?" It was Lucas, his voice low and muffled.

"Yeah, I'm fine."

She stood frozen for another minute, waiting for him to say something more, but only silence followed. Assuming he had left, she finished moisturizing her face and body, then pulled an extra large T-shirt over her head before stepping into the bedroom with the glass of water and phone in her hands.

Lucas was standing on the other side of the space, leaning back against the wall with his ankles crossed. She stopped abruptly in surprise.

"You've been in there for a while. I was starting to get worried," he stated.

"What's going on?" Alex asked, suddenly very self-conscious about her sloppy sleepwear.

She turned away from him to place the items she held onto the dresser next to the bathroom door. Then she reached up to undo her hair. When Lucas didn't reply, she looked over at him again, shaking out her locs so they fell heavily over her shoulders and around her face.

"I wanted to talk to you," he finally replied.

She let out a breath, now regretting her earlier impulsive and provocative question about them, together. Lucas may want her now, but his interest would fade eventually, so maybe it was all best left alone.

"Look, there's no need for us discuss it any further," Alex declared, turning her back to him again. "What happened in the hotel was nothing, right?

A few moments of something purely physical. And you're right. It shouldn't happen again."

Alex intended to make a simple statement to save Lucas from any further explanations about the topic. Prevent any more awkward, ego-bruising debates about it. But when Lucas didn't immediately respond, the seconds ticked by and she couldn't help filling in the silence.

"There's really no point to it, right? It's not like either of us wants a relationship. Sure, we could enjoy a few moments of pleasure, but what's the point? We both have jobs to do, and sex would just be a distraction."

He cleared his throat.

"Alex—"

His voice sounded soft, concerned, almost regretful. Alex hardened her resolve, and turned to face him in the shadowy space.

"I'm a big girl, Lucas. My ego heals pretty quickly. So, no need to feel bad about it—"

Her statement ended with a gasp as he closed the distance between them with two swift steps.

"Alex, stop talking," he growled low, his eyes blazing into her before his mouth fell onto hers.

Her heart pounded in her chest as his tongue slipped between her lips to entwine hers with hard, swirling insistence. His arms wrapped around her body and his large hands pulled her up against his hard length. Surprise made her hesitate, but only for a moment until the taste and feel of him quickly dominated her senses. Alex responded, matching his heat and intensity. All the very logical reasons she had just articulated as to why this was a bad idea now seemed like flimsy, lame excuses.

The tension mounted swiftly. The sounds of their kisses and soft moans vibrated in the dimly lit room.

"God, you smell so good," he muttered against her lips. "It drives me crazy."

Alex moaned low, incapable of responding coherently. He ran his mouth along the side of her neck, licking softly at her skin. His hands slid over the thin cotton of her nightshirt, down her back to cup the curve of her ass. She gasped at the feel of his thick erection branded against the base of her stomach. Then he pulled up the fabric to caress her naked flesh. He kissed her hard and deep, stroking into her mouth with his tongue like a promise of what was to come. Alex shivered in anticipation.

"Alex," he murmured in a low rumbling tone against her lips. "I didn't bring anything with me. Let me go get protection."

She shook her head while pushing up his shirt so she could touch his bare skin. Lucas pulled his head back from her and lifted her chin gently until she looked up at him with hooded eyes.

"What do you mean?" he asked with furrowed brows.

"You don't need to get any," she explained, finding it difficult to be articulate. "I have some."

"You do?"

Alex shrugged dismissively, realizing how it sounded for her to have come to this hideaway with a supply of condoms.

"They were in my bedroom, and it made sense that I would take them with me on an extended vacation."

Lucas paused, and then grinned with that slow, easy, panty-wetting smile.

"Makes sense to me, too," he replied simply. "Where are they?"

She turned in his arms and pulled open the top drawer of the dresser beside them. The small stack of condoms was right there next to her underwear. Alex tore one off the strip and closed the drawer. Lucas pulled her back around and took the packet out of her hand to place it on top of the dresser before kissing her thoroughly again. Then he stepped back and unhurriedly removed his clothes, tossing each item aside until he was only wearing boxer briefs.

Alex had seen him partially naked before, less than a week ago. Yet the site of his beautiful body still caught her by surprise. He was tall, lean, and perfectly contoured, like a performance athlete. The light from the bathroom highlighted every hard ripple and dip of his cinnamon skin.

It also revealed the rough, raw edges of a small wound on his shoulder, and Alex remembered seeing it bandage when they were at the hotel. She reached out one of her hands to trace lightly over the injured spot.

"What happened?" she asked, softly.

But Lucas was silent as he took hold of her T-shirt, bunching the cotton in his hands and easing it up her body. She raised her arms into the air so he could easily pull it over her head. He flung it in the direction of his clothes while they stared intently at each other.

With an unexpectedly gentle and tender touch, he stroked a hand along a path from her cheek, down her neck, and over the firm swells of her peaked breasts.

"You're incredible," he whispered while his finger swept lower across her stomach on down to the apex of her thighs.

She could only moan, clutching at his broad shoulders for strength when he finally touched her now-swollen nub.

"Yes," she gasped hotly.

Lucas stepped closer, so her breasts brushed against the upper part of his abdomen, and his touch reached farther, deeper. It was delicious. Her back arched and her legs quivered with sharp arousal as he stroked into her tender, wet flesh. Alex closed her eyes and her head fell back. The sensations were incredible, yet excruciatingly intense. He cradled the back of her head and bent his to kiss her neck and stroke his tongue along the rim of her ear.

"So hot," he whispered thickly, then brushed her lips gently with his while his fingers increased their sensual assault.

Alex was panting with urgent want. Her body was tight and quivering as a sharp orgasm curled tighter in the base of her spine.

"That's it," Lucas urged between nibbles to her lips and the sweep of his soft tongue along the tender inside of her mouth.

"Lucas," she sobbed, her eyes scrunched tight as

she clenched his shoulders, her nails digging in the hard flesh. "Yes!"

He stroked his finger into her wetness with firm, relentless pressure until Alex came hard and fast. Her skin was damp with sweat as every shattering vibration seemed to last an eternity. Yet it slowly faded away too soon. Once she could manage free movement, Alex opened her eyes to find Lucas holding her close to his body to keep her on her feet. She let out a deep breath and stroked down the length of his chest. He tangled his fingers within her locks.

"Are you good?" he asked softly against her temple.

"Yeah," Alex replied with a short giggle. "I think I've survived."

She felt his chest rumble with laughter. Then he stroked both his hands down her back and cupped firmly at her ass, suggestively rubbing her against the hard, insistent force of his naked arousal. His underwear was now gone.

Alex rotated her hips, loving the feel of his thick length. Her want for him was swiftly throbbing back to life, though she had felt completely sated only moments earlier. She reached between their bodies to cup the heavy sac of his balls. Lucas groaned deep in his throat. Alex smiled to herself, really liking the sound of it. She fondled him a little more until he bit her earlobe in protest.

"You don't like that?" she teased.

"Too much," Lucas murmured. "But there's something I want more."

Alex stifled a scream of surprise and he quickly lifted her up in the air and placed her legs around his hips. Then he took a few steps until her back was against the wall. His strong legs were braced wide to keep her balanced and stable.

"Hold on," he instructed as he grabbed the condom and slipped it on between their bodies.

Alex barely had time to think before Lucas gripped her hips and pressed forward, inch by inch until his hard, thick length was sheathed in her body to the hilt. He filled her fully, so completely, she felt merged with his flesh. They were both panting with acute arousal and anticipation for what was to come. But Lucas remained still for several seconds, his eyes closed and jaw clenched hard. Alex watched the sexy, masculine contours of his face, knowing she had never seen a man so perfectly beautiful.

As though aware of her stare, he opened his eyes to look back at her. They shone with deep fervor and something else she could not identify but really wanted to understand. Did it echo this feeling that was budding in her stomach? As though he was now closer to her than anyone could be, and ever was? That he might take a vital and irreplaceable piece of her with him when this was over?

"Hi," Alex whispered, feeling the need to fight the emotional lump in her throat, reminding them both that this thing between them was supposed to be fun, casual, and convenient.

Lucas gave her a strained smile before leaning forward to touch his forehead against hers. He gripped her hips, squeezing her soft flesh to create subtle friction. She felt his arousal thicken and lengthen within her, and her body pulsed in response.

"Jesus, Alex," he growled deeply, his lips so close that his warm, moist breath brushed her skin. "I want—"

He swore deep with frustration, then stroked hard into her, pinning her against the wall. Every nerve ending in her body tingled in response. Her body wanted and needed more of the same. He was now entering with powerful thrusts, touching her so deep that Alex moaned over and over with approval. His lips brushed her face in feathery soft breaths while his harsh breathing echoed around them.

"Lucas," she panted, loving every minute.

"Yeah," he gasped, increasing his speed and intensity until she could only hold on for the ride, craving whatever the journey would bring her.

Suddenly, he wrapped his arms around her waist to hold her still and carried her across the room. Within seconds, she was flat on her back and Lucas barely broke his pace. His driving rhythm had them both breathing hard and damp with sweat. The new position added more stimulation to her sensitive bud, and Alex was quickly climbing to ecstasy again.

"Alex . . . Alex . . ." chanted Lucas as his thrusts became wild and untamed.

She wrapped her legs tighter around him knowing they were at the edge together. Then another incredible orgasm swept through her body and mind.

CHAPTER 20

There was a long, still silence as their breathing calmed. Eventually, Lucas turned, taking Alex along so they were both lying on their sides facing each other. With his eyes closed, he stroked his hands along the length of her back, savoring the silky texture of her skin as their bodies cooled. He would be content to stay like this for as long as possible, even all night. But that wasn't possible.

When Lucas finally got up, it was too soon. Alex sat up on the bed also, sweeping her tangled mass of hair away from her face. He strode into the bathroom, feeling the warmth of her gaze against his back before closing the door. Lucas quickly cleaned up and washed his hands while his thoughts remained fixed on the woman he'd left naked on the bed.

How the hell had that happened? He had only sought her out to provide an update on the case. Yet, the moment she entered the room, smelling sweet and clearly naked under the thin loose T-shirt, Lucas was rock hard.

With his hands spread, he leaned on the counter of the sink to look closely at himself in the mirror. There were two things very clear to him at that moment. He wanted Alexandria Cotts with a hunger and ferocity that was now impossible to ignore, and her protection remained his single most important priority. Now, he just had to figure out how to ensure both those two things weren't mutually exclusive.

When he returned to the bedroom, Alex was dressed in her T-shirt again, and sitting cross-legged in the middle of the bed. She had also picked up his clothes off the floor and draped them over the footboard.

"I need to talk to you about something," he stated as he pulled on his underwear.

"I thought we already talked about it," she replied, watching him openly. "Though I guess we really didn't finish the conversation, did we?"

"That's not what I came here to talk about," Lucas explained, zipping up his black cargo pants. "I have an update on Cesar Hernandez."

"Oh," Alex stated, clearly taken aback. "Okay."

"We have a lead on who tried to sell him the battery design that Adam North had developed for you," he told her.

"It wasn't Adam, right?" she insisted. "He would never do something like that. I know it."

"No, it wasn't North. It was his wife, Susie."

"Are you serious? Why?"

"That we don't know yet, but we should have more information soon," he assured her.

Alex covered her eyes and let out a deep breath.

"I should call Adam," she finally muttered. "Does he know yet? He must be freaking out."

"Sorry, Alex, you can't say anything to him until we know all the details. Including what he knew about his wife's activities, and when," he instructed.

She looked back at him with her shoulders low, but finally nodded with understanding.

They looked toward each other for a few moments, until it became awkward. Lucas dug his hands into his pockets.

"Alex, about earlier," he started, knowing he could not just walk away without saying something to explain his unplanned behavior.

But she shook her head, swinging her legs over the edge of the bed to stand up across from him.

"Maybe we should just forget about it for now," she then stated.

She seemed confused and uncertain, and Lucas found himself frustrated at the knowledge that he had caused it. He stepped toward her, ignoring her stiff spine and raised chin.

"I'm not sure I can," he whispered before leaning down to kiss her softly. "Good night, Alex."

Then Lucas walked away while he still could.

Over the next week, they fell into a predictable routine. Alex still spent all day in the shed working, only taking breaks to eat. But each afternoon, shortly after lunch, they met out back by the steps down to the dock and took a walk into town for a coffee. Each night, when she returned to the house, Lucas watched her head off to her room and resisted the driving need to join her.

During that time, he and Fortis made great progress to reveal the full network involved in the

Magnus assignment. The follow Friday morning, Lucas called Marco Passante to provide a report on the assignment and Lucas's recommendations for next steps.

"Once the Optimal driver confirmed that Susie North was the woman who had approached him to sell her husband's new rechargeable battery technology, everything else fell into place. While North was building the battery for you and Alex, his wife was trying to sell it for more money through the racing club that North belonged to in Chicago."

"I have my lawyers reviewing the situation right now with North and his wife," Marco stated. "He thinks there is a good chance we can sue for damages."

"Well, the feds haven't charged her with anything yet. It will depend on what North provides in his official statement about what he shared with his wife about the technology. So far, he's not provided them with that information."

"So what about Cesar Hernandez?" Marco asked.

"Hernandez admitted that he wasn't interested in just a new battery, he wanted the whole new hybrid design that Magnus was rumored to have in the works, and hired a firm called Crow to steal it back in January," Lucas explained. "He claims they had three months to deliver and we know that Crow planted Timothy Pratt at the University of Illinois in Chicago to get into North's computer in order to hack into the Magnus network through his access rights. When Crow realized that Adam's access was limited to uploading encrypted files on the Magnus file-sharing server, they had to wait until he delivered the final battery design, to which

Pratt ensured that a Trojan horse was loaded along with it. Once we shut down the intrusion, Crow could not deliver the Cicada designs to Hernandez. Hernandez then cancelled the gig with them and hired Frank Nunez to have it destroyed.

"We know most of that is true based on the statements from Nunez and the Petrov brothers. So, he's now charged with a list of offenses, the least of which is the destruction of property, and conspiracies to commit theft of trade secrets and copyright infringement."

"Jesus, what a greedy prick!" Marco swore.

"Even if he manages to escape jail time, he's ruined financially. His partners in the venture capital firm, Red Stream, have already filed several lawsuits based on other shady deals they've now discovered," added Lucas.

"That's something, I guess. So, where does that leave us with Alex?" Marco continued.

"I would like to tell you that all is safe for her to return, but I don't think it is, Marco," Lucas explained. "We believe that this firm Crow that Hernandez hired is now after the Cicada design."

Lucas then explained that attempt to hack into their networks after the Crow contract was cancelled.

"Maybe it was just a mistake, a delay in communication?" suggested Marco.

"We considered that at first," Lucas acknowledged. "But early in the case, we made a copy of the laptop the hacker, Pratt was using. It had a copy of North's design, e-mail exchanges between him and Alex with technical specifications, then search strings on hybrid engine design. All of that would be beyond the gig that Hernandez hired them to do."

"Shit!" cursed Marco. "So what now? Can't we find these Crow people and shut them down?"

Lucas stood up and walked across the living room of the cottage to look out at the shed where Alex was working.

"That's the problem. They're a ghost organization of expert hackers. You don't find them unless they want you to," Lucas explained.

"But you guys know one of them. The one with the laptop you copied. Timothy Pratt, right?"

"Yeah, we did. But someone killed him after Hernandez cancelled the job."

There was a long moment of silence as the seriousness of the situation sank in on the other end of the phone.

"What are you proposing?" Marco finally asked. He sounded tired and spooked, and Lucas couldn't blame him.

"I would like to keep Alex here for the next three weeks until the engine is rebuilt," Lucas explained. "The good news is that we haven't seen any more activity from Crow since Hernandez was arrested, so there is the possibility that the threat has been eliminated. But it's a risk I'm not willing to take."

"Okay, I understand. Does Alex know all of this?"

"Most of it, but I haven't told her my recommendation. I wanted to secure your approval first."

Marco sighed.

"I spoke to her this morning and she seemed

optimistic now that Hernandez was charged. I'm sure she'll be disappointed not to be returning home until after the Sea-to-Sky race."

"I agree," Lucas added. "But I think she'll quickly realize it's for the best."

"Well, you now have my approval," Marco finally stated. "Let me know if you need anything else."

The call ended soon after, and Lucas spent the next couple of hours confirming logistics with the Fortis team, then analyzing all of the information they had gathered about Crow, Pratt, and the network attack over a week ago. He also called his neighbor, Kathy to let her know he'd need Lita's cleaning services for another few weeks.

Occasionally, he was distracted by thoughts of Alex in anticipation of their conversation about extending their stay at the cottage through June. He wondered how she would react to the news that they would be staying at the cottage for the long haul. Lucas expected that she would be disappointed. Who wouldn't be, cut off from friends and family and her real life? Yet he couldn't deny feeling a sense of relief to know she would be safe with him until the threat to her and her design was neutralized. And that they would have more time together for him to figure out what to do with the unnerving feelings she stirred in him.

He worked through the lunch that Ned made, then walked out to the edge of the lake at the usual time. Alex was sitting on the top of the stairs to the dock. They smiled at each other before starting their usual walk along the boardwalk.

"I spoke with Marco this morning," he stated

when they were a few houses down. "I gave him a summary on the case."

Lucas then quickly gave her the same information about Cesar Hernandez, Susie North, and the shadow organization known as Crow, but left out the murder of Pratt.

"What's going to happen to Adam's wife?" Alex asked when he had finished.

"It depends," Lucas replied.

They were approaching the edge of the town center.

"On Marco," she finished, with a sigh. "I spoke with him again this morning. He still wants to sue."

Lucas looked over at her, but she was staring blankly ahead

"It's more complicated, unfortunately. Marco can only sue her if it's determined that the nondisclosure agreement North signed with Magnus covers his wife. That he shared the information about his technology with her, under the expectation that she would also act under the stipulations of the nondisclosure," he explained. "Then they both breached the contract and could be sued for damages."

"If he didn't share it with her, then she stole it," Alex continued.

"Right," he confirmed. "In which case, it's criminal. And since Adam North isn't talking to anyone but his lawyer right now, it's hard to say which way it will go."

They sat in silence for a few moments.

"I wish I could talk to Adam, see how he is doing, what he's thinking," she noted wistfully.

"Alex, we've talked about that," Lucas warned.

"I know, I know. It's too dangerous. I get it," she conceded. "I just feel responsible, I guess. Like I talked him into working with us, and now his life is a mess."

"The only person responsible in this instance is Susie North," he reminded her.

She nodded and looked down at her feet.

"There is enough evidence to suggest that Crow might still want to steal your engine design. So, I've recommended to Marco that we keep you here until you've rebuilt the engine, and he agrees," Lucas stated finally.

Alex was silent for another minute or so.

"Okay," she finally conceded. "I was prepared for that anyway."

They walked some more, until they reached the coffee shop and ordered her usual latte. Lucas got a bottle of water, then they started back to the cottage.

"I saw you and Ned fighting this morning," she stated, looking up at him with a big smile. "What's that all about?"

"Not fighting, sparring," he corrected. "It's good training, keeps us sharp."

"Training for what?"

Lucas knew where she was going with the discussion. They had talked a lot over the last few days on these walks, about the investigation and her work on the Cicada. Sometimes just random things that they found funny or interesting. But he had not talked about Fortis beyond the work with Magnus.

"Training for what we do, Alex," he finally replied. "Fortis protects people and valued assets.

In order to do that, sometimes we have to engage with the threat."

The words hung heavy between them, and he wondered what she was thinking. Lucas also considered why it was so important what she thought of what he did for a living.

"I guess I knew that," Alex finally responded in a neutral voice. "You don't carry a gun as a fashion accessory, right?"

He stopped and gently took her arm so they were facing each other.

"Alex, we're not thrill seekers or adrenaline junkies out looking for the next battle," he told her firmly. "The best way to protect something is to secure it, keep it out of harm's reach. That's what my team does best. But if that's not possible, then the threat has to be neutralized. We're damn good at that, too."

They looked at each other for a while, until Lucas started to regret his outburst. This was not something that he'd ever told a woman he was with. He had never needed them to understand the inherent danger in his business and accept it. Accept him.

"Is that what happened with your shoulder?" Alex finally asked.

She brushed her hand along the top of his trapezius muscle. He had removed the stitches a few days ago, but the area was still sore. The sparring session with Ned that morning was the first since the incident, and his muscle would take another couple of weeks to fully heal.

"I was shot."

Her eyes widened and she took a step back. "What? When?"

"In Chicago, when we had a lead on who was hacking your systems," he explained.

Alex looked down, then back at him with sharp fear in her eyes.

"Oh my God! That's when you decided I needed protection, right? Lucas, why didn't you tell me?"

He reached to cup her shoulders reassuringly, hating to know she was scared. "Alex, it's going to be okay," he insisted. "All of this is still just a precaution, okay? We have no indication that anyone is after you directly. But these people are dangerous, and I will continue to do everything and anything to keep you safe."

She looked back at him with those deep, golden brown eyes.

"That's why we're here," he continued. "Out of harm's reach, remember?"

Her shoulder seemed to relax just a little. Such a small change yet he felt so much lighter as a result.

"Come, let's head back before Ned comes looking for us."

"Wait, Lucas," she stated, grabbing his arm. "Did I make a mistake? Is this all worth it? Should I just walk away before anyone else gets hurt?"

Lucas felt her frustration and understood what was driving it. It was really hard to be a catalyst without feeling responsible for all the change it brings. He urged her forward so that they were walking again.

"I started attending college at sixteen years old," he told her softly. "I was this weird, awkward, skinny kid who spent way too much time in front of a computer."

He chuckled at her doubtful expression. It was hard for him to believe also, sometimes.

"My two older brothers had always been the athletes in the family. Lead rushers in football, highest scoring points in basketball. That sort of thing. At some point, I figured out that I would never have their abilities. But I was smart, at least with math and computers. It all made sense to me. I started writing my own programs, focusing on cryptography. The next thing I knew, I was seeing encryption vulnerabilities everywhere, and it became a game to see how far I could go to break through them."

Lucas paused. It was very rare that he reflected on the decisions he had made as a young man.

"By the middle of my freshman year at MIT, I could access several government networks undetected. I had built an application, a malware or Trojan horse that gave me undetected access to whatever system I targeted," he explained with a neutral tone. "I wasn't after anything, I just wanted to prove that I could solve the problem."

"What happened? Did you get caught?" she finally asked.

"No. My professor contacted one of the cybersecurity agencies in the government after I handed it in as an assignment. I was pretty naïve about the whole thing, obviously," he admitted. "Thankfully, because of my age and the fact that I hadn't tried to access anything of value, they decided not to press charges. Instead, they convinced me that my programs could help the government tighten their security. Or maybe coerced is a better description."

He let out a deep breath. Only a small number of the men he worked with knew these details about his life. And now, Alex.

"Anyway, what I'm trying to tell you is that the hacker that Hernandez hired to steal your design used my Trojan software to do it. It was over fifteen years ago, and my intention at the time was just to challenge myself and build something noteworthy. I didn't take into account the possible ramifications. Like someone stealing my malware to use for a crime, which is exactly what happened. It's still happening."

"Lucas, that's unbelievable," she whispered. "But, you were just a kid."

"I know that now. But it took me a long time to understand that I can't own other people's evil actions or the tools they use to commit them," he continued. "That's what I'm trying to tell you. You can't be responsible for other people's actions, Alex. Only your own."

They had reached the cottage and walked up the steps and to her shed in silence. Inside, Alex walked over to the large worktable and stood looking down at the various machine parts strewn there.

"Are you okay?" Lucas finally asked since he could accurately read her mood.

"Yeah," she replied firmly. "I'll be fine."

"Good. Then, I'll leave you to get some work done."

"Lucas," she stated as he opened the door. "Thanks. For earlier."

He nodded, giving her a brief smile before he headed back to the house.

CHAPTER 21

For Alex, the days went by in a blur of work. She awoke each morning by seven o'clock, and was in her workspace before eight with a cup of coffee and a light breakfast. Lunch was a quick break to eat whatever Lucas or Ned had made, and dinner was much the same. It should feel difficult or stressful to focus on one specific task for twelve to fourteen hours a day, seven days a week, but it didn't. For Alex, it felt like a rare opportunity to get away from all the other aspects of life in order to complete what may be the most significant accomplishment of her career.

When Lucas told her that they wanted to keep her in upstate New York for the next three weeks, until the engine was rebuilt, she immediately sent a bunch of e-mails to Noelle, Shawn, her dad, and her brothers with a story about signing up for a series of European conferences on emerging technology, and it was just boring enough to be believable. She should have been upset about the situation, but Alex had actually felt relieved.

The effort to rebuild the entire Cicada drivetrain by herself was going quite smoothly at a pace that would have it completed well within the time frame they had before the road tests in Vancouver. Returning to Toronto and reengaging her team in the process at this stage could be more disruptive than beneficial. She had the design specs that Niles, Randy, and Bobby had recorded, all the necessary parts and equipment, and the autonomy to tweak things as she wanted in the process.

The one welcome interruption to her work was the daily walks with Lucas. They only lasted about an hour, but provided an opportunity for her to relax and clear her mind. Most of the time, they talked about everyday things. Lucas would keep her updated on the news, and they would discuss the details. He would also provide details on the case, though as the weeks passed there was less and less to tell. Sometimes, Alex would bounce ideas off of him about various configurations to the Cicada drivetrain. He was sharp and knowledgeable enough about cars to ask the right questions and ultimately help her make a decision.

They rarely talked about their personal lives, other than when Lucas told her about his freshman year at MIT. And they never discussed that evening when Lucas had come to her room.

Alex had been very tempted to bring it up on several occasions. She wanted to know why he had kissed her, then made love to her after insisting it shouldn't happen again. And why had he made no move to touch her again? Was it just an impulse that he later regretted? As much as she wanted to ask, Alex wasn't sure she wanted to know the answer. It would hurt too much to hear once again that she was cool to hang out with, but not the type of woman he was into for a relationship. Not that she wanted a relationship right now with him, or any man. The tenuous friendship they had established was just fine, despite the awkward and consistent undercurrent between them of something unresolved. So, Alex suppressed her natural urge to confront a situation, and for once left it alone.

It was Wednesday evening, over three weeks since they had arrived at the cottage, when she hit a major speed bump. While testing the power output of the new electric motor, Alex discovered that the stranded copper wiring used in the stator was defective. She wasted four frustrated hours that evening trying to figure out the problem, then another two hours after a quick dinner in an attempt to rethread the wires before she gave up. There was no other option but to order another supply. And this time, it would be from a manufacturer she trusted.

Alex sat slumped on the work stool with her iPad and went through the design documentation for the original motor, hoping she could track down the details of the wiring used. No such luck. She was racking her brain, trying to remember the name of the brand when the message indicator for her e-mail in-box caught her eye. There were new e-mail messages since that afternoon after the daily walk with Lucas.

Needing a mental break, Alex opened up the e-mail application, expecting another response to one of the ongoing message threads from Noelle, Adrian, or Shawn asking when she'd be back from her European adventure. Instead, it was a note from Jean Renaud, the Indy car driver she had dated for over a year, and hadn't spoken to in over eight months. It simply said: *Hi Alex, will you be at the Sea-to-Sky race next month? It would be nice to see you. Maybe for dinner?*

She stared at the note for a long moment, trying to decide how to respond. Jean was a nice guy who had been great fun while they dated long distance. Until it stopped being easy.

Last summer, about eighteen months into their relationship, he was in Toronto to race in the Honda Indy. After the event, Jean planned to stay for another few days with the expectation that he could meet her friends and family, and ultimately make their relationship more committed. Suddenly, her glib, generic comments about her life, job, thoughts, and opinions weren't enough for him. By the time he left for Chicago, their communication became strained and Alex knew they had hit a wall. It was time to move forward to the next level in their relationship, or end it.

Alex already knew she wasn't ready to reveal her full self to Jean. He liked the carefree girl with manicured nails who wore pretty dresses and sexy shoes. That's who he wanted to be with and get to know more about. Unfortunately, that wasn't who she really was, and it would be too complicated and uncomfortable to try to explain all that. So Alex ended it.

Though hurt and confused by her sudden decision, Jean had been a gentleman about it, only reaching out a few times to see if she would reconsider. His invitation to meet again now left her with mixed feelings. Jean was an attractive guy, fun to be around, and it would be nice to see him again. But, after the kind of intensive, all-consuming experience with Lucas, could Alex now settle for just casual but enjoyable sex?

She stared blankly across the work shed trying to find some answers. Maybe Jean was exactly what she needed after this whole Fortis case was over and Lucas was gone and back to his own life. Jean could remind Alex that relationships weren't her thing. That men ultimately wanted pretty, feminine girls by their side, not the assertive, ambitious, and sometimes competitive bitch she could often be.

Before she could change her mind, Alex sent Jean a reply, confirming she would be at the race and dinner would be nice. Then she went back to work until she finally found the name of the manufacturer for stranded copper wiring used in the original Cicada electric motor. She didn't enter the house until after eleven thirty. Ned was sitting at the table on the computer as she went through the living area toward the kitchen to get some water.

"I was about to check on you, Alex," he stated casually. "You're working later than usual. Is everything okay?"

Alex gave him a wry smile as she filled a glass from the tap.

"I'm fine, but I've run into a problem," she admitted, then explained the situation with the wiring. "Can you get me a new supply of a specific brand? I'm dead in the water without it, and we don't have any time to waste with another defective batch."

"Okay. Give me the details and I'll get the order placed," Ned stated.

She walked over to the table and sat beside him, then pulled up the details on her iPad. Ned launched a Web site for a distributor called DaCosta Solutions and typed in the specifics in the search window.

"This distributor supplies parts and equipment to the U.S. military and military contractors," he explained. "It looks like they have several grades of copper wiring by that manufacturer. Any preference?"

Alex looked at the search results, amazed at the options listed on the page.

"Is this site available to the general public? Can I use it in the future?" she asked.

"Unfortunately you can't, it's only available for approved organizations," Ned explained. "But, Fortis is well connected within DaCosta. I'm sure we could pull some strings to get you an account."

She looked at him speculatively, then back at the Web site. The name DaCosta did ring a bell—

"Isn't that the name of one of your owners? Evan DaCosta?" she asked. "Any relation?"

Ned grinned.

"He owns it."

"Ahhh," she mumbled, suddenly understanding their ability to get her equipment so quickly. "Let's go for that one."

She pointed to the option noted to have the lowest voltage drop, ideal to support high speeds and maximum horsepower from the motor. It was expensive, but worth every penny if it produced better results.

"You got it," confirmed Ned as he made a few clicks on the site. "Hopefully, we'll get it by tomorrow. Friday morning at the latest."

"Wow, that would be fantastic," she mumbled, standing up. "Thanks so much."

"No problem at all."

"It's late," she added, noting the time on the laptop. "Where's Lucas?"

"He's out for a run."

"Now? It's after midnight," she questioned with surprise.

Ned shrugged.

"He's out every night these days. Says it's the best time for him to clear his head," he explained. "I prefer mornings myself. But he should be back any minute. It's been over an hour."

Alex took a sip of water as she absorbed the information. Since Lucas was usually in the house when she returned from the shed, he must head out as soon as she went to bed.

"Okay. Well, I'm off to bed then."

"See you in the morning," Ned replied.

In her room, Alex headed right into the bathroom to take a long shower. Exhausted, she bathed, washed her hair, then stood for an extended period under the warm, beating spray of water. The decision to meet Jean at the race wasn't sitting well with her. The more she thought about it, Alex realized it was only an attempt to prove that she would be able to walk away from Lucas as easily as he would at the end of all this. That she could forget how good it felt to have been completely real and transparent with a man, and return to the preference of casual relationships that didn't interfere with her real life. Forget the feel of his hands and the imprint of his hard body against hers.

It now seemed like wishful thinking, made more foolish by that fact there was absolutely nothing between her and Lucas. Judging by his obvious lack of interest over the last three weeks, whatever had sparked his fleeting attention had faded, just as she knew it would. Unfortunately, she still struggled to contain her own attraction, and seeing Jean again wasn't going to change that. Only time and reality would.

Alex turned off the water and stepped out of the shower to dry off. She softly squeezed her wet hair with a towel and wrapped a second one around her body before brushing her teeth. *Maybe I should cancel with Jean now before he gets the wrong idea?* she debated while applying body lotion. *Or just wait until we meet?*

She was going back and forth in her head, trying to decide which approach would be less awkward, when she walked back into the bedroom and came to an abrupt stop. Lucas was standing in the dark, across from the bathroom door with his arms crossed at his chest and an unreadable look on his face. In the dim light, she could see that he was wearing sweatpants and a T-shirt.

"Lucas," she gasped in surprise. "What are you doing here?"

He didn't react for about ten seconds, until the pause became tense and Alex became worried that something was very wrong. She tentatively stepped forward, looking around.

"Is everything okay?" she finally asked.

He didn't move, nor did his intense stare waver from her face.

"Why are you meeting him?" Lucas finally demanded in a low, silky voice.

"What? Who?" returned Alex, completely confused.

"Renaud! Why are you meeting him in Vancouver?"

Her heart stuttered, then started pounding with a fast, heavy rhythm.

"Excuse me?" she stammered. "How do you know about that?"

He just looked back at her stone-faced.

"Are you spying on me? Reading my e-mails?" she demanded, striding toward him.

"Of course I'm reading your e-mails, Lex. How else am I supposed to make sure your communications are safe and within protocol?" he said dismissively. "Answer my question."

"Are you serious? It's none of your business," she told him, trying to keep her tone neutral, without any sign of her mounting anger.

"I'm making it my business. Fortis business," he clarified. "How do we know he isn't involved with trying to steal your Cicada technology?"

"What are you talking about?" demanded Alex, now standing directly in front of him, forgetting for a moment that she was only wearing a fluffy white towel. "I told you that Jean doesn't even know I'm an engineer. And you ruled out his involvement from the beginning."

"Maybe we were wrong. He lives in Chicago, he's connected to the same racing club as North and his wife, and the Optimal Racing driver the wife approached to sell the battery tech. Maybe *Jean* was involved the whole time," he shot back, uttering the name like a dirty word.

"Don't be ridiculous!" Alex scoffed back at the suggestion with a dark laugh.

He leaned down toward her much shorter level, suddenly looking menacing.

"You have no idea how many ridiculous things are actually true," he growled. "Why else is he reaching out to you now to meet? According to you, it's been months since you guys broke up."

Alex sucked in a deep breath. Is that what he thought? That the only reason a man like Jean would want to see her again is if he was after something? She stepped back, too angry and hurt to respond immediately. Then, she turned to walk over to the dresser in the middle of the room and slowly removed underwear and a clean oversize T-shirt.

"Is that what you think, Lucas? That he's using me for information? For access to my hybrid design?" she finally replied in a deceptively soft voice. "Maybe he just wants to use me for something much less complicated. And maybe I want to be used."

Suddenly, he was turning her to face him with a firm grip on her upper arms. She gasped with surprise and tried to shake off his hold.

"Is that what you really want, Alex?" he asked softly, ignoring her struggles like she was just a small child. "That puny kid?"

She looked into his face only inches from hers, and noted the hot fire burning deep in his eyes and the hard clench of his jaw.

"What can I say, Lucas. That puny kid really knows how to work his equipment."

The dark fire burned hotter and Lucas bared his teeth. Alex felt a small amount of satisfaction.

"Tell me the truth, Alex. Is that why you want to see him? To get back together?"

"I told you the truth," she whispered, leaning even closer so their lips almost touched. "It's none of your business."

Before she could take another breath, his mouth was on her in a deep, bruising kiss. His tongue delved deep and wet with dominating force as though staking claim. He wrapped his arms around her body, pulling her up tightly against his hard length. Alex couldn't move, couldn't breathe against the onslaught. Her head was spinning from the surprise and lack of oxygen. Yet she didn't want it to stop.

"Damn it, Alex!" Lucas muttered when he finally took a breath. "You're driving me insane."

Then he was kissing her again, softer, more seductively, enticingly until she was coaxed into meeting his tongue with hers. He let out a vibrating groan and lifted her off her feet. Alex wanted to smile at the sound but was too busy tasting his lips, enjoying the stroke of his firm tongue against hers. She barely realized that he had laid her down on the bed until his lips started a trail down her neck toward her collarbone. Then he reached the edge of her towel and Alex opened her eyes to look down at the top of his head. Common sense and self-preservation were both starting to penetrate her foggy brain.

"Lucas," she whispered as he slowly pulled the

towel loose to reveal her naked breasts. "What are you doing?"

He stilled, staring fixedly at the twin globes of generous, round, chocolate-tipped flesh.

"What is this?" Alex forced out, wishing she didn't need to know.

Lucas looked up at her with those beautiful brown eyes rimmed with silky long lashes. His sensuous mouth was pouted with desire.

"I don't know, Alex," he finally replied. "I just know that I want it."

He brushed his thumb across one of her puckered nipples, sending a shock wave of intense need down to the base of her stomach.

"No matter how many times I tell myself this a really bad idea, I still want you more than I did the day before," he continued with his gaze now fixed on her body's reaction to his touch. "At this point, being with you has to be less of a distraction than not. That's all I know, Lex."

He leaned forward to lick her tight nub, sucking it into his hot mouth and swirling his tongue over it. She squirmed under the stimulation. It was like incredible torture and she just wanted more of the same.

"I should probably have something more romantic to say," Lucas mused, looking up at her again, sheepish. "I usually do. I should tell you that you're incredibly beautiful and I can't stop thinking about you. All of which is true, but it doesn't change anything. Within a few weeks, this mission will be over."

He sucked on her nipple again while teasing the other with his fingers. Alex wanted to reply, ask questions, but she couldn't think straight enough to do so. Nor did she want him to stop.

"I want you now, tomorrow, and for as long as I'm here to protect you. I don't know what comes after that."

While he cupped her breasts with his hands, Lucas continued to kiss a leisurely path down the center of her stomach, right to her mound. Then he slid easily off the bed to kneel in front of her reposed, naked body. She watched, propped up on her elbows, challenged to breathe properly as he brushed his fingers along the inside of her thighs, spreading them wider.

Lucas leaned forward again to run his lips along the seam of her lower lips and Alex let out a shuddering moan.

"God, you taste good," he muttered, gripping her hips to pull her down to the edge of the bed.

Spreading her legs wider, he swept deep with his tongue, stroking her hidden depths and teasing the swell of her clit. It was so good that she had to bite her lips to hold back a scream. But still she watched, wanting to remember every second of the experience. He licked her again and again, then deeper, harder, delving into her wet well with relentless pressure. Alex could only gasp and shudder as he devoured her delicate flesh like a delectable dessert.

She was floating on a pleasurable plateau until Lucas adjusted her body by draping one of her legs over his shoulder. He moved the firm stroke of his tongue up to her erogenous bud before stroking into her with the long firm length of his finger.

"Oh God," she panted with explosive need. "Lucas."

"You like that?" he demanded breathlessly.

"Yes," she begged. "Yes!"

He stroked his finger again with a relentless, hypnotic pace while sucking and stroking on her clit. Alex fell back on the bed, completely overwhelmed by the hot, silky need that radiated out from the center of her body. On and on it went, building with consuming ferocity until finally, she peaked, shattering her mind and body into thousands of little pieces.

CHAPTER 22

"You like this position, don't you?" Lucas asked in a tight voice.

His was sitting in the middle of her bed with his back against the headboard. Alex was sitting astride his lap, and he was buried deep within her tight grasp.

"It might be my second favorite," she whispered back, flexing her hips to tease him.

He hissed, gripping her shoulders and fighting the never-ceasing need to pound into her with mindless abandon. Lucas was seriously wondering if he would ever regain the easy ability to make slow, leisurely love to a woman, if not this woman.

It was Sunday night, and they had been together every night since that irritating e-mail to her ex-boyfriend, yet his greedy hunger for her still seemed insatiable.

"What's your favorite?" he asked, though he already knew.

"There is something about the top of a hotel

credenza that really does it for me," she stated with a sexy smile.

Lucas groaned at the thought, though the image was never really far from his mind.

"I think I agree with you. But I'm not picky," he replied while she continued to drive him crazy with small thrusts and undulations of her hips.

"Good to know," Alex whispered, leaning forward to kiss him softly on the lips.

He took a moment to enjoy the soft, sweet feel of her touch. Until she stroked her tongue into his mouth to entangle his. His body shuddered with mounting arousal. Then she wrapped her arms around his neck and began to ride him with a slow, maddening canter. Jesus, she felt amazing, like every inch of her was designed to fit into his hands and house his length in a perfect, snug, incredible grip.

"Lucas," she gasped against the side of his neck.

"Yeah, baby?" He loved when she said his name like that.

"So good," she whispered, slowing her pace and lengthening her stride until she was sliding along every inch of his throbbing arousal.

"Good" didn't even begin to describe the need that was rushing through him. It took every ounce of control he had not to flip her over and drive into her soft wetness, take her, owning her so she could never forget the feel of his touch. Possessing her so completely that he'd forever be imprinted on her soul.

Lucas gritted his teeth against his primal instincts. But his wild thoughts spurred on his mounting climax until it was pounding relentlessly at the base of his spine. Whatever idea he had to allow Alex to move things at her own pace was now untenable. He took both her hips into his hands, driving up into her sheath with long, deep thrusts. She tightened the hold around his neck and relaxed into his embrace while moaning deep with his every penetration until his body finally reached the pinnacle of a staggering orgasm. Even as he shuddered with ecstasy, Lucas could feel every gripping pulse of her body as she joined him in completion.

It was long moments later before their bodies were cooling and their heart rates were back to normal. Alex was still sitting across his lap, running her hand along the back of his head with soothing strokes.

"Your new supply of wiring should arrive before noon tomorrow," Lucas finally stated. "We can pick it up during our walk."

"That's good. I was starting to get worried," she replied with a sigh.

"I know. We could have had it on Friday through the delivery company that DaCosta uses, and it probably would have been fine. But I arranged a private courier to a post office box in town to be extra safe. The last thing we need now is to tip anyone off about your work here."

"No, that makes sense," she conceded in a soft, lazy voice. "I got some work done on the power converter, so we're in good shape. Marco has booked time at a racetrack near Whistler for the road tests during the week prior to the race. So, I need to have the full drivetrain completed by at least June third."

Lucas brushed his hands along her back leisurely.

"I know. He's given us all the details, so we're planning to travel on the Friday or Saturday, at least a day before the Magnus team arrives in Whistler," he explained. "Do you have enough time?"

"That's two weeks," she confirmed with a sigh. "Assuming nothing else goes wrong, I think I'll be okay."

He finally turned them so they were lying down on their sides facing each other.

"Then I should let you get some sleep, shouldn't I," he told her, only half teasing.

"Yeah, you should," she replied seriously, but he could tell by the purse of her lips that she was holding back a smile.

He pushed a few stray locs off her face.

"I can do that," he whispered. "At least until tomorrow."

Alex grinned at that while Lucas rolled off the bed and pulled the bedcovers over her delectably naked body. Then he headed into her bathroom to shower and get dressed before doing a final security check for the night and returning to her bed to get some rest next to Alex's warm and already sleeping form.

The next morning, Lucas was up before her as usual, working at the computer when she strolled into the living area sometime close to eight o'clock. Though Ned was out for his daily run, they only smiled at each other while Alex made a couple slices of toast and headed out to the shed with a cup of coffee.

Ned returned a short time later, then joined him at the dining table after a shower.

"So, what do you think? Is it him?" the other agent asked.

Lucas looked up at the page of hacking programming code that was at the core of Ned's question and his own intense scrutiny for the past three weeks. It was a complicated yet very elegant script, designed to mask itself within any system or network administrator functions until it was triggered to take over by overriding all other access.

It was the code that was used to hack into the Magnus servers just days after the fire at the shop, and after Cesar Hernandez had cancelled the contract with the organization called Crow. Lucas had recognized the code within days of the hacking, but it had taken much longer to figure out why.

"Based on my contacts at the Secret Service, NSA, CIA, and Interpol, we know that this virus has been used on at least twenty-two known cases of cybercrime. Each of those cases has been a targeted attack on some kind of corporate data storage, and the hacker has never been identified."

"Crow," Ned stated.

"Crow," agreed Lucas.

"But, is it Purdy?"

Lucas pulled up another file.

"This is the source code that Edgar Purdy tried to sell to Russian representatives almost eight years ago," Lucas explained. "It's not identical, but it's close enough."

"So Purdy is Crow," Ned confirmed.

"It's either him, or a group of people using his

signature code," added Lucas. "Either way, we're dealing with some pretty unique skills."

"Yeah, well Edgar Purdy is one of the fathers of twenty-first century network intrusion detection systems."

"And he was a top expert in the Secret Service until he decided he could make a few million dollars selling virus technology on the international market."

"You mean until you discovered he had stolen the code from the lab you both worked in," clarified Ned. "It might explain why Pratt was using your Trojan horse. I think Purdy might have a hard-on for you, Lucas."

Lucas looked back at this laptop screen.

"Yeah, I'm thinking he might still be holding a grudge," he mumbled. "He always did have a massive ego."

"What if he knew you and your private firm were on the Magnus case from the time Hernandez hired him to steal the engine design?" pondered Ned. "He might see this as a way to finally prove that he's smarter than you."

It was the same idea that had been swirling in Lucas's head for the last few days. Edgar Purdy had been his supervisor and mentor in the Secret Service for about five years until Interpol began an investigation into a mole somewhere in one of the elite government network security protection departments, with the intent to sell a new, highly effective virus to the highest international bidder.

Lucas hadn't really been paying attention to the case. He had been too wrapped up in completing his various consulting projects successfully.

He certainly never suspected that Purdy was the mole. Not until several files in his own work appeared to be accessed by someone else. Lucas spent days tracking down the intrusion, until he finally discovered that the trail led right back to his supervisor. Purdy knew that Lucas had discovered the truth, and by the time Lucas handed over the evidence to Interpol, Purdy was long gone, never seen or heard from again despite his permanent presence at the top of several most wanted lists.

"He's managed to stay completely dark for eight years, now he's leaving trails of breadcrumbs everywhere," Ned continued. "He may want to steal Magnus technology, but looks like he wants to beat you even more."

"And if he's still driven by an insatiable need to prove he's the best hacker out there, maybe we can use his ego to our advantage," finished Lucas.

"Any ideas?"

"Nothing specific yet. But I tell you, Ned, no one has been this close to Purdy since he disappeared off the radar. This may be the only chance to shut him down, and his Crow organization."

There was a moment of silence until Ned cleared his throat. Lucas looked up as his friend and knew exactly where the conversation was going to go.

"You still think this thing between you and Alex is nothing?" Ned finally asked, reference their conversation from weeks ago in Toronto. "I mean, it's pretty obvious that you haven't slept in your bed for days."

Lucas sat back and ran all his fingers through the short crop of hair on his head.

"Whatever it is, I have it under control," he replied serious. "It won't impact the mission."

"I have no doubt about that," Ned explained. "But that doesn't make it an easy situation."

Lucas didn't reply and Ned dropped the subject. The two men went back to work through the morning. While things had been very quiet over the last few weeks since Hernandez was arrested, there was a building sense of concern that it wasn't likely to stay that way. Every day closer to the Vancouver race increased the chances that Crow or someone else would try to take the hybrid technology.

At one thirty in the afternoon, Lucas headed outside to walk with Alex into town. She was waiting for him out near the stairs down to the pier, and they took the usual route along the boardwalk. It was a mild but cloudy day in late May, and Alex wore a light jacket over close-fitting jeans and sneakers. Lucas couldn't help but notice how the dark denim hugged her lean limbs and soft curves.

"How are things back home?" he asked along the way to the town center. "You haven't asked for any pictures to send to anyone."

She laughed.

"I think that would have created more suspicion than anything else."

Lucas grinned back.

"Everyone seems fine. They've asked when I'm planning to be back, so I've just told them it would be after the race. Shawn was the only one who seems skeptical about my story."

"Anything we should be concerned about?"

"Nah, he just knows me really well, and is finding it hard to believe I would take off on an extended trip instead of trying to do everything possible to remake my engine."

He smiled down at her.

"He really knows you well."

"What about you, Lucas? How does your family deal with your long absences?"

"They're pretty used to it by now," he told her simply.

"You said you were from New Jersey originally? Do your parents still live there?" she asked.

"Yup. Along with my two older brothers. One is a cop and the other is a college football coach. Both are married and have a house full of kids."

"Do you get to see them often?"

"A few times a year, at least," he explained. "My parents come to stay with me at my house in Virginia Beach for a couple of weeks each summer."

"Sounds like you guys are pretty close," she stated.

"We get along pretty well, but they still don't really understand what I do. To this day, my mom thinks I was part of the security detail for the president," he admitted with a chuckle. "She seemed so disappointed every time I told her that wasn't the only thing the Secret Service did."

They walked for a while in silence.

"I have to admit I find it hard to imagine you were ever a skinny computer geek," Alex eventually stated.

Lucas shrugged.

"I was a very late bloomer, that's all," he mused.

"Then I met a few big, badass dudes that whipped my ass into shape."

"Like Ned?"

"Yeah, for one. And my partners, Evan and Sam," he added. "Those are two guys you don't want to run into in a dark alley when they're in a bad mood."

"I don't know, Lucas Johnson. I think you can handle yourself pretty well."

He only grinned back, but felt ridiculously pleased by her comments.

Shortly after, they walked through the lakeside park at the edge of town and up to the sidewalk.

"The post office is across the street from the cafe. We'll grab your latte on the way back."

Over the next five minutes, the skies gradually darkened, threatening a heavy rainfall. They ducked into the small convenience store that housed the post office and rental boxes in the back just as the first few raindrops started to fall. Lucas quickly retrieved the package of copper wiring from their rented box, then stood at the front of the store with Alex to watch the downpour.

"How long do you think it will last?" she asked.

There was a bright streak of lightning in the direction of the lake followed by the loud clap of thunder.

"Hard to say," he admitted. "Let's make a run for the cafe, then we can wait it out over afternoon coffee. Will you be okay?"

He tucked the box under his arm, then zipped up the front of her jacket.

"Maybe we should get you an umbrella. I'm sure they sell them in here somewhere."

Alex looked up at him seriously, then surprised him by rising up on her toes to press a soft, sweet kiss on his lips.

"I'll be fine. It's just rain," she teased.

Before he could stop himself, Lucas leaned down to kiss her again, savoring the pleasurable tingle that radiated through his body from the touch.

"Okay, ready?" he whispered when he finally pulled back.

"I'll race you," she stated quickly, then dashed out the front door to run across the street.

"Alex, wait!" Lucas immediately yelled, but she didn't even look back.

He ran after her, cursing under his breath and doing a full hasty security sweep along the way. Lucas entered the café only seconds after Alex, only to find her giggling as she declared her victory.

"Damn it, Alex! Don't ever do that again," he growled while pulling her with him to the back of the small bakery.

"What? What did I do?"

"I told you, never go anywhere without either me or Ned at your side. That's the protocol. That's the only way to keep you safe at all times," he snapped, still struggling to reduce his heart rate.

There were only a couple of other people in the store, and neither even looked their way.

"Sorry," mumbled Alex, her bright golden brown eyes wide with surprise. "I was just messing around."

He let out a deep breath.

"I know. It's okay," he finally acknowledged. "You just took me by surprise, that's all. Here, have a seat. I'll go get your latte."

She nodded, all traces of her earlier playfulness now gone. It made Lucas feel like an ass, but he knew that his reprimand was necessary. The potential danger was too real not to remain diligent at all times.

While he waited for the barista to make Alex's specialty coffee, Lucas scanned the street outside to note anything unusual or concerning. At first, it looked calm and quiet except for the pounding of the hard rainfall. Until he noted the car parked two stores down from the postal office. It was a dark blue sedan with rental plates, with one person sitting in the driver's seat, and it had been there fifteen minutes ago when they had arrived.

He took out his cell phone to call Ned.

"I think we have a problem," he stated immediately.

"What do you have?" the other agent asked.

"A stakeout in a rental car, near the post office for at least fifteen minutes." Lucas provided the license plate number. "Can you work with Laura at headquarters to find out who rented it? I'll keep Alex locked down in the café across the street."

"You got it. I'll send you what we find."

"Thanks, but be prepared for an extraction," Lucas added before they hung up.

"Is everything okay?" asked Alex when he returned to the table where she was sitting. He handed her the latte and took the seat across from her where he could still see the car on the street.

"I'm not sure," he told her honestly.

"Why? What's going on?"

He put a reassuring hand on her shoulder, wishing she didn't look so scared.

"Nothing for certain. I've just asked Ned to check something out," he told her. "Drink your coffee."

Though she looked around with concern, Alex did as he suggested. The text from Ned came less than five minutes later.

The car was rented with a fake identity. I'm on my way.

"Alex, we have to go. Ned is coming to take you back to the house," he stated, standing up.

"Why? What happened?" she demanded, lower her coffee cup and staring up at him.

"I think we're being watched. I want to make sure you and the package get back to the safe house without being followed," he explained briskly while his eyes remained fixed on the suspect outside.

"What about you?"

"Ned will stop the truck across the street in about three minutes. The second he gets here, we'll run to get you inside, okay?"

"What about you, Lucas?"

"Alex, did you hear my instructions?" Lucas demanded while escorting her to the front of the café as casually as possible. "Do you understand?"

"Yes! I heard you."

"Okay, good. I'll be fine," he finally explained. "I'm going to stay back and find out who this guy is and make sure he doesn't locate the house."

Within a couple of minutes, Ned drove up the street in their large SUV and came to an abrupt stop in the active lane right beside the dark blue sedan, effectively blocking it. Lucas put a protective arm around Alex's shoulders and hurried her across the empty street. He nodded at Ned as she quickly ducked into the backseat. Once her passenger door was closed and locked, Lucas withdrew his gun and crept low around the back of their truck and then between the two vehicles. Betting that the driver's side door was unlocked, he pulled open the door just wide enough to press the barrel of his gun into the side of the driver. The heavy-set man jumped in surprise, letting out a stream of curses.

"Move over," Lucas demanded while still crouching low at the driver's door. He poked into the man again with the gun barrel to reemphasize his command. "Now!"

"Who the fuck are you, man?" the stranger stammered while trying to maneuver his large size over the center console of the car.

"And don't bother trying to reach your weapon. I have no problem shooting you in the gut long before you ever get your hands on it," Lucas explained. "And don't make me run after you either. You wouldn't make it to the end of the block."

"Okay, okay!" the man yelled desperately with his hands up in the air.

Finally, after some awkward scrambling, Lucas

was able to enter the rented sedan in the driver's seat. Ned immediately drove away with Alex and the package secured.

"Give me your wallet," Lucas instructed with his pistol still discreetly pointed at the man's midsection. "Slowly."

The guy took out a leather billfold from a pocket on the inside of his jacket and handed it over to Lucas before putting his hands up in the air again.

"Who sent you?" demanded Lucas softly as he flicked open the wallet to read the identification displayed on the inside. ROBERT MALONE.

"I don't know. I was just given instructions to come here."

"What instructions exactly?"

"Just to wait for someone to pick up a package from this post office today, and track where they went and provide the location," Malone explained.

"How did you get the instructions?"

"By phone, at my office in Syracuse. I'm a private investigator, so it's pretty standard stuff."

"And how were you to send back the information you gathered?" Lucas asked.

"I have an e-mail address. It's inside my wallet."

"Good." Lucas tossed over the wallet so it landed in the other man's lap. "This is what's going to happen, Bobby. You're going to wait until tomorrow to e-mail your client, saying that you did not see who picked up the package at this post office. Got it?"

"You can't do this!" stammered Malone. "I'm a legitimate professional."

"Unfortunately for you, I can, Bobby," replied

Lucas in a patient and patronizing voice. "Word of advice: I don't take cases from faceless clients who pay more than the job is worth. There's a big chance that they're on the wrong side of legal. Do you get what I'm saying?"

Robert Malone swallowed a big lump in his throat.

"What about my payment? I have a business to run!"

"I can't help you with that, unfortunately."

Lucas could see the desperation in Malone's eyes and knew immediately that the man was going to do something stupid. They stared at each other for three seconds before the private detective lunged across the center of the car, trying to hit Lucas's right arm with his elbow and knock the gun out of the way. But Lucas saw his slow attempt coming from a mile away, and followed Malone's momentum with a swift, fierce jab into the big man's right jaw with his left elbow. Malone immediately slumped down in the middle of the car, knocked out cold.

It was still raining pretty hard, with no one on the street to see the struggle. But Lucas remained cautious of anyone who might see him step out of a car where an unconscious guy could be resting for a good twenty minutes or more. And since Malone seemed reluctant to follow his instructions and take his advice, Lucas took matters into his own hands. He turned on the dark blue sedan with the keys in the ignition and drove it and the PI out of town about four miles north, stopping on a rural side street. Then, he took Malone's wallet, the car keys, and the small pistol he found after a quick search. He left the cell phone, to allow for some tracking. Satisfied that would slow him down sufficiently for the day, Lucas started back to the cottage at a steady jog.

About a mile outside of the town center, he tossed away the keys, gun, and wallet, minus the driver's license and a small note with an e-mail address on it, just as Malone had detailed. Lucas then called Ned to provide an update and plan for reinforcements.

CHAPTER 23

That evening, Ned left in the seaplane to pick up Samuel Mackenzie and another Fortis agent, Renee Thomas, from LaGuardia Airport in New York. They were back at the lakefront cottage in Skaneateles before midnight. Lucas met them in the backyard as they crossed the lawn.

"Hey, Renee," he stated as he patted the tall, lean woman on the shoulder. "Thanks for taking this assignment so last minute."

She grinned at him with white teeth that shone brightly against the cool, milk chocolate tone of her skin. As the newest member of the Fortis ground team, this would only be her second mission.

"No problem, boss. You know how much trouble Sam can get into if I'm not around," she replied with a strong British accent.

"I think it's the other way around, young lady," came the deep, burly response as Sam stepped up to them.

Both Lucas and Renee raised their eyebrows.

"Let's get inside, and I'll show you around the

house," continued Lucas. "Renee, you can take the bedroom I've been using. There's a fourth room with two beds. Sam and I can share that one while Ned and Alex can stay where they are now."

"No concerns from me," Sam stated. "I can sleep anywhere."

"That's for sure," Renee added. "He was asleep the minute we were seated on the flight from D.C. to New York. One of the flight attendants dared to wake him up when we were about to land, then ran away scared after the look he gave her."

Sam just shrugged. He was a big guy, about six feet four inches and all carved, rippled muscle. There were few people who would risk their lives to point out any of his less endearing qualities. But Renee never seemed to hesitate. Probably because they had a history working together in MI5 prior to Fortis.

They entered the living room area, where Alex was still awake, sitting at the kitchen counter with a cup of coffee. It had been a long, scary afternoon and evening for her. Lucas gave her a small encouraging smile and watched as she took a deep breath before standing up to meet the new agents.

"Alexandria Cotts, meet one of my partners, Samuel Mackenzie," Lucas stated.

"Nice to meet you in person, Alex," Sam added as he stood forward and shook her hand. "Call me Sam."

"Hi, Sam. Thanks for coming here so quickly," Alex told him, craning her neck to look up at him.

"And this is Renee Thomas, our newest recruit," continued Lucas.

"Hi, Alex," said Renee with a wide smile.

"Hi," she replied as the two women also shook hands.

"Why don't we get settled in for the night," suggested Lucas. "Then we can meet in the morning at O-eight hundred hours to review the security plan."

He and Ned then showed the new agents where they could put down their travel bags. Lucas left them a few minutes later to do a perimeter inspection of the property. All was secure. Back inside, the house was quiet. He paused in the hallway to the bedrooms, knowing the smarter choice would be to join Sam in the fourth bedroom and get a good night's sleep. But after the events of the day, Lucas didn't try to resist the need to hold Alex securely in his arms. He strode purposefully to her room at the end of the hall and quickly stripped out of his clothes to join her under the sheets.

The next morning, Lucas was up before the rest of the team and ready with an operational plan before the others joined him for coffee and a light breakfast. Alex walked through the space a few minutes later, grabbing coffee and a bagel on the way out to her work shed.

"You guys had a chance to review the updated mission report, including the threat assessment based on yesterday's events," he stated to the other three Fortis agents who now stood around the table. "I'd like to confirm our protection plan for the next two weeks."

"We remain at this site until next Friday while Alex finishes off the motor and other components of her Cicada design," Ned explained. "Then we will meet with the Magnus racing team in British Columbia so they can put the car together and complete the road test and final calibrations.

"The challenge is we now have confirmation that someone is still trying to get the hybrid. And they are running out of time. Once the product is launched publicly by Magnus at the race in less than three weeks, the window to steal the designs will be closed. Which is why we've brought on additional security support. We need to be prepared for anything, and the threat will only increase as we get closer to the race."

"How confident are you that it's Crow that's after the design now?" Sam asked, standing with his legs spread wide and his arms crossed against his massive chest.

"From everything we've gathered about the cyber intrusion tactics used on North's computer by Pratt in Chicago, then directly on the Magnus servers, I'm ninety-five percent certain Edgar Purdy is involved. And you're all now up to speed on the various incidents of corporate hacking over the last seven years that have been attributed to the ghost organization called Crow. The code signatures are pretty damn close," stated Lucas. "So either Edgar Purdy is Crow or he is closely affiliated."

"This is also the first time where Purdy has blatantly used virus algorithms that we know he developed while with the Secret Service," Ned added. "He's shown his face and we have to assume it's because of Lucas."

"Yeah, well, from what we read in the mission

files, it's not surprising," rumbled Sam. "He taught you everything you knew about developing solutions to secure the country against electronic crimes, and you turned around and ruined his plans to make millions from the Russians."

"I think you're overstating things a bit, Scotsman," Lucas scoffed. "I had learned a few things on my own before joining the Service."

Sam smirked. "All right, all right, don't get your knickers in a twist."

"The point is that Purdy has always been driven by his ego, and he now thinks he has something to prove," continued Lucas. "Let's take advantage of it."

"You want to bait him to come after the Cicada," stated Renee. "Do you think that will work? I mean, this is a guy that's managed to stay completely off the grid while wanted by several government agencies. Seems pretty stupid to risk all that just to prove that he can steal something out from under your protection, Lucas."

"You would think so," Lucas agreed. "Yet here we are. If our friend Robert Malone was hired by him, Purdy's spending a lot of energy to get the Cicada long after his contract has been cancelled by Hernandez. And he wants me to know it."

"Whatever his motives are, it's stronger than staying off the grid," Ned summarized.

"Exactly," Lucas agreed. "So let's see if we can use it to draw him out."

Ned pulled up a map of British Columbia.

"The Sea-to-Sky race is an open competition that runs along a fifteen-mile stretch up Highway

Ninety-nine from Daisy Lake to the ski town of Whistler. Last week, Marco Passante confirmed accommodations in Whistler, with plans to arrive with the racing team and meet us one week before the race to conduct a final road test with the new hybrid," Lucas outlined. "He's also booked time at a racing track about thirty minutes north of Whistler, in a town called Pemberton, to try out the Cicada."

"Won't that make us the perfect target?"

"It would, which is why it makes the perfect decoy," replied Lucas.

"Since the Magnus racing team thinks Alex's Cicada was destroyed, they've built another gas engine for the race, loaded in one of their other Mitsubishis," Ned told them. "We're going to suggest they continue with those plans, but only arrive in Whistler a day or two prior to the race like all the other teams."

"So, what about Alex and the Cicada?" Sam asked.

"We'll go with her and stay in Pemberton for the road test, using aliases," explained Lucas. "Magnus has a few spare car frames. I'm sure Alex can recommend one for the Cicada that can be shipped there for her to use. And if we fly to British Columbia on a private charter out of Toronto, there will be no online record of the trip."

The other three agents thought about the plan for a long moment, trying to uncover any weak spots.

"What about the road tests?" Renee asked. "Won't Alex need other engineers to help?"

"That's our only gap in the plan right now," Ned admitted. "We'll need one, maybe two engineers to help complete the car and do final tuning and calibrations."

"I'm sure we can find someone good with the Fortis or DaCosta networks," Sam suggested.

"Yeah, I've asked Evan to see who he can come up with," Lucas agreed. "Alex has suggested Adam North."

"North? The guy whose wife started this whole thing by trying to sell the Magnus battery tech to another buyer?" Sam asked incredulously.

"Yeah, that was my reaction also," added Lucas. "But if you think about it, it makes sense. He's a well-respected physicist with a solid knowledge of auto design according to Alex, and he's the expert on the battery. He also has a vested interest in making sure the Cicada has a successful launch, especially now that he's provided an official statement confirming that he had shared the battery specs with his wife. Whether that's true or not, it means that there are no criminal charges. The lawyers confirmed that the wording of the non-disclosure agreement does in fact extend the restrictions to his wife, so Magnus can sue them for damages. If North gives us a week of his time to complete the road tests, we can probably talk Passante into only suing them for out-of-pocket costs, like our fee."

"Hmm . . . When you put it that way, it does have some merit," mumbled Sam.

"Any other questions about the plan?" Lucas asked, but the others shook their heads. "Good.

I'll provide Alex and Passante with an update this morning and we'll confirm all the logistics. In the meantime, we'll double up on our security rotation, add a rotating night shift. This house is wired like Fort Knox, but I'm not taking anything for granted. Purdy had the same protocol training as Ned and I, and was in the Service for far longer. If he manages to figure out where we are, I want to make sure we have the manpower to stop him."

The others nodded in agreement.

"What about our new friend, Robert Malone?" Ned asked.

Lucas leaned over and opened a tracking application on his laptop.

"He was pretty resourceful. Based on his cell phone records, he managed to get back to Syracuse late last night."

"Has he reached out to Crow yet? Or anyone else of interest?" Sam asked.

"Nope. Looks like he may be taking my advice after all," Lucas surmised.

"That's encouraging," Ned noted. "Purdy has to be using a fairly complicated algorithm to search the Internet for any component orders that could suggest we're rebuilding the Cicada. He might not back off just because Malone failed to pinpoint our location, but he'll have enough similar queries popping up every day to keep him busy for a while."

"Maybe," Renee conceded. "But based on the mission report, don't we have to assume he already knows about our initial order of parts and components? That puts a pretty big bull's-eye on our back."

"It would if there were any accurate records of where it all was delivered," said Lucas with a cocky smile. "That's why I had all the fabrication tools and equipment delivered to the post office box in Syracuse, which Ned picked up. And, I made sure that the paper trail for the engine parts had a delivery address of an auto shop in Akron, Ohio. Only the truck driver knows different, and we paid him pretty generously to forget this address."

"Well, with any luck, we'll make it to Vancouver without having to repel a siege," added Sam, looking almost optimistic.

"Now, let's work out the important stuff," Lucas stated, looking seriously at the other three agents. "The housekeeper comes on Tuesday and Friday to clean and restock the fridge. Which of you is going to take over the cooking?"

They managed to figure out an acceptable schedule of the task, then moved on to implementing the new plan. For the next twelve days, Sam, Ned, and Renee focused on surveillance and reconnaissance within a five-mile radius of the property and small town. Memorial Day weekend brought a crowd of tourists to the lake, and plenty of noise and rowdiness with it. The Fortis team knew it was an ideal opportunity to create diversion for an attack, and they were prepared for anything. But the holiday came and went with only bursts of loud fireworks and a couple of drunk college kids who tried to steal the seaplane.

Midafternoon on Wednesday, two days before

they were scheduled to travel to British Columbia, Alex sent him a text message asking him if he could stop by the shed when he had a moment. Lucas was in the middle of building an online identity for their alias racing team that would arrive in the small town of Pemberton to do the road test. But, he was ready for a break to stretch his legs, particularly since he and Alex were no longer able to take their daily walks. After the incident with the private investigator, it was too risky for her to be seen in the town.

As Lucas made his way through to the back of the house, Sam was coming in from his surveillance of the immediate vicinity. Ned was doing a similar scan of the broader area, while Renee was still asleep after her overnight security detail.

"Did you speak with DaCosta yet," Sam asked.

"About the tech company in McLean? Yeah," replied Lucas. "I told him I'll need another week after the Magnus engine launch to wrap things up before I can take on a new client."

"Doesn't sound like they can wait that long," Sam stated. "And they'll need both you and Raymond to help them with their network security problem. I can finish off this mission in Toronto after the race."

Lucas knew it was a great solution. The final objective for Magnus would be to install a sustainable and scalable security plan, particularly if the Cicada engine fulfilled its potential. And there was no one more capable than Sam to do that. But it also meant that Lucas would be heading back to

Virginia in less than two weeks. It didn't seem like enough time to figure things out with Alex.

"Sounds like a plan," Lucas finally conceded, knowing it was the right decision for Fortis. "I'll give Evan an update later today."

"Good," his good friend replied. "How's Cotts making out with the engine? Are we still on schedule?"

"As far as I know, but she's been pretty tight-lipped over the last few days."

Sam nodded while looking at Lucas intently.

"What about things between you two? Anything for us to be concerned about?" he finally asked.

Lucas scratched the back of his neck with a little discomfort. This was uncharted territory for him, since he usually had a clear line between his personal life and business, as did Sam. But he knew it was only a matter of time before they had this conversation in one form or another. Quite frankly, he was surprised it had taken so long. Though he and Sam shared the bedroom with two beds, Lucas hadn't slept in there once since Sam and Renee had arrived.

"Everything is cool," he answered. "She and I are—"

"Hey, don't feel like you have to explain anything to me," interrupted Sam, throwing up his hands. "I'm the last person to have an opinion about who you fall for. Shit happens, right?"

Lucas shook his head.

"I haven't fallen for her," he insisted. "We're just—" He couldn't find the right words to explain exactly what they were doing.

Sam gave him one of those hard stares that said they both knew Lucas was full of shit.

"Let me give you a little advice," returned the Scotsman with a rich rumble in his accent. "Don't kid yourself about what you want. By the time you get your head out of your ass, it might be too late."

Lucas wanted to scoff at the comments, laugh it off as an overreaction, but the earnest seriousness in his friend's eyes made him pause. For a moment, it looked like Sam was talking from experience. Painful experience. Yet for the seven years that they had been close friends, Lucas had never heard him talk about a woman who could have caused that kind of damage.

"I don't know what it is, or what I want, to be honest," Lucas finally admitted, digging his hands into his pants pockets.

"We'll, don't take too long to figure it out."

Then Sam was gone, walking into the house and leaving Lucas with more to think about than he really wanted to. He walked purposefully across the lawn and opened the shed using the security code. The space was brightly lit by overhead lights and the large wall of windows facing the lake. It was also warm and a little muggy, though he could see that all the windows were open. Alex was standing near the back of the space wearing a tank top and yoga pants with her sneakers. Her skin glistened with moisture from the heat. She was standing in front of a large workbench, but looked up when the door closed behind him. Her eyes were bright with girlish excitement.

"You should have told me how hot it is in here.

I would have gotten you a fan," he said walking toward her.

"It's fine," she dismissed with a wave of her hand. "You're just in time."

"For what exactly?"

"It's done," Alex stated, turning back to the bench. "I've finished it."

Lucas stopped beside her and looked down at the collection of machinery on the work surface.

"Here it is, the Magnus Cicada 2.0. I've just finished a fourth round of bench testing for everything; the gas engine, generator, charger for the batteries, the power converter, and the electric motor," she explained, pointing to each component along the drivetrain.

"Wow, Alex! That's fantastic," he replied, wrapping an arm around her shoulders. "You're done ahead of schedule."

"I'm actually behind schedule," she countered, looking up at him with those sparkling brown eyes. "I had planned to be finished last weekend, just to be safe. But the defective wiring set me back a bit. I was a little panicked over the last few days, to be honest."

"You have been buried in here since the new supplies arrived. Only stopping to eat and sleep."

Alex turned to face him, pursing her lips mischievously and placing her hand over the hard slabs of his chest. Lucas couldn't contain the shiver that tingled down the center of this stomach at the light touch.

"I've made time for other things, too," she noted.

"Very laborious, time-consuming things. Maybe you need a reminder?"

Her exuberance at finishing the project was great to see and very infectious. Lucas had been very careful to keep their intimacy confined to her bedroom at night like a clear line between business and personal. But now he found it very hard to resist her teasing, tempting smile and the feel of her hand on his body. It was so easy and natural to wrap his arms around her back and pull her into a deep, arousing kiss. She responded immediately, using her lips and tongue to skillfully pull him deeper into a thick cloud of arousal.

"Hmm, that does ring a bell," he groaned while pulling her even tighter against his body.

Her abdomen rubbed deliciously against the hard throb of his erection.

"How about this?" she whispered before reaching down to stroke over his fullness with the palm of her hand.

His knees weakened. *Shit, she is dangerous.*

Lucas kissed her again with hot intensity, losing himself in the spontaneous moment, forgetting everything around them, including the dangerous threat lurking in the shadow. A threat hell-bent on destroying everything Alex had worked so hard to build.

"Alex," he muttered, pulling his mouth off hers in a moment of sanity. "We can't do this. Not here."

His words didn't stop her lips from trailing over his chin and down his neck, or still her hands from an effective exploration of his rigid length through his clothes.

"Lex," he repeated, part groan, part plea.

"Okay, okay," she finally conceded reluctantly. "I was hoping we could celebrate, that's all."

He smiled at how cute her disappointment sounded.

"How about I have Ned pick up some pastries from the café and we'll crack open a bottle of wine. There's a few good options in the pantry," he suggested, tilting her face up by her chin. "And we can have our own private celebration after hours."

"I suppose that will do," she accepted with a big, dramatic sigh.

CHAPTER 24

Pemberton, B.C., was located about twenty minutes north of Whistler. It was a quiet, quaint village at the base of Mount Currie that somehow managed to maintain the look and feel of the Old West. Alex, Lucas, Ned, Sam, and Renee arrived late Friday afternoon over one week later, after a quick flight back to Toronto on the seaplane, then a long haul on a private chartered flight right into the local airport. When they landed, there were two big, rented pickup trucks waiting for them in the parking lot, providing transportation to one of the rustic chalet-style hotels.

The Magnus racing car arrived just after noon on Saturday in a fully outfitted race team transport truck. It was a Subaru WRX STI, painted yellow and black. Alex met the delivery at a local auto shop in which Lucas had arranged the use of one of their service bays and equipment to assemble the car. Lucas, Sam, and Renee traveled with her for security while Ned stayed back at their hotel to monitor the area for potential threats. They had checked in under the aliases that Lucas has set up, but the Fortis team remained vigilant just in case.

Adam North arrived at the hotel on Sunday morning. Though they had communicated frequently through the design and build of the lithium-ion batteries, Alex hadn't seen him for almost a year. It was an awkward reunion under the circumstances.

"Did you really share our design with your wife, Adam?" Alex finally asked several hours later.

They were both standing under the hoisted car, connecting the drivetrain to the control units. Adam was a quiet, intense man who listened more than he spoke. He continued to work on the wiring, until Alex thought he wasn't going to respond.

"Never mind, it's none of my business," she eventually added. "This whole thing must be a nightmare for you. The last thing you need—"

"No, it's okay," he finally stated, letting out a deep sigh as he lowered his arms to place them on his hips. "You deserve an answer, Alex. The truth is, I don't really know. Susie knew I was working on a project for you, and we talked about what we'd do with the fee. We wanted to move out of the city and buy a house, and at one point she questioned whether I had negotiated for enough money. But it's not like I sat her down and showed her the design specs."

He looked so confused and despondent.

"I talked about the battery a little, but she's never shown any real interest in my work," he continued. "She's a product manager for a marketing firm. Physics and engineering stuff usually made her fall asleep. It never occurred to me that she would understand the value of the battery design beyond racing. I didn't even realize that she knew people at the racing club. It always felt like she was going to the events reluctantly."

"So, she did steal it," Alex confirmed.

"Yeah, I guess that's what it boils down to," Adam finally agreed. "She had a copy of the early concept and figured that if she committed to another buyer, I would have no choice but to build them a prototype also."

"Wow, Adam. That sucks."

"Yeah, it does," he agreed in a quiet voice.

"What are you going to do?"

He let out another deep sigh.

"Beyond this week? I have no idea. We've had to pay you guys back the original fee to cover the damages Susie caused. But at least she's not going to jail over it."

"Well, the battery you built for us is just the tip of the iceberg, Adam," Alex assured him. "That's part of the reason I wanted you to help me prep for the race. Once you see it perform in my hybrid, I have no doubt you'll be able to come up with other configurations that will drive the market forward."

"Maybe, but quite honestly, that's the least of my worries," he replied.

Alex nodded and decided to leave the man alone with his concerns as they went back to work.

What did you do once your spouse was so driven by greed that they violated your trust so completely? Could a relationship survive something like that? She was the last person to have answers for a question that big. Alex hadn't even been able to figure out how to let down her guard and be her true self in a relationship.

Lucas knew exactly who she was, almost from the beginning. And he continued to want her, weeks later, now sharing her hotel room in Pemberton. Alex wasn't certain their situation could be described as a relationship in a meaningful sense. But it wasn't purely casual anymore, at least not for her. At some point during the stay in the lakefront cottage, their time together became a friendship, somehow enhanced by their intimacy. She was completely honest and genuine with him, in a way she had never been with anyone before, including Shawn. It was an unnerving realization.

Almost as uncomfortable as the thought of what would happen in a week, after the Sea-to-Sky race and the official product launch of the Magnus Cicada electric-drive hybrid. Was there the chance of something more between them, or would they politely go their separate ways? Alex had no idea. She was just starting to accept her own feeling and desires, and had never developed instincts to read what Lucas may want.

Since Niles, Randy, and Bobby were still working on the Magnus gas engine race car, Fortis had arranged for a hired driver to join the Cicada race team. David Ferguson arrived Sunday night. He was a DaCosta Solutions employee with extensive experience providing logistical support in combat zones around the world. From what Lucas explained, this assignment was more vacation than work. Even though he was a little cocky, Alex couldn't find fault with his knowledge or capabilities.

The road tests started on Monday, right on schedule, and went smoothly through the week. The first few runs were rough, requiring extensive tweaks to the drivetrain and connected mechanics. But, by Wednesday, Adam was recording results similar to their first tests almost eight weeks earlier. Friday afternoon, the Cicada had surpassed Alex's projections. The reduction in weight along with a new power converter and higher-grade copper wiring provided higher torque and maximum speed capabilities.

Friday morning, the day before the racing event, Adam and David drove to Whistler in the transport truck with the Subaru, while Alex rode with Lucas and Ned in one truck. Sam and Renee followed in the second. They arrived in the town before eight o'clock, joining the dozens of other racing teams that were already parked and ready to register for the event.

"Marco arrived last night," Alex stated as she watched their racing trailer stop to park a few blocks from race headquarters in the convention center. Sam and Renee pulled their truck up beside it, while Lucas drove her and Ned to a large hotel complex farther into the center of the village.

"Yeah," Lucas agreed. "They have the Magnus trailer stationed in the north parking lot of the main building. We're going to meet Marco at the hotel. He has arranged a press conference for three o'clock this afternoon to announce you're entering the Cicada."

Alex turned to face him from the passenger seat, looking confused.

"Is that a good idea? What about the people trying to find me, or destroy the motor?" she asked.

"That's exactly why Marco needs to go public sooner rather than later," Lucas explained, looking around at the crowded streets. "I guarantee you that the threat is already here. And they have exactly twenty-four hours to either steal the designs or destroy your hybrid again. Now that we have the motor here, and you've proven its capabilities, we have a short window to release some details. Then it will be much less profitable for anyone to pass the stolen technology as their own."

"I guess that makes sense," Alex agreed reluctantly. "But it won't stop it from being destroyed."

Lucas parked the truck in the parking lot at the back of the hotel and the three of them got out.

"Well, that's where our decoy comes in," explained Lucas as he and Ned took their overnight bags out of the cab. "As far as anyone knows, the only car registered to Magnus is sitting in their branded trailer, along with the design schematics stored on a virtual private network. Once we get you checked in here, Ned will stay with you, and I'll be at the Magnus trailer to provide visible protection."

Alex stopped, grabbing his arm while Ned walked ahead of them into the rear entry of the hotel. He seemed casual but she knew that he was armed and alert, just like Lucas and the other Fortis agents.

"You've set a trap," she gasped. "Lucas, that's crazy. You're drawing them right to you!"

"They are here anyway, Alex," he told her earnestly. "It's been quiet for the last couple of weeks. Too quiet. I know the way these people think. While they may not have known where we were up to this point, they know exactly where Magnus is now. All we've done is point them in the direction that we want."

She turned away, scrubbing her hands over her eyes, wishing Lucas was wrong but knowing deep down that he was right. Her stomach rumbled with fear of what seemed inevitable. What if Lucas and his team couldn't stop them? What if someone got hurt or worse? What if it was Lucas?

"Alex, look at me," he asked, taking her gently by the arm and turning her to face him. "Everything is going to be fine, I promise. This is what we do, and we've planned well for this day, and you'll be safe here at the hotel. You have to trust me."

"I do trust you," she whispered, looking up into his face. "But promise me you'll be careful?"

Lucas smiled.

"Does that mean you're worried about me?" he teased, brushing his hand along her cheek.

"What can I say, you've grown on me," Alex admitted, swallowing against the tight lump in her throat.

"Have I?"

They stared at each other for a long moment with the weight of unsaid words hanging heavily between them. Finally, Lucas leaned forward to brush his lips along hers in the softest kiss.

"Let's finish this conversation later tonight, when we have a little more privacy," he murmured while his mouth hovered a breath away from hers. "Now come. Let's get you inside. You've just returned from an extended European vacation, remember?"

She let out a deep sigh, then walked with him into the hotel. Her mind was filled with everything he had told her about their plan, and her heart raced at the danger they all faced. It also drummed in her chest at the moment that had passed between them. Could Lucas feel the way she did? Like this thing between them was something deeper than they had been seeking? Like something long-lasting? Alex felt dazed by sudden, blinding clarity. She had fallen in love with Lucas Johnson.

In the hotel, they had booked a room for her on the eighth floor with connecting doors to a second room where the Fortis team would be based until after the event. Lucas put both their bags on the bed.

"Why don't you stay here and relax for a bit. Maybe order up some coffee?" Lucas suggested as he followed Ned into the other room.

"Okay. Are you leaving now?"

"No, not for about thirty minutes or so. Ned and I are going to check in with Fortis headquarters to review the surveillance in the area," he explained with a reassuring smile. "Don't forget our security protocols, Alex. They apply here, too. Don't go anywhere without Ned and keep your phone with you at all times."

And then he was gone, leaving her alone with her tangled thoughts. She put her purse down on the dresser and turned on the television to a local news station broadcasting the lead-up to the races. After a few minutes, she took out her phone, reading the messages from Shawn, Noelle, and her brothers, all confirming that she was back in Canada. Alex also finally sent that e-mail to Jean Renaud letting him know she would have to turn down his invitation to dinner.

She was then exchanging texts with Marco when Ned returned to her room.

"Is everything okay?" she asked as he looked out the window down the busy center of the village.

"All's quiet right now," Ned replied.

"Marco says he and the racing team have rooms on the second floor. Are we going to join them?"

"We will later, before the press conference. It's happening in one of the meeting rooms on the first floor," he explained. "But we'll stay here until then."

"Did Lucas already leave?" she asked.

"No, he's on a call," replied Ned. "I need to get some more equipment from the truck. He'll stay here with you until I'm back. Lock the door behind me."

Alex put her cell phone down on the bed, then walked across the room to do as he instructed. She could hear the faint hum of Lucas talking from the other room and walked over to the connecting doors. Maybe if his call ended soon, they would have a few minutes alone before he left on this crazy mission.

She meant to knock on the door between the rooms but it was already open a crack and Lucas's voice was more clearly audible. Alex paused for a second, uncertain of whether it would be rude to walk in. Just as she turned away, intent on waiting patiently until he was done, his words registered in her brain. She backed up to hover near the doorway.

"It was just supposed to be for the duration of this assignment. I thought I made that clear," he stated, sounding a little annoyed. "I never agreed to any sort of commitment. Once this assignment is done, I'll just have to tell her our arrangement is over."

She leaned closer, pushing the door a little wider until she could see him standing across the room.

"Look, even if I wanted someone long-term, I'm not sure it would be her."

He listened for a little.

"Maybe someone less difficult, for starters," he shot back with exasperation.

Alex stepped back several steps, not wanting to hear any more. She turned toward her room without seeing anything except for a way to escape from Lucas and the sound of his voice ringing painfully in her ears.

"*. . . if I wanted someone long-term, I'm not sure it would be her.*"

With her blood pounding loudly in her head and her heart splintering into pieces, she grabbed her purse off the dresser and rushed out the door of her room. Alex didn't have a plan but she was smart enough to remember the danger of their situation. She just needed a little space to think things through and figure how she had managed to read something between them that was clearly not there. And the last thing she needed right now was to have to see Lucas and pretend she didn't know how anxious he was to end things between them.

Out in the hallway, she walked quickly toward the staircase, looked behind her repeatedly to ensure she wasn't being follow by Lucas or anyone else. Once she got to Marco's hotel room, she would send a text message to Ned and he could meet her there. Sure, he'd be mad, and so would Lucas, but Alex really didn't care what either of them had to say at that moment.

Once through the heavy metal exit doors, she started jogging down the stairs, staying alert to any sign of movement around her. But the only thing she could hear was the echo of her footsteps and the sound of Lucas's dismissive voice in her mind.

"Maybe someone less difficult . . ."

Alex stopped on the landing of the second floor, when the lump in her throat became too constricting to breathe around. A deep sob escaped her lips before she could cover her mouth and stifle it. She was not going to stand here and cry over a man. Not now.

Determined to get herself together, Alex bit down hard on her bottom lip and pressed the heels of her hand into her eyes, trying to suppress any tears that still threatened to escape. Once she was with Marco, everything would be fine. She'd have time to think things through and hopefully remember what was real.

Alex took another deep breath and reached out to open the stairwell door. But it suddenly swung toward her, causing her to stumble in alarm. She tried to step back, down to the lower step, but she missed it in her haste and faltered backward wildly. Arms flailing, she tried to grab the handrail to prevent herself from falling. Then, rough hands were gripping her arms, pulling her back onto the stair landing.

"Whoa," said Bobby Chiu, the Magnus race-team driver. "You okay?"

She let out a deep breath of relief.

"Yeah, you just caught me by surprise. For a second, I was sure I was heading down those stairs, ass first."

"You're lucky I have quick reflexes," the younger man declared with a cocky grin.

"I suppose so," Alex agreed.

"When did you get in town?" he asked.

Alex paused for a moment, remembering that Marco was not going to update her team until just before the press release, so Bobby still thought she had been on vacation in Europe for the last six weeks.

"Late last night," she lied. "I was just on my way to see you guys. How are the road tests going?"

"Pretty good. We've been given an hour window to do trials on the highway along the race route, so

I'm headed there now," he explained, looking at his watch. "Why don't you come along?"

Alex was ready to say no. By now, Ned and Lucas must have realized that she had left and would be looking for her. Marco's hotel room would be their first stop, and all hell would break loose if she wasn't there.

"Niles and Randy are prepping the car right now," added Bobby, as though sensing her reluctance. "At least go over to say hi to them. They'll want to hear all about your trip."

She sighed. What could be the harm, as long as the Fortis team knew where to find her?

"Yeah, sure I'll come along. Can't wait to see what you guys have put inside the Evo," she finally agreed with small nod. "Just let me tell Marco where I am."

Alex reached into her right pocket, but it was empty. So was the left one. She tapped the pockets of her jeans. No cell phone. She then searched her purse, but already knew it wasn't there. In her haste to leave the hotel room and get away from Lucas, she must have left her phone on the bed. She groaned with frustration. Lucas was going to kill her for breaking all of his security protocols.

"I left my cell phone back in my hotel room," she explained.

"No worries, I'll send Marco a note now," Bobby offered cheerfully. "We can grab your phone when we get back."

She didn't want to explain why she didn't have a room key, so Alex just agreed. He quickly tapped in a message on his phone, and they both heard a ping as it was sent.

"Okay, we're all set," he stated, then they both headed down the last flight of stairs and out the side entrance of the hotel.

CHAPTER 25

"Lita is a great cleaning lady, Lucas. What more do you want?" asked Kathy Anderson, Lucas's neighbor.

"Maybe someone less difficult, for starters," he shot back with exasperation.

"She's not difficult, honestly," she insisted.

"This is the fourth time in three weeks that you've called me about this," Lucas reminded her, striving to keep his voice even.

"Weeell—"

"Well what?"

"Maybe I exaggerated a little. To Lita about how long you needed her."

"Kathy—!" Lucas growled.

"Just a little!" Kathy stammered quickly. "It was the only way that she'd stay."

Lucas sighed and rubbed the back of his head. Who on earth spent this much time discussing housecleaning?

"Kathy, I really don't have time to deal with this

right now. I'll speak with Lita when I'm back in town next week, and you will likely need to find yourself a new maid."

"Come on, Lucas. I know you're annoyed with me, but just think about it a little more."

"Kathy, I'm hanging up the phone."

"Okay! Okay, I'll talk to you when you're back."

They said a brisk good-bye and Lucas shoved his phone into his pocket, wishing he could get back the last five minutes of his life. He walked swiftly across the room and through to the connecting room where he and Alex would be staying until after the races. Since the door to that room had shut just a couple of minutes earlier, Lucas assumed that Ned had returned from the truck with their extra weapons and supplies. Yet no one was there. The room was empty. He walked around, thinking that maybe he had missed something while talking to Kathy.

Then, he spotted the cell phone on the bed, almost hidden between the pillows. Lucas leaned over and picked it up, just as the room door opened. It was Alex's.

"You all set?" Ned asked as he carried their locked trunk inside and put it down on the desk across from the bed.

"Where's Alex?" Lucas asked, standing up and looking around.

"What do you mean? I left her here," Ned stated. "Did you check the bathroom?"

The door was closed, but something at the base of Lucas's stomach told him she wasn't in there.

But he checked anyway, pushing open the door and finding the dark room empty.

"She's gone," he declared sharply. "We need to find her, now!"

Ned had the trunk popped open, and they each started to load up on concealable weapons.

"Where would she go? And why would she leave her cell phone? She knows the protocol."

"I don't know. Maybe she just forgot it."

"Or someone took her?" asked Ned, and the two men looked at each other, trying to gauge the threat level.

"I don't think so. Not forcibly. It was too quiet. I only heard the door close and I assumed it was you returning," Lucas replied. "Call Sam and get him up to speed. I'll call Marco. And let's check both staircases and meet up at the truck. We need to find her fast."

Lucas pocketed Alex's phone, then took out his own as they strode out the door. He called Marco Passante while Ned was already talking to Sam.

"Is Alex with you?" he demanded as soon as his client picked up the phone.

"No. Should she be? I thought you guys were lying low until the press conference," Marco stated with obvious surprise.

"That was the plan. But she's left the hotel room by herself and doesn't have her phone," Lucas explained as he ran down the stairs, two at a time. "Call me if you see or hear from her. Tell your team to do the same."

"Of course. They're working on the Evo in the

trailer. We have our practice run at ten thirty," added Marco.

"Okay, my men with be there shortly," Lucas confirmed. "I'm headed there now. I'll keep you posted."

Ned was already in the truck with the engine running.

"Sam and Renee are heading to the Magnus trailer, leaving the driver, David Ferguson, with the hybrid," Ned provided. "No sign of Alex yet."

"Passante hasn't seen or heard from her either," added Lucas. "There is no way she would just wander away without her cell phone and not go straight to the Magnus team. She knows where they are."

"Which means that someone has her against her will."

Lucas swore viciously, while his heart pounded with an erratic drum. He quickly made another call to Raymond Blunt, the Fortis tech wizard.

"Raymond, I need your help," he demanded briskly when the line picked up, then quickly provided the pertinent details of the immediate situation. "I want a full search of the Whistler area over the last hour. Utilize every surveillance option, open source portals, and government assets. Pull in any people or resources you need and send anything remotely useful to the ground team."

"You got it," Raymond acknowledged.

"This is a diversion," Ned stated the second that Lucas hung up the phone. "They want us looking for Cotts, leaving the Cicada car and design vulnerable."

"Yeah, I know," agreed Lucas.

Every fiber of his being was vibrating with the instinct to tear this town apart to find Alex. The idea that people had her, were threatening her, or planned to cause her any harm made him sick to his stomach. And he tried not to think of what he knew they were capable of or how far they would go to get what they wanted.

Then minutes later, they arrived at the Magnus race team trailer, sandwiched between two similarly sized car haulers with enough space between to fit a race car for quick repairs. Lucas jumped out of the truck and ran up to meet Sam and Renee who were approaching him from the side entrance. Ned joined them.

"We just missed her," Sam stated gruffly. "She's left with the Magnus driver to start the trial run for the Evo."

"What?" Lucas growled. "Why would she do that? It doesn't make any sense."

"The guys here were surprised to see her. But there is no evidence she's under threat," Sam continued.

"Damn it!" muttered Lucas. "Who's the driver? I want to know everything about him."

"Bobby Chiu. He had checked out in our original security evaluation, along with all of the Magnus employees."

"Then something must have changed since then. They've sent in someone familiar to lure her away—"

"What the hell?"

The exclamation came from inside the trailer.

Lucas ran forward to look inside the long space. The two Magnus engineers whom Lucas remembered as Niles and Randy were standing in the middle of the long space, looking at all the equipment display screens that were now flickering as though the power was being disrupted.

"Purdy is here. He's going after the Cicada," Lucas growled, turning back to his team that now surrounded him. "Sam, you and Ned have to go after Alex. We don't have much time. You have to get her back."

"We've got it, Lucas," his friend stated firmly. "The trials run south on the highway. We'll head in that direction, and we will get her back safely."

The two men ran back to the truck that Ned had been driving and took off again. Lucas ducked back inside the trailer to wait for the network attack he knew was coming.

"Lucas!" called Renee from outside, and the alarmed tone of her voice said everything.

He stepped outside with his pistol drawn. Three big henchmen were approaching walking shoulder to shoulder, with big guns barely concealed under their shirts.

"Any ideas?" prompted Renee as the men slowly walked closer.

"Let's start by improving the odds," Lucas stated, then fluidly pulled a small knife out of his belt and flung it at the thug closest to him, embedding the blade deep into the side of his neck. The man stumbled back from the force while his companions paused in surprise, trying to figure out what happened. Lucas and Renee both leaped forward to attack the remaining two, as the first guy fell forward onto his knees, clutching at his neck and trying to breathe.

The opponent Lucas faced recovered quickly and struck out at him with a big right hook. But Lucas saw it coming and ducked low, then came up with a hard punch to the guy's kidneys. The thug groaned in pain and backed away while reaching for his gun. Lucas used the back of his left elbow to knock away the guy's arm and the weapon went flying out of his grasp to land a few feet way. Lucas then rammed the heel of his hand into the guy's face, crushing his nose. He repeated the hit two more times to ensure the pain was debilitating. The attacker dropped to the ground, grabbing his face and cursing in low, muttered whispers.

"Guys!" yelled one of the engineers from inside the trailer. "Something's happening!"

Lucas turned around to assess the situation with the other assailants. Renee was dominating her opponent with a series of hard elbow hits into the side of his jaw, then she finished him with a roundhouse kick, catching his temple with her heel.

"Renee, I need you to locate Edgar Purdy," instructed Lucas. "He's here, somewhere close enough to access the computer system in the trailer through the Wi-Fi. I'll counter his attack into the network, but we can't let him get away."

She nodded swiftly, then turned to jog down the side of the trailer into the busy crowd that passed steady in front of it. A few people did a double take at the sight of the three men strewn haphazardly on the ground.

Lucas went into the big hauler, pulling the side door closed and locking it from the inside. He sat down on a work stool in front of the onboard computer, quickly absorbing the rows and rows of code script than ran across the screen. Then he got to work. There was no doubt the hacker was highly skilled and sophisticated, using an incredibly fast spidering malware that was slowly breaking through the virtual personal network firewalls. Lucas immediately tried to stop the intrusion, but already knew it was too late. The hacker had a big head start and was only minutes away from breaking through. So, he changed his tactics, and focused his energy on wiping the system of all of the valuable design information with a custom, highly efficient data destruction software he had preloaded.

"Did you stop it?" asked Randy as Lucas pushed the stool back while clenching and unclenching his cramped fingers.

"No, I had to wipe the data instead," he replied.

"But what about our information?" Randy probed.

"It was the only way to stop the attack," Lucas explained patiently. "But we've only lost any modifications you guys have done since last night. I have your backup on a secure drive."

The two men looked at him speculatively.

"This is about Alex's hybrid, isn't it?" Niles asked. "They're still trying to steal it."

Lucas's phone beeped with a call.

"Renee, any luck locating Purdy?" he quickly asked after answering.

"I've got eyes on the target in the conference center, boss," she confirmed. "He looks a little different from the pictures, with a full beard and his hair dyed dark brown. But it's him. There are very few people in the foyer working like crazy on a very expensive piece of hardware, while a racing event is going on."

"Keep your eyes locked on him. I'm on my way."

"He's sitting in front of the left fireplace, and I'm standing just inside the closest entrance doors," she explained before they disconnected.

"What's going on?" asked Niles as he and Randy followed Lucas as he unlocked the door and strode out of the trailer into the morning sunshine.

"We've identified the hacker. You two need to stay here and lock the door behind me," Lucas instructed, then he was running through the parking lot toward the big building that was also headquarters for the Sea-to-Sky race.

It was a fast, three-minute sprint, yet it felt like an hour. All Lucas could think about was whether Sam and Ned had located Alex. Was she okay? Was she safe? Maybe he should take the time to call them for an update? But Lucas knew he couldn't allow the distraction. If they hadn't found her yet, and she was still in the hands of Purdy's people, Lucas honestly didn't know if he could stick to the mission plan. Magnus and Alex would only be safe if Fortis took down Purdy and his Crow organization. That had to be his main priority, and there was no room for any other focus.

He found Renee positioned exactly where she had indicated, and Edgar Purdy was still working on his intrusion attempt. She was right, his appearance was a little altered from the last picture they had, but it was definitely his old boss and mentor.

"Any change?" he asked right away.

"Negative."

"Well, get ready for him to make a move," suggested Lucas. "Any second now, he'll be deep enough in my network to realize he's too late, and there's nothing there."

They watched him silently for another couple of minutes.

"Any word from Sam or Ned on Alex?" Renee asked quietly.

"Not yet," he replied in a neutral voice. "Okay, looks like it's showtime."

Purdy had just shut his laptop with enough force to suggest he was frustrated. He then looked around as though he suddenly realized his distractions may have been thwarted.

"You stay here, and I'll flank him on the right," he told Renee. "Then we'll follow his exit, and take him down while he's still on foot."

"You got it, boss," she agreed, and they split up.

Purdy stood up just as Lucas passed his position across the room. But their eyes locked for a couple of seconds from a gap in the crowd, and it was enough to spook his target. The hacker took off in a dead run away from him, pushing his way through a path of people, directly toward Renee's position. Lucas sprung forward in pursuit, his eyes fixed on the top of Purdy's head, only losing sight when the other man rushed outside through one of the exit doors, looking pretty agile for someone in his midforties.

When Lucas got outside, he was only a few paces

behind Purdy who was sprinting hard across the grass in front of the conference center. Renee was even closer. She was breathing down his neck, when Purdy twisted his upper body and fired a gun straight at her. The loud bang echoed across the open area, and several people screamed. Lucas watched with alarm as his agent ran for a few more steps, then fell flat on her face. More people screamed, running away from the scene in fear.

"Renee!" he yelled as he approached her lying body, gently turning her over to check how badly she was wounded.

"It's okay," she gasped, coughing and clutching her side where her fingers were now coated with blood. "It's just a graze."

"Are you sure? Let me see?" he demanded, trying to move her fingers.

"You don't have time," she insisted urgently. "He's getting away. I'll be fine, I promise."

Shit! She was right. Already, he could hear police sirens. He needed to take down Purdy now before they lost him for good.

"Stay still, and try to stay calm. Help is on the way."

"Go," she urged again, and Lucas finally stood up.

For a couple of seconds, he thought Purdy had managed to disappear, until he saw people pointing in the direction of a shopping plaza. Lucas took off in that direction, but drifted to the right to avoid being detected. About a half a block later, he finally caught sight of the hacker as the other man cut down a main street toward a block of high-end resort hotels. Lucas stayed low, running along the storefronts until he was almost parallel to Purdy, who had slowed his pace to a light jog. Then when the moment was right, Lucas dashed forward and tackled the older man around his waist, effectively immobilizing him. They flew onto the street with a hard thud on their left sides, sending even more spectators running with screams.

Lucas didn't pause to catch his breath. He rolled forward so Purdy was lying on his stomach, then he pressed his forearm into the man's neck so the side of his face squished roughly against the bricked laneway.

"Where is she?" demanded Lucas in a low growling voice.

Purdy started laughing. It was the deep, crazy cackle of a madman.

"Where is she, Edgar?" he shouted, slamming the hacker's head into the ground with a loud crack.

"You're too late, Lucas," Purdy finally replied once he'd caught his breath again. "I knew you'd come after me. You were always so dedicated to the job. So predictable."

He started laughing again, this time higher and even more gleeful.

"It's over!" Lucas exclaimed, leaning close to the other man's ear. "You lost, Edgar. Now tell me where she is?"

"Oh, Lucas, my boy. Don't you get it? I don't give a shit about files or that fucking car," Purdy gasped. "I just wanted to see your face when you realized you went after the wrong asset."

Lucas pulled back, his brain working through the meaning behind Purdy's words.

"It's over, Lucas," Purdy added in a stronger voice. "And you lose!"

Within seconds, the haunting sound of fire-truck sirens grew louder until it drowned out Purdy's shrieking giggles.

"What did you do?" Lucas growled, bashing the other man's head to the ground again.

His former boss only looked back with eyes wide with hatred and satisfaction.

"I think your pretty little asset has just gone up in flames!"

CHAPTER 26

"Why are you taking this route?" Alex asked Bobby as he turned left onto the Sea-to-Sky Highway, heading north of Whistler and in the opposite direction of the race route.

"I heard about this really great stretch of road just past the city that I want to try out," he replied, looking around with searching eyes.

"Are you sure we have time? Our trial time is in fifteen minutes," she added with concern.

"We'll be fine," he assured her, but his posture and furrowed brows suggested Bobby was not at all as relaxed as he tried to appear.

Alex sat back in the passenger seat of the Evo and tried to relax. She had bigger problems than whatever was bothering the young driver. By now, Lucas would know that she had taken off on this reckless joyride and he was going to be pissed. Even though she was still very raw with hurt and disappointment at his words about her and their relationship, Alex was already regretting her rash actions. After weeks of hard work and sacrifice, she had risked their project over rejection and stupid pride.

"Bobby, I have to go back to the hotel," she finally stated, rubbing her hands into her eyes. "I shouldn't have come with you."

At first, Alex was too wrapped up in her misery to realize that Bobby hadn't replied to her request. They continued north on the highway at over eighty miles an hour.

"Bobby," she said more sharply. "Did you hear me? I have to go back."

He turned to her with a strange look of sadness mixed with resolve.

"Sorry, Alex," he mumbled, looking away from her eyes. "I can't go back."

"What do you mean? We have to go back, now!"

He went quiet again while checking all the mirrors repeatedly.

"Bobby! What the hell is going on?"

"It's almost over," he replied cryptically just as he slowed the car down through a sharp turn in the road.

At the next intersection, Bobby then made a sharp left turn off the highway onto a rough, unpaved road into what looked like a construction site adjacent to one of the many mountainsides. Alex gripped the door handles as the race car bounced along the rough terrain until he pulled to a stop with the transmission in neutral, about twenty feet away from a silver sedan.

"Bobby, what's happening?" she demanded again.

He didn't reply. Fear was building in her chest, though she tried to stay calm and focus on her surroundings. Two men stepped out of the other car, and neither looked friendly enough to ease her increasing panic.

Bobby took a deep breath and finally looked back at her.

"Sorry, Alex. I had no choice," he told her in a quiet, thin voice.

"What do you mean? No choice for what?" she demanded, grabbing his arm. "Bobby, what did you do?"

He pulled his arm away roughly and popped open his door.

"Sorry," he whispered again, and stepped out of the car.

"Bobby," she yelled at him as he walked up to the strangers.

She could see one of the men talking but couldn't hear anything. Then the man who had spoken calmly took a gun out from under his jacket and shot Bobby in the head. Alex jumped at the sound, but couldn't believe what had happened right in front of her eyes. The young man's body collapsed lifelessly to the ground and the shooter stepped right over him, striding toward her.

"No!" screamed Alex, clawing for the door handle so she could go help Bobby. "No, no, no—"

Confused by shock for several long seconds, Alex struggled to comprehend the situation. The two men were steadily approaching, now with two guns pointed at her. They were halfway to the car when her survival instincts kicked in. Remembering the last time she had been stuck in that car, she pulled on the seat adjuster and almost screamed with relief when her seat slid back. It created enough room to quickly climb over the component configured in the center console and into the driver's seat.

The men were almost at the front of the car when she pressed her left foot down hard on the clutch and pushed the shifter into first gear. Alex eased off the clutch and jammed on the gas just as the first bullet punched through the windshield and whizzed by her ear. She screamed, letting go of the steering wheel to cover her head while the tires squealed on the gravel and the car shot forward out of control. A volley of gunshots followed, shattering the windows and pummeling the side panels. Alex curled low toward the still-open driver's-side door. The wind velocity increased with her speed, and Alex could see the ground rushing by out of the corner of her eye.

Finally, the bullets stopped, and she grabbed the wheel to try to control the direction of the car. Then, Alex sat up straighter in order to quickly get her bearing. Through the rearview mirror, she could see that the two men were still running toward her, but their forms became smaller and smaller. She felt a small dose of victory, before she turned to look out the windshield and saw that she was rushing toward the edge of a cliff at over twenty-five miles per hour.

There was no time to think. Alex felt the front of the car tip forward just as she pushed down hard on the floor and dove out the open driver's-side door.

She hit the side of the steep incline hard on her shoulder, then rolled uncontrollably for what felt like forever. While the world spun wildly around her, Alex could hear the sickening sound of metal crunching as the Evo crashed down the side of the mountain. Her body was moving fast and picking up speed, hitting mounds of hard dirt before banging into a tree stump. It slowed down her descent until she slid on her stomach and finally stopped at a short landing.

The last thing Alex heard was a loud explosion that seemed to shake the ground beneath her. Her vision began to blur around the edges, and everything was fading into darkness until only a small coin-sized ray of light came through. Somewhere, miles away, she heard a deep voice yelling her name. Or maybe it was just wishful thinking.

The ringing of sirens pounded loudly in her head, pulling her back into consciousness. Alex blinked against the bright morning sunlight for a couple minutes while breathing deep, then slowly turned her head toward the sound. For a few seconds, she didn't understand where she was, or why she was lying on her back, spread-eagle on a rocky surface.

"Alex!"

It all rushed back with a sudden cascade of horrific images. Bobby, the two men, the Evo now lying in a burning wreck at the base of a steep slope.

"Alex!"

Someone was here to find her. She had to let them know her location.

"Help!" Alex tried to yell, but it came out as a deep, gravelly croak and led to a series of dusty coughs.

"Help!" The second attempt was more effective, and she closed her eyes with relief to hear her voice echo around her. "I'm here!"

Fearing it still wasn't enough, Alex tried to move, testing each of her limbs before crawling forward on her elbows. Her head swam with dizziness and her stomach rolled with nausea. Every part of her body felt bruised and battered, but it all seemed in functioning order. Feeling more confident, she pushed up on her hands and knees and shuffled into a more visible area on the shallow landing.

"I'm here!" she yelled again.

"Over there!" someone yelled from above. "I can see her!"

"I'm here," Alex repeated in a hoarse whisper, suddenly too exhausted to hold her weight up any further.

Alex collapsed flat and managed to roll onto her back, only able to focus on breathing without throwing up. She closed her eyes and listened to the constant sounds of urgent activity above her without any sense of the passage of time. Finally, one voice got closer and closer.

"Hang on, Alex. I'm coming to get you. Just hang on."

She meant to nod, but she actually hadn't moved. All her energy was going into staying conscious. It was another excruciatingly long wait before she felt the touch of firm hands on her shoulder.

"Alex, can you talk?" It was Samuel Mackenzie, Lucas's partner. "Are you in pain?"

Alex opened her heavy lids to look into his brilliant sky blue eyes.

"I think I'm okay," she managed to whisper. "My hip hurts the most, but I think it's just bruised."

"Okay, that's good," he told her with a smile that was so charming she blinked with surprise. "We're lowering down a stretcher, and we'll have you out of here before you know it."

She nodded and let out a deep, shaky breath.

"Lucas?"

Sam took her hand, seeming to understand what she was trying to ask.

"He'll be here any minute," Sam assured her. "Just relax, it's all over. And I'm staying right here with you the whole time."

Her vision blurred as her eyes suddenly watered. It was all over. Alex squeezed her eyes shut while hot tears streamed down the side of her face. She felt Sam's gentle whispers and consoling words while still holding her hand in the big, firm grasp of his. Then she passed into a soft cocoon of darkness with only shadowy glimpses of the world around her.

Once she had been located lying precariously on the rocky, narrow ledge along the face of a steep slope, it took almost an hour for the rescue team of firemen and local police, led by Ned and Sam, to slowly pull her out. Lucas arrived with Renee and Marco Passante almost forty-five minutes into the operation, feeling like his world had collapsed around him. After Edgar Purdy finally revealed his sick plan—to destroy the most valuable asset in Lucas's protection—Lucas held him securely for the local police, but immediately called his partner.

"Sam, we got Purdy," he yelled urgently, striving hard to stay focused and clear. "You need to follow those fire trucks. I think it's Alex."

"We're right behind them," Sam confirmed. "Raymond had found the race car on a satellite feed about ten miles outside of town, heading north on the highway."

"He played me," added Lucas in a harsh growl. "Alex became his target in the end, once he found out about our relationship. This whole thing wasn't about stealing the hybrid design, it was just to beat me. And the network attack was the diversion. He knew I would stay with the target I thought he was after. He played me."

"Listen to me, Lucas," stated Sam in a firm, calm voice. "We only know that the car crashed down the edge of a cliff, but Raymond says he has a satellite image of a person lying about twenty feet down from the edge. You have to believe it's Alex. We've just arrived at the site. I'll have Ned call you back in five minutes and keep you posted."

"Okay. I have to wrap things up here. There's a mess of injured people, including Renee. But don't worry," Lucas quickly added at his friend's sharp intake of breath. "She was grazed by a bullet, but it doesn't look serious. I can see paramedics attending to her now."

"We'll keep you posted on our end," Sam growled before they disconnected the call.

There was no time to pause for the wave of intense relief that flooded through him. The Whistler police arrived within a minute, guns drawn, and they demanded explanations. Once Lucas cautiously and calmly provided his identification and credentials, the cooperation level increased dramatically. They willingly took Edgar Purdy into custody with some medical care for his injuries, and the arrival of Interpol, the FBI, or the RCMP—the Canadian Federal police—was pending, based on who won the battle over jurisdiction. But not before Lucas had a chance to update the traitor on the fact that Alex had survived the attack. The older man wasn't laughing anymore.

Lucas called Marco Passante to let him know the final threat to Magnus Motorsports had been neutralized and outline the situation with Alex. They agreed that Marco would drive his rental car into the village from the hotel to pick up Lucas so they could join the rescue operation. Then he gave David Ferguson an update, asking the DaCosta contractor to stay with the Cicada and Adam North.

As she promised, Renee's wound was only a superficial graze to her side. The paramedics dressed it and provided some mild pain relief medication, but she firmly refused to go to the hospital. When Marco arrived, she also insisted on traveling up to the accident site with them. Lucas already had Ned on speakerphone for several minutes as the three of them started the tense drive fifteen minutes north of town. Marco swore loudly in relief when the agent confirmed that Sam had reached Alex and she was conscious and appeared lucid. Lucas could only look out the window at the mountain views, very aware that everything he wanted for the future had just come sharply and vividly into focus.

They arrived at the deserted construction site shortly after, driving by members of the local coroner's office as they zipped up a body bag, and stopping by the collection of emergency vehicles about half a mile away. Ned was waiting for them, but it was another twenty minutes before Lucas saw Alex as the fire and rescue team pulled her up on a stretcher. Her clothes were torn and dirty, and her face had several scrapes and lacerations, but there were no other signs of injury. He immediately took her hand and felt her light, responsive grip.

"Alex," he whispered over the lump in his throat. "I'm here. I've got you."

"Lucas," she replied softly, finally opening those bright, golden brown eyes.

"Yeah, I'm here," he confirmed, gripping her fingers tighter than he should. "It's over, baby. You're going to be fine, and I'm right here with you."

"I'm sorry," she added, followed by a series of rough coughs.

"No, baby," he whispered back, hating the mix of failure and regret that would haunt him for a long time. "I'm the one who's sorry. I failed you, and it will never happen again. I promise I will never allow anyone to hurt you again."

Lucas wanted to say more, but the ambulance had arrived and the paramedics were ready to transport her into the back for the trip to a local medical center. He stayed with her for the ride, while Marco and the rest of the Fortis team followed behind them. Once identified, the body of Robert "Bobby" Chiu was transported to the coroner's office for an official autopsy in relation to the rapidly expanding criminal case against Edgar Purdy and his Crow organization.

At the small hospital, Sam managed to charm their way into a small meeting room where they set up a makeshift control center needed to manage the many moving parts still in play. By one o'clock in the afternoon, Alex was resting under the influence of sedatives while they waited for her exam results to return, Renee was feeling comfortable and relatively pain-free, and they had a video-conference set up on Ned's laptop with Evan and Raymond at the Fortis headquarters, and Michael and Lance at the Magnus offices in Toronto.

"What do we know about Chiu's involvement in all this?" Lucas asked Raymond.

"We know he was clean at the start, but I found a five thousand dollar cash deposit in his bank account the day before the fire in the Magnus shop," Raymond explained.

"He sold information to the Petrov brothers," Michael concluded. "That's how they knew where exactly to hit the brake line and plant the combustible materials for maximum damage."

"It looks that way," Evan added. "I had Laura and a couple of other analysts go through the files again, and we found Chiu's face in two of the photos you guys had taken from the bar the Petrovs managed. One at a party in the bar, and the other at a racetrack. Looks like they've been in the same circles for some time."

"Jesus Christ!" swore Marco. "I can't believe this."

"It makes sense, Marco," Lucas added. "We know that Optimal also used that bar for their race events, and the track in the pictures is the same one you guys use for your road tests."

"That explains his role in the sabotage with Cesar Hernandez. But the guys today worked for Crow," Sam continued. "Do we know why Chiu would hand over Alex and the car to them?"

"We won't know for sure until Purdy or one of his hired thugs tells us something of value," Raymond explained. "The two men that killed him and attacked Alex were arrested about an hour ago by the RCMP. And it looks like the FBI will be taking custody of Purdy."

"My guess is that Purdy found the same info we did on Chiu, that he took a bribe for the arson, and used it to blackmail him," Lucas surmised. "Alex told me he only said that he was sorry, but he had no choice."

The group was silent for a few moments.

"So what happens now?" Marco finally asked. "I still have a press conference happening in a couple of hours."

"Well, it looks like you have a new hybrid engine to reveal for the race tomorrow," Lucas stated without hesitation. "That's what Alex would want you to do."

"Yeah," the other man agreed with a wry smile. "She'd be pretty pissed if I didn't."

"We took Purdy's laptop before the police arrested him," Lucas continued. "And I'll spend the next twenty-four to forty-eight hours analyzing the stored data. But, we're now fairly confident that all threats to Magnus have been eliminated, and our main mission will conclude on Sunday after the race."

"Wow," Marco sighed. "I can't believe it's finally over."

Lucas patted him on the shoulder, knowing exactly how he felt.

"I have another mission starting on Monday that requires me to return to Virginia Sunday, so Sam will take over to implement your long-term security plan back in Toronto."

"That's fantastic," acknowledged Marco as he reached out to shake Lucas's hand in a firm grip. "I can't thank you and your team enough for your work."

"You may take that back when you see the bill," Lucas replied with a quick grin.

Marco and the others laughed.

"Okay, let's iron out the logistics through the race tomorrow afternoon," continued Lucas. "Some of it will depend on Alex's test results. But we'll set up three teams. Renee and I will stay with Alex. Ned, you stay with Marco through the press conference and any interaction with the various police organizations. Sam, can you work with David to secure the Cicada and move it to the Magnus racing trailer? They have a bit of work to do to get it ready for the race."

Less than twenty-four hours later, the Magnus Cicada hybrid made its official launch into automotive history.

CHAPTER 27

Alex woke up slowly and a warm, hazy dream faded away. She lay still for a few moments, with her eyes closed trying hard to remember the details that left her feeling happy and content, but only fragments remained. The rich and intoxicating sound of Lucas laughing. The blindingly beautiful image of his face looking down at her. The sparkling view of Lake Skaneateles from the long wooden boardwalk. Everything else about the dream had dissipated, except for the smile in her heart.

She shifted on the soft bed, pushing against a heavy weight resting on her hip.

"Hmmm," came a deep rumble from behind her head.

Her eyes popped open as the heavy weight pulled her closer to a very warm and very hard body behind her. It was Sunday morning, the day after the Sea-to-Sky race, and Lucas was still asleep in the same bed.

The day and night before had progressed fairly

innocently. After Friday afternoon, when her
various test results had come back confirming her
only injuries were minor abrasions and contusions,
the health center had released her with a small
supply of prescription-grade pain reliever. Lucas
and Renee and taken her back to the Whistler
hotel where she was able to continue resting
through the worst of the aching, bruising pain. On
Saturday, Alex felt much too stiff and banged up
to take a shower on her own, much less get dressed
and make the trip out to watch the race. The two
Fortis agents stayed with her to watch the event
broadcast on local television.

They all cheered with surprise and delight to
see the Magnus Cicada win first place by a big
margin in the electric-drive vehicle class, and time
a very close second place overall.

She had done it. Alexandria Cotts had succeeded
in designing the fastest long-range hybrid-powered
vehicle on record with applicability in the passenger car industry. It was a heady and emotional
moment, filled with cheers from Renee and tender,
intimate hugs from Lucas, then a string of phone
calls and e-mails from Shawn and her family. But
she could not ignore the bittersweet knowledge
that along with an achievement so long pursued,
she was also about to lose the only thing that
would have made it all the more meaningful:
sharing it with the man she had fallen in love with
so deeply and unexpectedly.

After the trophy presentations and various
media interviews, Marco, Niles, and Randy eventually brought the celebration back to her hotel
room, along with Adam North, David Ferguson,

Sam, and Ned. They spent the rest of the evening talking, laughing, and making plans for what would come next for Magnus, the small racing-components shop that had rocketed into the big leagues overnight.

Lucas finally kicked them all out sometime before midnight, insisting Alex was overdoing it. No one disagreed since she had already dozed off on several occasions. Once they were alone, he helped her in and out of a hot bath and wrapped her in a warm towel with clinical efficiency, and she was too tired and grateful to argue. The last thing she remembered was having him carry her back into the bedroom, despite her insistence that she could walk, and tuck her under the thick covers.

Now he was spooning her from behind in a perfect fit that was achingly familiar.

"Good morning," he finally whispered in that sexy, sleepy voice. "How are you feeling?"

Alex cleared her throat, trying hard to remember what had to come next.

"Okay, I think," she replied simply.

"Good."

His hand touched her hip and then slipped over her stomach through the robe, and pulled her even tighter against his heat, until the hard length of his erection felt branded against the curve of her ass. Lucas then stroked his flat palm up along her torso and slipped his fingers between the edges of the robe until they found the full mound of her breast.

"Hmm, I miss you," he groaned softly. "I had a very hot dream about all the things I want to do to you when you're all better."

He tweaked her nipple, sending shock waves of intense desire right down to the delicate bud between her thighs. Alex gasped, trying hard to find the strength to stop him.

"Until then, you'll have to stop teasing me," he added playfully, pressing a soft kiss to the side of her neck. "Now rest for a bit longer. The charter flight to Toronto leaves at one o'clock this afternoon, and we have a lot to get done before that."

Then his touch and heat were gone as Lucas rolled off the other side of the bed and walked across the space to the bathroom, deliciously and blatantly aroused in his boxer briefs.

The reality of what the day would bring became so much harder to face. Lucas Johnson was leaving today. His mission was over, along with their time together. That was the simple truth, and she had made the disastrous mistake of forgetting that. He and his team had saved her life and her career more than once over the last two months. The least she could do was make this separation as uncomplicated as possible.

By the time Lucas came out of the bathroom with a towel wrapped around his waist, it was almost eight o'clock. Alex was on her feet and organizing her clothes for the day.

"Hey, what are you doing?" he demanded, immediately coming to her side.

"I'm fine, really," Alex insisted, backing away from him and managing not to wince at the sudden movement. "I'm a little stiff, but it's not bad."

"Are you sure?"

"Yeah. Honestly, I can manage," she continued with a small smile.

"Okay, but just take it slow. And make sure you use the grab bar in the shower if you're going to take one."

Alex nodded, then turned away from his stern expression to walk slowly over to the bathroom. The intensity of his inspection was easily felt along her back the whole way. Once inside, she closed the door and took a deep breath. She hadn't lied. The bruising and stiffness felt much better today, and would very likely be manageable with some Extra Strength Tylenol. Her battered heart would take a lot longer to heal.

When she came out of the shower about twenty-five minutes later, Lucas was on the phone, but there was a room-service table over by the window with two chairs at either end, coffee, orange juice, and two covered plates on top. Alex put her nightclothes in her travel bag, then walked over toward the food. It smelled wonderful and her stomach growled, reminding her of how little she had eaten in the last two days. She lifted one of the lids to find a western omelet underneath.

"You're just in time," he stated as he hung up the phone and stopped beside her. "Marco, Sam and the others have gone downstairs for breakfast, but I thought it would be nice for us to have a few minutes alone."

Alex swallowed. It was time.

"Okay," she agreed, sitting down in one of the chairs as he held it out for her. "Thanks for this. I didn't realize how hungry I was."

"That's a good sign," he stated, taking the seat across from her and removing the metal covers off each plate to stow them on the shelf under the tablecloth.

Alex ate three bites of the hot, tasty eggs before she realized that Lucas wasn't eating. He was looking at something metal in his hand as he ran his thumb over the surface. It suddenly occurred to her that he may be as uncomfortable about this discussion as she was, though for obviously different reasons. He might not have feelings for her, but wouldn't want to hurt her either.

Despite her sadness, she knew that her feelings of rejection and betrayal were unfair. He had only ever been honest and clear from the beginning about what they were sharing, even before he knew her real identity. It was time for Alex to put on her big-girl panties and respect that, even if that meant lying to him in return.

"I just realized that I never said thank you," she stated, filling the silence. "For saving my life, protecting my design. For everything you and your team have done for me and Magnus."

Lucas finally looked back at her, but his eyes seemed clouded with something very different from satisfaction and triumph. *Regret?*

"You have no reason to thank me, Alex. I was doing my job. And despite the outcome, I'm not sure I can be proud of how it all unfolded," he told her in a serious tone, so unlike his usually light-hearted temperament. "That's partly what I wanted to talk to you about."

She put down her fork, her appetite evaporating as suddenly as it had appeared.

"We've never really talked about what would

happen after this assignment," he continued, looking back down at the object in his hand.

"I think we did," Alex stated in a clear voice that disguised the lump clogging her throat. "I know your leaving today means that things are over between us, Lucas. We never intended for this to be anything more than it was. Two people taking advantage of a moment in time. I didn't forget, and I don't regret it."

"You don't?" he replied, his fingers pausing over the metal in his hand.

"Of course not," she said dismissively. "And you shouldn't either."

Alex forced herself to resume eating, though the food now tasted like dry chalk. Lucas cleared his throat and stood up abruptly so his chair flew back and hit the wall behind him with a thump.

"Okay," he muttered. Alex peeked up at him beneath her lowered lids as he clenched his jaw tight before striding across the room. "So, what are you plans then?"

Her chewing slowed as he threw the object in his hand into the garbage bin near the television console, then began packing his various things into his small duffel bag. His movements were stiff and jerky, as though he was agitated, or maybe even angry. Alex looked back at his untouched meal. What was going on? What was she missing?

"I'm not sure yet," she replied honestly. "I told Markie I need a little time off. Maybe I will take that extended European vacation after all."

She had meant to lighten the tension in the room, but it only thickened. Lucas was standing tall, legs wide and hands placed firmly on his hips. There was no trace of his easygoing nature now.

"By yourself or with someone?" he seemed to growl. "Like Renaud, maybe?"

Alex could only blink with confusion for several seconds. Renaud? Jean Renaud? Why would Lucas think she would suddenly go on a vacation with the ex-boyfriend she hadn't seen or spoken to since last year, despite the couple of e-mails before the race?

"What?" she finally managed to ask, lamely.

"He's here, you know," continued Lucas, with his arms now crossed aggressively in front of his chest. "He was asking the race team about you. And he didn't seem at all surprised that you were the engineer behind the now-famous Cicada design."

"Lucas, what are you talking about?" Alex demanded again as his words sounded more and more like accusations, but for what, she couldn't fathom. "What does anything about this conversation have to do with Jean?"

He only looked back at her with an unreadable expression for what felt like an uncomfortable length of time. And just when she was about to press him again for clarification, Lucas smiled at her and shook his head in that arrogant, cocky way that she had seen on many occasions. But this time, it didn't reach his eyes.

"Good luck, Alex, with whatever you do next," he finally stated.

She nodded, swallowing hard, then watched him finish packing his things.

"You haven't eaten any of your breakfast," Alex stated after another few minutes of silence.

"I'm not as hungry as I thought," Lucas stated, picking up his bag. "But stay and finish yours. Have some coffee. Renee should be back in about half an hour or so. She'll help you with anything you need for the flight back."

"You're leaving now?" she asked with surprise. This was it?

"Soon. But I have a few calls to make in the other room." He paused stiffly. "Good-bye, Alex. And, congratulations again."

Then he opened the connecting doors between the two hotel rooms and shut hers firmly behind him.

Alex threw down her fork with frustration, then pressed hard on her eyes with her hands. The clog in her throat was now coupled with a heavy stone at the pit of her stomach. She had prepared for it to be difficult, and emotional. But now she felt physically sick.

Too frustrated to remain seated, Alex pushed back her chair and strode cautiously across the room. Nothing about their conversation made any sense to her. Based on his phone call she had overheard on Friday morning, he should be relieved that she was clear about the fleeting nature of their relationship. So, why did he seem angry? And what was that whole thing about Jean? In another situation, his reaction would look like rejection and jealousy. It would be hard enough to move forward with her life after amicably ending their time together, but this cold, awkward, abrupt end felt unbearable.

Finally, she stopped pacing and tried to face reality. Like it or not, affable or not, it was done.

Now it was time to answer some of those questions Lucas and others had asked. What was she going to do now?

Alex collapsed on the edge of the bed, suddenly very exhausted.

It was true that as of Monday, she was officially on a four-week vacation. But what was in store for her after that? Did she continue in her role at Magnus? Already, Marco had received calls from several agents representing motor companies that wanted to talk more about access rights to incorporate the Cicada into their prototypes, and a couple wanted to discuss buying the full patent outright. In either case, her role with the project was essentially over and it was time to rethink her career path and the many new options now open to her.

At the very least, she now had a month to think through all of the possibilities.

While she pondered her future, Alex's gaze landed on the garbage bin only a few inches away from her feet. Perplexed, she stood up to look inside to see the metal object Lucas had tossed out so forcefully. There it was, an oval, silver-colored disk nestled between a few paper napkins. She picked up the lightweight can and pulled it out.

It was a key chain. The kind that was sold in the various gift shops in the village, with WHISTLER BLACKCOMB SKI RESORT carved into the front. Alex ran her finger over it, much the same way that Lucas had while they sat at the table. She turned it over in her palm and paused in confusion. The initials A.C. were carved into the back in large, italic letters. *Her initials?*

Her sore and aching heart started beating like a drum. Why would Lucas have a key chain with her initials carved in it? Was it meant as a gift, a token of their time together? Then why had he then thrown it in the garbage?

Alex took a deep breath and made a decision. Enough of this stupid guessing and questioning of someone else's motives. She had always prided herself in being the person to confront any issues, even the most uncomfortable, and not hide away, afraid to face the truth because it hurt. This was not her, and it wasn't the person she wanted to be.

With a purpose and resolve that she hadn't felt in days, Alex walked up to the adjoining doors and swung through them with as much dramatic force as she could manage.

CHAPTER 28

Lucas was leaning with his left shoulder against the wall in the other room, staring blindly out of the window. The mountains around Whistler were very beautiful in the summer, providing a dramatic backdrop to the small resort town.

But he barely noticed. He was too busy feeling like a coward and a complete asshole.

Nothing that morning had gone the way he had envisioned it, and he had been too arrogant and sure of himself to even imagine an alternative outcome. So instead of manning up and telling Alex how he felt, or acting like a gentleman by accepting her decision and wishing her well, he had behaved like a jealous prick.

Jesus Christ! If only he could rewind the last thirty minutes. He would still have to move on without her, but at the very least, he could have the chance to hold her close one last time.

Lucas rubbed at the dull irritation behind his sternum. Maybe it wasn't too late. There was still time. He could walk back into the next room, lay his cards on the table. So what if he looked like a total idiot? It couldn't feel any worse than what he felt right now.

Feeling a little lighter, Lucas turned around and started back across the room, only to stop in his tracks as the person who seemed to constantly occupy his thoughts strode in through the connecting doors.

"What is this?" Alex demanded, holding out the key chain he purchased for her just yesterday.

He was so glad to see her, all assertive and demanding, that Lucas found it hard to hold back a goofy smile.

"It looks like a key chain," he stated mildly, sliding his hands casually into his pockets.

"Yeah. That's what I thought," she agreed, but her golden eyes flashed with sarcasm. "And, why do you have a key chain with my initials engraved in the back? Sorry! I meant *'did have,'* since I found it in the garbage."

He did smile at that.

"Why does it matter, Alex?"

"Why are you answering a question with a question?"

"You're right," he conceded. "It's rude."

She rolled her eyes and let out a deep deflating sigh.

"Look, I should apologize about our conversations earlier," she added, looking down at the inexpensive souvenir. "I feel like I handled it badly."

"Really? I was just thinking the same thing," Lucas admitted, stepping a bit closer to inhale her sweet vanilla scent. "That I handled it badly, not you—"

Alex cocked a brow at his hasty clarification. *Shit,* he was messing things up all over again.

"I bought the key chain for you and had your initials engraved in it," he finally continued.

She straightened, rubbing her fingers over the shiny metal.

"Why?"

Lucas took a hand out of his pocket, to show her the key that he had removed from his own key ring on Friday night.

"So I could put this on it," he explained, with a sad chuckle. "It seemed like a good idea at the time. But that was before I understood that you and I are not really on the same wavelength about us."

Whatever Lucas had expected from his grand declaration, it wasn't for her to throw the monogrammed gift at him. It bounced off his chest and landed on the floor between them.

"Are you kidding me?" she demanded. "You have no interest in a relationship with me, Lucas. So why are you pretending you do? Does it make you feel better to play this game, where you string me along, suggest we try to make it work? So you can get a couple more rounds of hot sex before you realize it's just not going to work?"

Lucas couldn't keep up with her questions. He was still stuck at the beginning.

"Let me guess. It's the distance, right? It's killing our relationship?" she continued in a low mocking tone. "Or it's your job? You don't have time for a relationship? I know! You suddenly realized that you're not looking for long-term commitment.

And if you were, it wouldn't be with someone like me. Someone so difficult?"

Something about her words sounded off tiny alarm bells in his head, but Lucas wasn't listening.

"What the hell are you talking about, Alex?" he finally demanded.

"Really?" she whispered back, looking at him like he was a slug to be squished under her shoe. "Why can't you just be honest with me?"

He was about to answer, but Alex cut him off.

"I sat there earlier, pretending I didn't care that things were over between us," she stated in a quiet voice that vibrated with emotion. "Because I knew you didn't want the same thing and I didn't want to make it awkward. I lied about the way I felt so you could walk away. And you want to play me?"

"Alex," Lucas uttered with frustration, reaching out to her with his hands.

"Don't touch me!" she demanded as her lips quivered.

Lucas felt like he was watching a train wreck about to happen and was powerless to stop it. Until it finally clicked in his head that this wasn't just a clever debate, or a way to bust his balls. Alex truly believed that he didn't want her anymore. How was that possible?

He bent low and picked up the key chain. She was now standing more than an arm's length away with her arms wrapped protectively around her stomach.

"You asked me earlier why I had bought this for you," he finally stated. "I don't know what comes next for us, except that I don't want it to end. When we first met, maybe I would honestly say that I wasn't looking for something long-term, and my job is too demanding and the distance would kill us."

She looked away.

"Then somewhere over the last few weeks, I couldn't make those statements anymore," he continued. "I started thinking about what I could do differently so that none of those things would make this thing between us have to end. But I never told you that things had changed for me. And for that, I'm sorry. We should have talked about it long before now."

Lucas slowly worked his house key onto the silver key chain until the two were attached.

"So I wanted to give you the only thing I could. My commitment, and open invitation into my home and my life."

The words hung in the air around them.

"I don't understand," she finally whispered. "What exactly does that mean, Lucas?"

"It means that I've fallen in love with you," he told her simply. "That's it. But you have a life and an exploding career. I would never ask you to give any of that up. But whatever you decide to do, you can also have a home with me."

He extended the key toward her, but she only looked down at it as though it were a trick. His stomach made a sudden two-story drop and he lowered his arm. *All the cards on the table.*

"Does that mean we're done, Alex? That you don't have the same feelings for me?"

Her bright eyes locked with his in that intense stare that always seemed to penetrate his soul.

"You're serious," she murmured. "You're asking me to move in with you?"

Lucas smiled.

"Yeah, I guess I am."

"Okay, then," she replied stepping closer to him. "My answer to your first question is no."

"No?" he shot back.

She rolled her eyes.

"No, Lucas Johnson, this doesn't mean we're done," added Alex as she stuck out her right hand, palm up. "And yes, I do have the same feelings for you."

His lips spread into a big grin.

"Good to know, Alexandria Cotts," he told her, putting the key into her hand and then using it to pull her close. "It saves me from kidnapping you and spending the next four weeks convincing you that we were made for each other."

"You wouldn't do that," she gasped. "Would you?"

"I needed a backup plan," he lied.

Lucas wrapped his arms gently around her back and pulled her into a deep, lingering kiss. And like always, the taste of her made his knees tingle with electricity.

"So, do you want to explain that whole thing earlier?" he asked when they pulled apart. "Where would you ever get the idea that I don't want you anymore?"

Alex groaned and put her forehead against his chest.

"I overheard you say something like that," she mumbled into the fabric of his shirt.

"What? When?" he insisted, pulling back to look down at the top of her head.

"Friday morning."

He backed up one step, so he could see her face until it all clicked.

"Christ, Alex. Is that why you left the hotel room?"

"I was hoping that wasn't going to come up again," she sighed.

"I was talking to my neighbor about a housekeeper I didn't want to hire long-term," Lucas explained, adamantly. "How could you believe that I would be talking about you? Why didn't you say something?"

She only shook her head with her face still looking down.

"Alex, look at me." When she did, her eyes were full of tears. "I adore you. Everything about you. Do you understand? I don't care what anyone has ever told you in the past. You are what I want. All of you. Including your honesty."

She nodded, trying to smile by not quite managing it.

"Promise me that you will never do something like that again, okay?"

"Okay," she finally whispered.

Lucas pulled her close again, trying not to think of all that could have gone wrong because of a misunderstanding.

"So what happens now?" Alex eventually asked.

"I don't know," he admitted again. "But I'm thinking we could spend the next four weeks at my place figuring it out. It's not a European tour, but I do have a nice hot tub."

"Hmmm . . . A wine tour through France or a hot tub with the man I love . . . What to do, what to do?" She drummed her fingers on the top of his shoulder. "Is the hot tub clothing-optional?"

Lucas grinned.

"Always."

"Then it's a no-brainer. I'll take you, naked in the hot tub any day."

Don't miss the next book in the Fortis series,

Hard to Handle

Available in June 2016!

CHAPTER 1

"Come on, you can do better than that!" taunted the silky female voice, laced with a cultured British accent. "Looks like you've gotten soft lounging around on this side of the pond."

Samuel Mackenzie grit his teeth and hammered the punching bag with two quick left jabs and a hard right upper cut. His friend and employee Renee Thomas chuckled at his obvious annoyance.

"What are you doing here, Thomas," Sam demanded in a deep, rich Scottish accent while his focus remained on his boxing workout. He wore long, loose workout shorts low on his lean hips, but his thickly muscled upper body was naked and slick with sweat.

"I work here," replied Renee as she walked across the expansive gym inside the Fortis headquarters near Alexandria, Virginia. At almost six-thirty on a Friday evening, the building only had a handful of employees still at work. The gym was empty except for the two of them.

"Not right now you don't," he retorted, still pounding at the heavy-duty, leather bound apparatus. "You were shot less than two weeks ago, little girl. You're not approved to be back for at least another week."

The tall, lean woman stopped next to him, with a teasing smile on her milk chocolate face, and not the least bit put off by his gruff reprimand.

"Yes, I know. But I'm not an invalid. It's just a flesh wound," she insisted. "I was just in today to help Raymond with a bit of research in the UK. Nothing the least bit strenuous. So, don't worry. You still have a little more time to train before I knock you on your ass."

Sam snorted, and gave her a quick glance. Renee was five feet, eight inches tall, but at six-feet, four inches and a solid two-hundred and forty pounds, he was close to half her size.

"Not in this lifetime, sweetheart," he dismissed, working through another combination of boxing moves.

"Any problems in Toronto?" she asked, watching him with a mix of respect and amazement. For a big guy, Sam was surprisingly fast and almost graceful in his moves.

"Nope. Smooth as silk," he stated, throwing a powerful uppercut before finally stepping back, gripping the punching bag to still its swinging movement.

Sam owned and managed Fortis with his two best friends, Lucas Johnson and Evan DaCosta. It was a full solution security and asset protection firm of twenty-three specialized field agents, technicians, and operations analysts with elite government experience and training. He was in Toronto, Canada for two weeks on his last assignment, implementing a cutting-edge, virtually impenetrable security solution for their client, Magnus Motorsports. He had flown back to Virginia that morning, heading straight to the Fortis compound to finish out some paperwork.

Renee handed him a clean towel from the stack on the supply cart nearby. Sam used it to wipe off the moisture dripping from his face and head, leaving the dark blond mop of damp hair in a tousled mess. He draped the towel across the back of his neck, soaking up even more sweat as he picked up his discarded T-shirt from a bench nearby.

"Lucas says you're off for the next two weeks?" she questioned as she walked toward the gym entrance doors that led outside near the parking lot of the building.

"Yeah," confirmed Sam, sounding less than thrilled about it. "My mum was supposed to come for a visit, but she had to cancel at the last minute."

"Wow! Stood up by your own mum. That definitely explains your relationship issues."

"I wasn't stood up. She closed a big deal with a new corporate client for the inn and spa she runs near Inverness, and they needed some immediate accommodations," he explained, tossing the used towel into a laundry basket nearby. "And I don't have any relationship issues."

"You mean, you don't have any relationships,"

Renee shot back, shaking her head. "Probably also due to your generally sour disposition."

Sam pulled on his cotton T-shirt, effectively hiding a smirk. He and Renee had worked together for several years as Security Advisors within MI5, the UK Security Services before he moved to the US five years ago to join Fortis. They had stayed in touch since then, until Sam successfully recruited her to join the team earlier in the spring. He was glad to have her around, even if she was one of the few people who easily saw beneath his bad-ass exterior, and took every opportunity to tease him.

"So, what are you going to do with all that time off," she asked.

"Not sure yet," he admitted, grabbing his car keys and cell phone from the counter along the wall. "There's some work needed on the house that I haven't had a chance to do for months now."

"Well, try not to do anything interesting. You might actually have fun," Renee shot back, rolling her eyes with exasperation.

"Not bloody likely," declared Sam, grinning broadly with his blue-green eyes sparkling in amusement. "Are you leaving now? Do you need a lift home?"

"I just have a couple of things to finish off at my desk, but I'm fine to drive. It's only a twenty minute drive to my place."

"You sure? I can wait for you and drop you off."

"I'm fine, Sam," she insisted. "Almost as good as new."

Sam looked at her hard, clearly skeptical that

she was telling the whole truth. "Okay, but send me a note when you get home," he insisted.

"Sure, old man," teased Renee, punching him hard in the shoulder but he didn't even flinch.

He watched her turn and walk across the gym toward the entrance to the Fortis offices, then he pushed through the heavy exterior door and stepped outside. It was a warm evening in late June, with a cool breeze that carried the smell of a brewing rain storm. Sam strode smoothly to his car in the small parking lot, unconsciously noting the other cars. One was unfamiliar, and stood out as a luxury rental with darkly tinted windows. Seconds later, as he was about to pass it, the driver door opened causing the muscles in his stomach to tingle with caution. It was like a sixth sense telling him he wasn't going to like what came next.

Two shapely legs swung out from inside, smooth as melted caramel and wearing very sexy, very high black stilettos. And Sam immediately knew exactly who they belonged to before the rest of the woman emerged from the car interior, draped in a body hugging black dress and oversized dark sunglasses. Her thick, shiny chestnut brown hair brushed over the top of her shoulders.

For a brief moment, Sam thought about ignoring her. He could just walk a few more steps to his car and drive away as though she didn't exist. It was what he had been trying hard to do since the last time he saw her four years ago, but it had never actually worked. So he strode right up to where she stood, stopping just out of arms reach.

"What are you doing here?" he demanded bluntly.

Her full, pouty lips parted but no words came out. Sam could feel her nervousness and apprehension but refused to care.

"Well?" he growled, leaning forward.

She straightened her shoulders and lifted her chin. "I need to hire a security team."

Whatever he had expected her to say, it wasn't that.

"Then you've made a wasted trip. Evan is out of town until Monday," he told her, then made a move to walk past her.

"I know. I want you," she added in a soft voice.

Sam stopped and clenched his fists tight until his keys were cutting into his flesh. "And why the hell is that?"

"My boss needs protection. He's in the middle of a big real estate bid and he's been getting threats from one of our competitors."

"Your boss," Sam repeated, turning back to face her. "Who is he?"

"Terry Antonoli. He's a developer with a North American head office in New York, and project bids in several cities in the northeast."

"Never heard of him. Does your father know you're here?" he asked.

"This has nothing to do with him," she replied, evasively.

He looked down into her face, still a good six inches from his, despite her heels. Though her dark brown eyes were covered by shades, Sam knew exactly what they looked like. Sparkling bright, and rimmed with long, silky lashes.

"Tell your boss that we don't do babysitting," he finally stated with a dismissive sneer. "Call Evan on Monday and I'm sure he'll refer you to several good bodyguard services based in New York."

"Sam, wait. I need your help," she insisted as he turn his back to her and walking away. "I think Terry is in real danger."

"Call Evan," he snapped back without pausing or looking back.

Mikayla Stone-Clements was still standing beside her rental car as he drove out of the Fortis parking lot.

Sam was on autopilot for the drive to his house just a few minutes south of the office, his thoughts fixed on this complication he would prefer to forget. His mind wandered between the memories from the past and her pretty pleas for help now. Both made his blood boil with anger.

He had met Mikayla over four years ago while on a mission in Maryland for her father, George Clement, and his newspaper and magazine empire, Clement Media. It was a random encounter, and seemingly innocent at first. While completing an investigation into suspected corruption at one of the smaller Clement newspapers, Sam had found a very pretty and slightly injured woman lying in the alley outside the offices of the *Baltimore Journal*. She had introduced herself as Kaylee Stone, a staff writer who had sprained her ankle on uneven concrete while rushing to do an errand. Of course, Sam helped her get immediate medical care. Then one thing led to another, and he found himself at her place over the next few days as they got to know each other better.

By the time he discovered her real identity, an unforgivable line had been crossed. Not only was she his client's daughter, she was Evan DaCosta's fiancée.

Mikayla Stone-Clement was the worst kind of trouble four years ago, and judging by how damn hot she was looking tonight, she was even more trouble now.

Sam parked his car in front of his house and entered the cozy, secluded cottage situated on a large wooded lot along the banks of the Potomac River. Once inside, he headed straight into the bathroom for a long, hot shower. After towelling off, he walked naked back into his bedroom to get dressed in jeans and a gray shirt. It was only seven o'clock and he felt a nervous energy to do something or go someplace where he was less likely to spend the next few hours thinking about a woman he could never have.

He picked up his cell phone, intending to call Lucas, but paused when the phone vibrated with a new e-mail message. It was from Mikayla.

Please listen to this message left for Terry this afternoon. I hope you'll reconsider. I'm staying at the Hilton Crystal City hotel until tomorrow.

Her phone number was listed beside her name at the end of the note. Sam paused for several seconds before he clicked on the audio file she had attached.

"We've warned you to keep your foreign money out of our business interests. But you don't seem to be listening. So we'll just have to make it real clear for you. Pull out now or your bitch will pay the price. And she won't be so pretty when we're done with her."

Sam listened to the deep, distorted voice on the recording three times, trying to assess the seriousness and viability of the threat to the woman indicated. Who in Terry Antonoli's life was the intended target? His wife? Girlfriend?

Mikayla?

Sam quickly called Michael Thorpe, a Fortis agent with a background in the FBI.

"What's up, Sam?" the young man asked as soon as he answered the call.

"I need your help," Sam stated bluntly. "Are you near your computer?"

"I can be in about ten minutes. Why?"

"I need you to pull up any information you can find about Terry Antonoli, real estate developer."

"Okay. What's going on?" Michael asked.

"I'm not sure yet, but we might have a new client."

"I thought you were on vacation?"

"Yeah, supposed to be. But looks like I might have to postpone it," Sam explained. "Send me whatever you find on the developer."

"You got it," confirmed Michael before he hung up.

Then Sam called Mikayla at the number she provided. After three rings, it went to voicemail. He didn't leave a message. Instead, he went into the walk-in-closet in his bedroom and opened a concealed cabinet at the back of the space. From it, he took out a Berreta 9mm pistol, checked the magazine, then tucked it into the back of his pants. He called Mikayla's number two more times as he strode out the house and got into his car. She still did not answer, and the tingling in Sam's stomach was now an incessant warning that something was wrong.

GREAT BOOKS, GREAT SAVINGS!

When You Visit Our Website:
www.kensingtonbooks.com
You Can Save Money Off The Retail Price
Of Any Book You Purchase!

- All Your Favorite Kensington Authors
- New Releases & Timeless Classics
- Overnight Shipping Available
- eBooks Available For Many Titles
- All Major Credit Cards Accepted

Visit Us Today To Start Saving!
www.kensingtonbooks.com

All Orders Are Subject To Availability.
Shipping and Handling Charges Apply.
Offers and Prices Subject To Change Without Notice.